# TOMB OF FAITH
## A GABRIEL DE SADE THRILLER

ERIC MEYER

ISBN 978-1-909149-18-2

Typeset by Swordworks Books
Printed and bound in the UK & US
A catalogue record of this book is available
from the British Library

Cover design by Swordworks Books
www.swordworks.co.uk

# TOMB OF FAITH
## A GABRIEL DE SADE THRILLER

ERIC MEYER

# PROLOGUE

She stared at the window. A man was there, backlit by the streetlamps outside. He raised a gun, and her muscles tensed ready to roll away from the bullet. Before she could move, there was a shot, and then another. But incredibly, she wasn't hit. The man started to pitch backwards into the street. And then there was someone else there, standing on her balcony. Galina! Her long-term friend, a former member of the Russian Spetsnaz who'd joined the Orthodox Church. Yet she was anything but orthodox, and when the church discovered her martial talents, she became a troubleshooter, able to deal with frequent threats to the security of the Church. As now, her solutions often involved the application of deadly force.

"Galina? What are you doing?"

"This guy was sent to kill you. We need to hide the body quickly before anyone sees it. Otherwise they'll just send someone else if they know what we've done. Hurry!"

"But the cops will be here soon. And Gabriel is in the next room. He must have heard."

"Never mind, we must hide the body. I believe this is the last one. If we can make him disappear, you should be safe, but we need to get him away from here."

She looked outside the window. The body was on the fire escape, lying at an unnatural angle. A small pool of blood had seeped out, and Galina ripped off the man's coat to wipe it away.

"What do you want me to do? I'm not even dressed. I can't go like this. I'm only wearing my PJs."

"No time! Come and help me. It's essential that no one sees the body, not even Gabriel."

She didn't ask any more questions. Faith climbed out of the window onto the fire escape, and between them they manhandled the body down to the next floor. The window was open, and the apartment empty. Galina indicated they should take the body into the apartment. They carried the dead man through to the hallway.

"What if the occupants come home?" Faith objected.

"They won't, they're away for a few days."

"How did you know that?"

"Your father checked out everyone who lives in the apartment block. He keeps an eye on things. You know Jonas, my partner, works for him. Well, Jonas looks at the daily logs to see who's coming and going. We're just trying to protect you."

She nodded, her father, of course. The Director of CIA, he made an irritating habit of discreetly watching over his daughter. She hated it but couldn't stop it. And maybe it had saved her life on this occasion.

"Okay, and then what?"

"We dump him," Galina replied. "It would be best if he was disposed of a long way away. The Appalachians would be a good bet. You could lose a hundred corpses in that place."

"Galina, I still don't understand why. Who sent him?"

"That business down in Mexico, the Church never forgave you for what they thought you did to them."

"You mean the Vatican? Surely not."

"Not the Vatican as such, but some rogue elements inside the Vatican, yes. I hope that when this one disappears they'll give it up, just in case he's been caught, maybe turned State's evidence. They'll think twice before they do anything more."

Faith nodded. It made sense. They rolled the body into a rug from the living room. Faith managed a smile when she saw it was a handmade Kurdish antique, probably worth thousands of dollars. They carried the heavy bundle to the elevator and pressed the button for the basement. Galina's car was parked out back, so they carried the corpse outside and lifted the weighty load into the trunk and drove off into the night.

They dumped the body in an abandoned mineshaft. Galina pulled out the supports so that the sides collapsed inwards, covering the body for eternity so that it would never be found. Galina watched the dirt and dust settle, and then turned to Faith.

"It's time to get you home."

"No, I can't go back, not yet. I don't know why, but I need some time on my own."

The Russian girl looked at her sharply. "Are you okay?"

She shook her head. "I just don't know. All I do know is that I need some time."

"Where will you go?"

"There's an Orthodox retreat just outside Bridgewater.

They'll take me in for a while."

Galina nodded. "Yes, of course they will. How long do you plan to stay away?"

"I don't know, Galina, really. But listen, this is important. There is something I need to think through, and I don't even know what it is yet. I just know."

"Some kind of a vision? Something that is going to happen in the future?"

"Yes, it is. And it is something that involves Gabriel. He is not to know where I am, it is important. I wish I knew more, but I don't."

The Russian girl gave her a tight smile. "I don't like it."

"No, I suppose not, but it is important. If I don't resolve this, something will happen to Gabriel."

"Like what?"

"He'll be killed."

# CHAPTER ONE

She tossed and turned, trapped in the throes of the nightmare that haunted her dreams for night after night. She was in a complex and dark labyrinth, a maze of tunnels. The walls pressed in on her, causing a claustrophobic sensation as if they were trying to suffocate her. Behind her, she heard footsteps as her pursuer drew near. She ran, but the footsteps ran too, nearer and nearer. A shot cracked out, splinters of stone hissed around her head, and she looked around. He was near, much nearer. She had to get away. Where were the others? Why didn't they come down here to save her? She ran faster, knowing that she was even further away from aid. Suddenly, the lights went out, and she was plunged into darkness. She could hear breathing, hers? Or his? She crept forward, feeling her way along the tunnel, touching the stones to find an opening, a way out, anything. Her hand touched something different, wood, iron. A door. She felt around the surface until she found the handle. It opened, and she slipped through, closing it behind her. Would he know she was in here? Except that she didn't know where she was, only that it was a dark chamber. She felt the fear, a terror that leeched all of her courage away and left her weak and helpless. There was only one way she could help herself. She prayed. It was a silent prayer for help and deliverance. She closed her eyes, even though it was dark, and said the familiar, comforting words. When she opened her eyes, she felt calm, at peace, her mind clear, and even more important, she knew what she should do. Why she should do it she had no idea, only that it must be done. She looked around and saw a faint gleam of light on the far side of the dark chamber. She walked towards it. The light came from small hole in the stonework, as if someone had constructed a peephole. She peered through and stifled a gasp. Directly in front of her was the man who had tried to kill her. He was facing away from her, looking towards the brightly lit stone steps that led down into the labyrinth. As she watched, a man emerged from the dark of the stairwell. Her stomach flipped over. Gabriel, her lover, had come to save her. He was holding a gun, yet because he was backlit against the steps, he couldn't see the man who waited to kill him. He started forward, and the man raised his gun to kill him. She tried to scream, but no sound came out of her mouth. Her vision blurred, and a mist started to obscure the terror that was unfolding in front of her. There was the sound of a shot, but the flash of the explosion left her even more blinded. She closed her eyes and re-opened them. They were gone, the men, the stone steps, and instead, there was nothing, just a black emptiness. She twisted her neck to look sideways at Gabriel de Sade, her lover, who slept peacefully beside her in the bedroom of their New York apartment. Thank God, he was safe. But what did it mean? She felt her fear beginning to surface again. She knew that it more important than anything in her life. It had a meaning that would become clear at some time in the future; it was a portent of an event that had yet to happen. She would have to work out what it meant, and what was even more important, to answer terrible question. Could she save him from being murdered? She pictured that terrible nightmare and suddenly realized there was something else, or rather, someone else. Behind Gabriel was yet another dark form, another man. She couldn't make out what he was doing, only that his intent was to hurt, to maim, and to kill.

* * *

It was a fall evening, and that time of the year when dark shadows mingle with the faded rays of the sun to make it difficult to see across the city. Carlo Estevez, Gabriel de Sade's partner, strapped on his vest, took out his piece, and checked the load on the Police-issue Glock 17.

"Damn, this place is dark. It'll be difficult to see anything when we go in, let alone the perp."

They were outside a boarded up warehouse close to the Hudson. Carlo had recognized the guy as they drove through a nearby street. They'd followed him when he ran away and disappeared into the building, moving aside a sheet of plywood to gain access. He was wanted for a brutal series of knock-ins, smashing into apartments, and stealing the occupant's property while he held them at gunpoint. Three women had reported that he raped them during the process of the crime, forcing them to carry out obscene acts. He threatened to shoot them if they refused to obey. So far, he hadn't killed anyone, but the profile showed he was escalating, and it was only a matter of time before he graduated to murder.

"Take it easy in there, Carlo. We know he's armed, and he'll be desperate. Assuming it's our guy. We need to make a positive identification."

"It's him. I saw him," Carlo muttered as he slammed the clip home. "It's time to nail this sucker and haul his ass off to Rikers. You ready?"

"All set. Do you want me to go first?"

It was a sore topic between them. De Sade had a heap of Special Forces experience in Afghanistan. Carlo, the macho, Latino male, was always conscious that he was the junior partner, in age, experience, and military training.

"Nah, I'm good, I'll take this. Watch my back, okay?"

"I've got it."

Carlo moved the wooden board aside, and they climbed into the dark building. A rustling noise above made him jerk his flashlight upwards, and they saw the staircase.

"Up there," Carlo whispered. "They always go for the high ground, stupid bastards. I'm going up."

Gabriel followed him up the dusty staircase, and a slight noise made them both look down, but it was a rat. They made the second floor landing, a wide, open loft space, and one of the few that hadn't succumbed to the gentrification of the property developers.

"Did you hear that?"

"No." Gabriel hadn't heard anything, but his concern was to get a firm identification on the suspect. "Play your flashlight around to try and see him."

"Yeah, I was about to do that."

Carlo shone the beam into the far corners and recesses

of the open space. Almost immediately a pair of eyes were lit up and stared back at them.

"Christ, it's him. Police! Come out with your hands up!"

"I ain't done nothing! The place was already open. Don't hurt me."

The voice was weak, pitiable. Either the suspect was a good actor, or it wasn't the guy they wanted.

"I said come out or I'll shoot."

"Please, no, don't hurt me."

Carlo fixed the dark shape of the man in his beam and started forward. "Put your hands where I can see them, buster. You're under arrest."

"No, no, I didn't do anything. It wasn't me."

The man finally got up and lurched forward.

"Stop, stay right there or I'll shoot!"

"I've got ID! I'm a vet, look, I'll show you."

He put a hand into his shabby raincoat, and the room exploded into noise and a blinding flash as Carlo fired. Two shots. They hit the suspect and threw him to the ground. They both ran up, and Gabriel put his fingers to the man's neck.

"He's dead."

"I got him," Carlo exclaimed. "That'll save the city a few dollars."

"If it's our guy. What was he reaching for?" Gabriel felt inside the pocket and drew out a wallet with a veteran's ID card. Carlo's face fell.

"I told him to stop and put up his hands. The stupid bastard, he kept coming. It could have been a gun."

"But it wasn't, Carlo. I'll call in the ME, and they can take it from there. We'll need to fill in a report, and I'd be ready for Internal Affairs. They may want to talk to you about an OIS."

"Yeah, I guess they will."

An Officer Involved Shooting meant that there'd be many questions to answer, and the fact that the guy wasn't armed would raise more than a few eyebrows. The guy should have done as he was ordered, but who knew what his mental state was? A lot of Vets were seriously damaged after involvement in the war in Iraq and Afghanistan. If this proved to be one of them, it could be a major embarrassment for the department. They waited for the ME to arrive and then left to return to the Precinct to fill in the paperwork. As they walked in, Captain Kruger was waiting for them.

"I want your reports on my desk ASAP, and that means an hour ago. What were you thinking of, Estevez?"

"I gave him a fair warning," he defended himself. "Besides, he could have been the perp. Have you thought about that?"

"No, I haven't, Carlo. While you were shooting that poor guy, he struck again. This time, the woman is on life support in the emergency room. You killed the wrong man."

Carlo went white and turned away, muttering that he'd shouted for the guy to stop and put up his hands. But he knew he was in trouble. The citizens of New York expected their police to protect them, not gun down the innocent. Two suits entered the detectives' room and walked up to them.

"You the detective who killed that guy tonight?"

"Yeah, what of it?"

"Internal Affairs Division, we need you to make a statement. Now!"

It took the whole night to finish, talking to IAD, writing up the reports and going over the same ground again and again until the men in suits were satisfied. Almost.

"Listen, Detective Estevez. You're off the hook on this one, but you're on notice. If it happens again, you could find yourself up on manslaughter charges. Do you understand?"

"Yeah, yeah, I got it," Carlo replied, trying to maintain some of his macho bluster. And failing.

They turned to de Sade. "And you, Detective, you're the senior man. You should have made sure it didn't happen."

Gabriel nodded. They were right. "I got it," was all he said.

"That's it then, you're free to go and continue on duty."

Gabriel felt a bitter taste in his mouth. Killing a man, an innocent man, was not something they'd ever be free from. He knew they'd both see that guy in their nightmares for a long time to come.

\* \* \*

His mind flashed back to Afghanistan, to a skirmish that cost three marines their lives. During long patrol miles from the American controlled area, a group of Taliban insurgents set an ambush that caught them in crossfire as they walked along a narrow ravine. They were pinned down in an area of broken ground, strewn with loose rock that protected them from the worst of the enemy fire. Gabriel recollected the sweet smell that hung over the whole area, like an invisible cloud. They were next to an opium field, one of the thousands that were increasing in numbers across the countryside. He called in a helicopter gunship that came in with its guns blazing and rockets firing and drove off part of the enemy. However, some of them were entrenched in a village less than four hundred yards away, an inhabited village. They poured fire onto Team Bravo, knowing that the RoRs prevented them from firing back. Technically. One of their men, new to the unit, had protested when shots were fired in the direction of the village.

"That's against orders, Sergeant! There'll be women and children in there, you know that."

"I know it," Gabriel replied. "If you want to obey orders and die here, that's okay with me. I want six of the team to lay down a curtain of small arms fire on those stone huts. No grenades, just bullets. If any of those civilians haven't had the sense to get their heads down, they deserve what they get. I'll take four men and go right, Jonas, take another four and go left. Let's kill those bastards."

They attacked hard and fast as they'd been trained, and the insurgents never had a chance. When they went through the village to search for any enemy hiding in the huts, they found the civilian inhabitants were all dead, killed by the Taliban. The Afghan press blamed the Special Forces, of course. There was no mileage in trumpeting the incessant butchery of the Taliban. It was not the rules of war, more the application of brutality to achieve an objective. Yet always, it was the innocent who suffered, no matter what the justification.

* * *

The early snow had turned to slush, and few people bothered to even look as they hurried home in biting, cold wind and wet, ice-covered sidewalks. Cabs and trucks drove through the pools of melting water, sending sheets of spray soaring into the air to drench cursing commuters trying to make their precarious way home. The water company was repairing old piping by the look of the fenced off section of street with a tent place over the manhole protecting the workers from the elements. As he watched, a man in a yellow hard hat ran out of the tent, talking urgently on his cell. The man was amused at his gestures, the way his face moved, eyebrows raised, and lips stretched as he described what his team had uncovered. From his comfortable office on the eighth floor, he needed no description of what was down there. He already knew. Skeletons, more than twenty of them, the result of a nineteenth century battle between Presbyterians and Mormons. He sighed. Why did these fools still fight when the truth was so obvious? There was only one true faith. And yet even his fellow believers sometimes left the true path, or else there would be no need for his organization; the pilot that steered the ship through stormy waters and put it back on course. He sat and browsed through his work schedule for that day. There was nothing that could not wait, and what was going on outside was much more interesting. He watched the ME's minivan draw up to the tent. Two people climb out, both wearing dark blue insulated coats with ME stenciled on the back, a middle aged woman and a young man. Would they find more than just the skeletons? He wondered. It would be a shame, for it had been such a useful place to place the bodies. After all, it was already a tomb for unbelievers. But now that they were investigating the site, he'd have to find somewhere else. It was an elementary precaution. They disappeared into the tent, and for almost a half hour there was no further activity. Then the young man with the ME's coat emerged from the tent and vomited into the gutter. They'd found them, so be it. A few minutes later, an unmarked car drew up. He recognized the type, and without doubt it was the police. Why did the plainclothes detectives always use vehicles that were so obvious? Strange. Two men climbed out, the first, a Hispanic in his late twenties. He had a thin, pencil moustache and was dressed in what the man would regard as 'gangsta chic'. Cheap suit, cut slightly too small, a thin tie, and a hairstyle that owed more to pomade than it did to a barber's scissors. The second man was altogether different. He was dressed more for the weather, in a thick leather coat. His hair was black too but cut in a more conservative manner. He walked like a soldier, looking around his immediate environment, moving with a smooth economy of motion that almost hid an inner strength that men would be wise to beware of. Without doubt a powerful man, he could have been a soldier in Special Forces, even an athlete, or maybe an Olympic pentathlete. He was the lead detective. There was no question, and this was about to get interesting. He'd wondered when the bodies may be found, and who he'd have to cross swords with. He knew he was seeing that man now. He sat back from the window. Even eight floors up, he didn't want his face to be seen watching developments.

* * *

"Jesus Christ, Gabriel, it stinks!"

De Sade smiled at his partner, Carlo Estevez. He hadn't a great deal of experience with homicides, and this was obviously his first attendance at a corpse cache. But he was right. The stench was appalling. The ME came out of the tent, and Dr. Margot Reese's face was paler than normal. She nodded to Gabriel and Carlo.

"Hi, guys. If you're going down there, you'd better wear a facemask. It'll stop some of the worst of the stench."

"You got any spares?" Carlo asked.

She smiled, dug into her bag, and passed them out a mask apiece. "It's not going to be easy to give you much information until they bring them down to the morgue. We've got about twenty skeletons, and I'd guess they've been there more than a hundred years. One of those city guys pulled away two of the skeletons and found the more recent bodies stacked in a corner behind a false wall that was probably constructed to hide them."

"How many, Doc?" Gabriel asked.

She stared at him. "Between ten and fifteen."

"Recent?"

She nodded. "Probably, and some of them certainly in the past few months. The rest not so recent, but this one's bad. He's been active for some time, too."

Then he realized the importance of what she'd said. "Between ten and fifteen? What does that mean? They're not..."

But she nodded. "Oh, yeah, they are. Butchered, and this guy is one mean killer, believe me. There are so many body parts that it'll take us some time to put a number to it. I'd guess the victims are prostitutes in the main. Their clothes, at least the pieces I can see, high boots on the legs, short skirts, plenty of vinyl, you know what I mean. It fits the image."

Prostitutes, they were so often a target of the crazies.

Their profession took them out of sight of mainstream society, and when they disappeared, they were rarely mourned.

"Okay, Doc. Let us know when you have anything." He turned to his partner. "Carlo, fix that mask. We need to take a good look down there. You bring your flashlight?"

"I'm kind of wishing I hadn't. Can't we do this from the crime scene photos?"

Gabriel grinned. "Believe me, if there was, I'd call it like that. We have to see this, so let's go."

* * *

He watched them fix their facemasks in place and go through the doorway of the tent. When they'd disappeared, he cast his mind back to the last salvation. She'd been like the others, cheap clothes, skinny, almost emaciated. Standing on the street corner, touting for trade. He used the minivan, like he always did, and made sure that his face was in shadow when he stopped next to them. This one was just like the others, a face once pretty, a mind that had once dreamed of a golden future, and a soul that was pristine and unblemished. But no longer, drugs and whoring, the life on the streets, had put her beyond redemption, in this life, anyway, but not in the next.

"Your place or mine, Mister?"

He turned his relaxed fatherly smile on her. "I'd prefer to use the back of the minivan, if that's okay with you, my dear. How much?"

"You want a blow job, or all the way? Maybe something special, I can do most things?"

"Oh, I think we'll go all the way, don't you think?"

"Yeah, well that'll set you back fifty dollars. And I'll need it up front."

"That's no problem. I'll find somewhere quiet, and we can park up and go in the back."

He drove to the Brooklyn Bridge and found his usual place empty, an abandoned builder's depot. He opened the door and walked around to her side of the vehicle, but she sat tight. He smiled, "Of course, the money."

He handed her five tens, and she climbed down and followed him to rear doors. He struggled with the lever to unlock it and then turned to her.

"Would you mind? I can't seem to work out how to open it."

"Yeah, my folks hired one of these minivans once. I can do it."

She grinned and stepped forward to open it. As her hand touched the lever, she smelt something pungent, and the odor overwhelmed her as a rag was clamped over her face. She blacked out. When she came to, she couldn't move. She glanced around. She was bound in the back of the minivan, but it was no ordinary vehicle. It was a torture chamber, lit by battery lanterns hung from the roof. The walls were streaked with dull red marks. She was lying on some kind of a table, her limbs fastened down, and a strap around her neck. She couldn't move. A gag was fastened around her mouth too. She felt the panic start to overtake her body, but she forced herself to relax. She'd need all of her wits if she was to get out of here, and she'd do whatever he wanted. The john came and stood over her.

"Ah, you're awake, that's good. Do you know why you're here?" She shook her head.

"No, you can't speak, but I'll tell you anyway. This is not

for kinky sex, so I'm going to do you a favor. You've taken a wrong turn, and your life is in ruins, am I right?"

She stared at him. What the fuck was he talking about? She shook her head wildly.

"No, you don't understand. They never do. I'm going to save your soul, my dear. Redeem this awful life you've fallen into. I'm going to make things better. But first, you must confess your sins. You may use this rosary as you pray for forgiveness."

She hadn't got a clue what he was talking about. But it was when he produced the filleting knife that she understood. Her life would end here, and he was going to kill her. Thoughts flashed through her mind; other girls like her who'd disappeared from the streets. Had they ended up here with this wacko? She shook her head from side to side, "Please, don't kill, me, I'll do anything!"

But it came out as "mmmggghhh".

"Don't worry, your misery is about to end, and you're going to be redeemed in heaven. I commend your soul to the everlasting glory of God. In nomine Patris, et Fili, et Spiritus Sancti."

He could see the agony flare in her eyes as he started to cut, but it was essential. She had to suffer the way the Lord had suffered, so until the shock stopped her heart beating, she'd have to endure, just as He did. He took off a leg first, avoiding the spurting of arterial blood and urine that pouring out of her bladder as fear released it. Then the next one, but she was in her death throes now, weak and perhaps she wasn't feeling the pain quite so much. She continued to writhe as he started on the second leg, but then the movements stopped as her heart gave out. He patiently carried on cutting, doing the Lord's work.

When he'd finished, he went to the front of the minivan, unzipped his pants, took out his penis and started to masturbate. Some would see it as sick. He knew that. But it wasn't, this was simply a reward he was entitled to for doing something that so few men would be capable of. He made a mental note to hose out the interior of the vehicle when he'd disposed of the body parts. It was really much too messy for such a sacred task. After all, the Lord was looking down on everything he did.

The man suddenly came back to the here and now. The two detectives were emerging from the tent. Good, so now the hunt would begin. He took out a pair of binoculars from his desk that he sometimes used to observe people as they passed by. He focused on the Hispanic and then on the other one, the lead detective. He thought he'd seen that face before but couldn't be certain. He smiled as he saw the disgust on the detective's face. Yes, sometimes it was necessary to dirty one's hands to carry out the Lord's work. Then he moved the binoculars to look down on what he was holding, and his smile disappeared. The man had the medallion, the medallion that meant more to him than anything else in the world. The hand of Josemaria Escriva, Saint Josemaria Escriva, and the Spanish founder of the organization that he served had touched the medallion in this very building on East 34th Street.

He'd only been here for eight months since being forced out of the Vatican in disgrace. But in that short time, he'd already uncovered the road to fame and fortune, and to salvation. Now his plan was threatened with ruin. One of the whores he'd saved must have taken it from his pocket, stolen it at an opportune moment. He had to have it back! It was a vital part of the jigsaw he'd been working on for so long, and the puzzle that would lead him to immortality in the ranks of the righteous. After he'd solved it, of course, and that medallion was a vital to part of the solution. He had to know the answer, had to have that medallion, but how?

* * *

It had been a scene that would haunt his and Carlos' nightmares a long time. A heap of old bones, mostly intact skeletons. To one side, a pair of skeletons had been moved aside to expose a narrow opening in the hard, flagstoned floor of an ancient, long forgotten New York dwelling, lost beneath many yards of landfill and development. It must have been a root cellar, or storage cellar for some kind of foodstuff. Now it was used to store bodies, or body parts. The smell was terrible, yet the scene revealed in the beam of Carlos' flashlight was even worse. A death house, a butcher's shop, like something from a medieval painting that depicted the awful agonies of hell, except that this was only feet beneath the teeming sidewalks of one of the mightiest cities in the world. The killer had hacked the bodies to pieces and tossed them into this dark place. It was only by counting the heads that the ME would have been able to form an estimate of the numbers. There was a weird characteristic they needed to check out. Many of the arms with hands attached clutched a rosary, so a religious killing? He stepped back, and Carlos joined him, glad to move from the overriding stench of death. As the beam of the flashlight played over the skeletons, he saw it pick up a glint of light. He bent down and retrieved a metal disk. On closer inspection, it was a medallion of some sort.

He showed it to Carlos. "What do you think this is? Do you think it came from these skeletal remains, which would make it a nineteenth century artifact? Or from the bodies in the lower chamber?"

Carlos bent over to look at it. He shrugged. "Could be anything, could be nothing."

"Yeah, I'll get it to the lab. Let's see what the technicians make of it." He pulled out an evidence envelope and inserted the object, and dropped it into his pocket. Then he forgot about it. They went gratefully out into the fresh air and removed their masks, breathing deeply. The New York pollution had never tasted better.

"I don't want to see that again for a long time," Carlos exclaimed.

"Yeah, it was one of the nasty ones. You know we've got two crimes there, my friend? The old and the new."

"That's true, but only one for us to investigate. The doer that dumped those skeletons would have died over a hundred years ago, maybe two hundred years. It's those body parts we need to look into."

"Unless they're linked, both crimes."

Carlo stared at Gabriel. "Linked, what do you mean? It's impossible. The gap between them makes them entirely different."

Gabriel nodded. "Yeah, maybe you're right."

* * *

The sight of the body parts reminded him of a grisly episode during his time in Afghanistan. Their Humvee was racing away from a fight at a river crossing outside

Jalalabad. They came across a Marine Bradley M113 APC that had taken hits from heavy machine gun and cannon fire. Two bodies were lying on the hull, unmoving. Jonas was about to call in a Medevac helo to take away the wounded. But as he spoke, an RPG rocket hit the vehicle. A soldier fell out into the road, rolling in the dust, his uniform on fire. They raced level with the Bradley and saw to their horror a severed leg of a marine lying on the vehicle's ramp. The injured soldier lay nearby, and as they reached him, blood spurted out of his mouth and nose, and he sighed his last breath. They pulled another casualty out of the Bradley, but as they pulled him out of the smoking vehicle, his upper torso separated from the rest of his body. They had a motto in Team Bravo; they never left their dead and wounded on the battlefield, everybody came home. They wrapped the body parts in a shelter-half and explored the wreckage. One of the Team started to look nervous.

"It's going to blow any moment. There's a lot of ammo on board."

Jonas fixed him with a cold stare. "These are our men. When we leave this place, they're coming with us. These boys're going home."

The man calmed down. He was new to the team. He'd learn.

"Yeah, you're right. I'll check for any survivors."

He went digging around inside the still smoking hull and found a live marine underneath two bodies. They were lying on top of him. So he called Gabriel over, and they pulled the bodies off him. They stacked up both dead and wounded together in the cramped interior. Even the leg was carried away, for it belonged to some mother's son.

As they drove away with their gristly cargo, the ammo in the Bradley detonated with an explosion that blew the Humvee two feet into the air, and it settled back with a crash. Apart from bruises, there were no further injuries, and they hit the gas pedal to rush the wounded to the base hospital. But at least on that occasion they had survivors. This time, there were none, just the dead, and a testament to one man's unending capacity for life.

\* \* \*

Something made him look up then, but he couldn't describe it. An instinct, possibly, but in front of him loomed a tall office block and just another New York skyscraper. And yet there was something that had caught his eye. Maybe it was someone looking down, a lookyloo taking a break from his work, probably. Or was it someone else entirely?

"Carlo, that building there. Do you know who owns it?"

His partner smiled. "Yeah, of course. Every Catholic knows what it is. Opus Dei."

Gabriel nodded, of course, Opus Dei, literally the 'Work of God'. Opus Dei was an organization within the Catholic Church that taught that ordinary life was a path to sanctity. It was founded in 1928, and approved by no less a person than Pope Pius XII. Also known as Hitler's Pope, after his reputed support for the Nazi leader. An interesting and colorful outfit, but that was all. There was no link he could see to the murders.

For the rest of that day the question of the connection between the old and the new haunted him. Could it be possible? And if it was, what could possibly link them?

"Religion." His girlfriend Faith handed him a stiff measure of Bourbon. It wasn't his normal drink, but he felt the need for something to smooth away the horrors of the day's crime scene. He'd told her the rough details and mentioned his hunch about a connection. "If they are linked, it could only be that someone sees that site as a kind of tomb for their victims. Consecrated ground, maybe. It's possible a church once stood on that place."

He smiled as he looked at her, wondering as ever how he'd been so lucky as to have such an exotic partner with whom to share his life. She was petite and slim with an elfin face framed by her trademark pageboy haircut. Underneath her dark brown hair and eyes she had smooth, creamy skin and full lips that were just made for kissing. He brushed her lips with his.

"I think you should be the detective, as you seem to know so much about it. But I guess an FBI Special Agent would know more about homicide than the average Joe."

She sat down and leaned over to kiss him back, a gentle peck on the cheek.

"Former FBI Special Agent. That's all behind me now. I'm more than happy to just run my business and let law enforcement take care of itself."

She put her hand around him and nuzzled into his neck. She pulled back as she touched the outside of his pocket.

"What have you got in there, is it jewelry? You haven't bought me a present, have you?"

He jerked upright. "Oh Christ, the medallion. I should have put it in the evidence locker overnight."

He put his hand inside his pocket and drew out the plastic baggie containing the artifact he'd retrieved from the crime scene.

"It's some kind of a…"

Faith was staring at it, and her face had gone pale.

"What's up?"

She grimaced. "It's that thing. It feels evil. You said it came from the place where the bodies were found?"

"Yes, it did. I found it on the ground, but I've no idea which particular crimes it is associated with, the old or the new."

She took hold of the bag and examined it carefully.

"It came from the newer crime. This is from the 1930s. There's a Christian symbol engraved on one side, and it looks to be Latin which makes it Catholic." She looked closer. "I'd guess the origin is Spain. These designs are classic for that part of the world. The Moorish influence is unmistakable." She handed it back to him with a shiver. "I can feel a kind of vibration from that thing, and it's unpleasant. You take it back."

He stared at her for a few moments and took back the baggie. "It came from a repository of homicide victims, so I'm not surprised it gives off evil vibes. But your analysis of the medallion takes my case forward. I may be hunting a Spanish Catholic serial killer running around New York, bumping off the street whores. All I need to do now is find him."

\* \* \*

So it was another manhunt. His mind went back to when he'd been on the wrong end of a manhunt, and hunted by someone who would kill him. It was autumn, at the foot of the Hindu Kush, and he was hiding under a log, pretending to be part of the terrain. He pulled branches on top of him and smeared mud on his face. At the time, he was twenty miles inside Pakistan, returning from a solo mission to escort a friendly tribal leader back to his territory after a meeting inside Afghanistan. The Pakistan Taliban fighters who hunted him were not friendly, and a group of them had passed close by, unaware of his presence. But if they did stumble onto his hiding place, the end would come very quickly. He estimated the enemy strength at forty or fifty men, too many to outshoot. The only way to survive would be to outwit them. Except that he was betrayed when a stray bird screeched out of a nearby bush and flew away. The Taliban returned, and with scores of submachine guns and rifles pointing at him, he was forced to put down his weapons and come out with his hands up. He expected to be killed out of hand, but they tied him and led him on a long journey that lasted two days. He realized he was being taken inside the badlands of Afghanistan. The trip took him over the Hindu Kush, battling along snow-covered trails thousands of feet above sea level; his limbs numb and aching from the thin line they'd used to bind him. Whenever they stopped, they beat him, and he remembered shutting off his mind to the pain of the blows.

When they reached their destination, the Afghan Taliban camp, he was pushed into a deep, dark, stinking hole in the ground, but this time his limbs were unbound. They considered that escape was impossible as the hole was fifteen feet deep. But de Sade was Team Bravo. They'd given up on the word 'impossible' a long, long time ago. At the bottom of the pit, the reason for the stink became obvious. He could make out the skeleton of an animal that had been thrown down there a long time ago and been picked clean by rats, probably a small dog. Gabriel had ripped off pieces of skeleton and used them to make rudimentary climbing hooks. It took him three nights of patiently working at the stinking carcass until he was ready. When the camp was quiet in the early hours of the morning, he'd used two hooks to climb up the sheer, earth sides to the wooden frame that penned him in. The rope that secured it was rotten, like most things in Afghanistan; except their weapons that they treated as if they were a treasure beyond price. The rotten rope had been easy to chew through, and he climbed out of the pit and fell on the guard who was sleeping nearby. He'd taken the man's weapons, an AK-47 and more importantly, a long, razor sharp hunting knife. He had to silence the sentries who were looking outwards from the camp for possible attack, not inwards. There were four of them, and he crept silently behind each one and slit his throat. He found enough food, water and ammunition to equip him for the trek back through enemy territory; and crawled away from the camp. Two days later he was back at the Team Bravo base in Kabul, inside Camp Phoenix. Whenever he was inside somewhere dark and dangerous, that stink came back to him. And the memory that despite the odds, he's got out, and he'd survived.

\* \* \*

He stared at the medallion as if it was about to give up its secrets. He didn't know for certain that it was linked to the crimes. It could have been dropped and lost by anyone. But somehow he didn't think so.

"You could try Opus Dei."

He looked at her sharply. "Opus Dei? Why do you say that?"

"Well, they're a Catholic organization which has their main office in New York."

He thought about the office building opposite the crime scene. "Yeah, they're right next to the site, but what's the Spanish connection?"

"Well, they were founded in Spain, by a Spaniard, Josemaria Escriva."

"I didn't know that."

"He was a controversial guy. Speeches in support of Adolf Hitler, political involvement with right-wing causes like the Francisco Franco, and Augusto Pinochet in Chile."

"So he was a Nazi, so what?"

"I didn't say he was a Nazi. I only said that he leaned that way. But it doesn't mean that Opus Dei believe in that stuff. Last I heard, they were more into self-flagellation, you know, whipping themselves for real or imagined sins."

"Or getting a prostitute to do it for them?"

She smiled. "I doubt it. It would miss the whole point of it. But look, why don't you bring the medallion to the gallery, and let Galina and I run some tests on it?"

He thought about that. It should go to the Precinct to maintain the chain of evidence, but if it disappeared into the system, it could take weeks to get the answers he needed.

"Okay, would you do that for me? You may as well take it."

He made to pass it back to her, but she flinched away.

"I don't want it, Gabriel. You bring it in tomorrow morning. You know I have a kind of feeling for these things."

He knew. She had demonstrated on many occasions a power to hear and see things that others were blind to. He nodded. "Okay, I'll drop by tomorrow."

"It will be interesting to see what Galina makes of it." Galina Polotsova, her partner, had an encyclopedic knowledge of religious history and artifacts.

"Yeah, that would be helpful, thanks."

"Thanks? Is that all the gratitude I get?"

"What did you have in mind?" But he had already guessed.

Her expression was lascivious as she ran a delicate tongue across her red lips. "Probably the same as you, Gabriel de Sade."

"Right."

They made love there and then, on the couch. Faith had an innocence about her that concealed the real person underneath. Indeed, she'd spent a short stint in an Eastern Orthodox convent as a novice nun, even if it was to hide from the Russian mob at the time. But the experience had changed her views forever, and she had become, like Galina, a member of the Orthodox. Whatever that meant. But this was no time for religion, she was like a fire lit beneath him, and he had to use every ounce of his self-control to keep himself from exploding. This was an experience to be savored, like a fine wine, smooth and memorable. The fragrance of her body surrounded her, a faint, musky, animal odor that mingled with her expensive perfume to overcome all of his reason, as it always did. These times were for him a taste of an exotic and erotic paradise. Yes, he was indeed a lucky man, for Faith Ward was unique, an elegant young woman on the outside, and the mind and body of a skilled courtesan inside.

"What are you thinking?"

He opened his eyes, to see that she was staring at him, eyebrows raised, waiting for an answer.

"Mm, I guess I was thinking you're a tasty piece of tail." He grinned as he spoke, for she knew what she meant to him. All he received in return was a sharp punch to the kidneys from an FBI trained unarmed combat expert.

"Hey, that hurt."

"Yeah, it'll be harder next time, Mister. Tail indeed!"

"I did use the word tasty."

"So you did, but next time, come up with something more flattering. Unless you want this particular piece of tail to start rationing it."

"I'll think of something more flattering."

"You'd better believe it."

He reached for her and held her to him. They kissed, and he tasted the warm sweetness of her breath. When she moved her head back, he saw she was still watching him carefully.

"What? What is it?"

"It's that medallion from the crime scene. There's something about it. I don't know, but it makes me feel uncomfortable."

"I guess that it's a vibe from all of those murders."

She didn't answer at first, and he thought she was dozing. But then she spoke.

"No, it's not that. What happened is terrible, but it's what is going to happen. Something bad."

He didn't reply. He'd found her premonitions were accurate, most times. He hoped this wasn't one of them.

When he called into the gallery the next morning, Faith and Galina were talking to a client, so he and Carlo looked around at the displays. Crucifixes, relics in tiny decoupage frames, icons, statues, even pieces of rock. And paintings; every possible representation of the agonies of the crucifixion and the Stations of the Cross that foretold that event, together with many scenes depicting the discovery of the empty tomb.

"This sure beats all," Carlo exclaimed. "It's like some kind of a weird museum."

"Except that here you can buy the exhibits, if you've got the dough," Gabriel replied.

Carlo looked closer and inspected some of the price tags. "Two hundred thousand dollars for that little daub! Damn, it's not even very good."

"A little daub that was painted by a renaissance master nearly seven hundred years ago, Carlo," Gabriel laughed. "I'd guess that'd make it pretty rare."

"We could offer you a discount, Detective."

Both men looked around to see that Galina Polotsova had come up behind them. Where Faith kept her exotic character hidden, the Russian girl hid nothing from the world. Her thick, brunette curls dangled past her shoulders, worn over a sharp business suit that only served to emphasize the lush richness of her hair. She wore just enough makeup to enhance her perfect, oval face and compliment the suit. Rich, flashing, dark brown eyes smiled out at them, and both men had to work hard to avert their gaze from the tiny necklace hanging in the V created by her cream silk blouse, like an arrow pointing directly at the firm swell of her breasts. She wore, as she always did, elegant shoes with just enough high-heel to give a perfect arch to her spine. She was one, classy lady. She was also the partner of Gabriel's best friend, Jonas

Savage, with whom he'd served in Afghanistan. He kissed her on the proffered cheek.

"Hi, Galina. You've met Carlo, I believe? I don't think he's too impressed by your painting."

They shook hands. "Hi, Carlo, yes, of course we've met. That painting is believed to be by Sangallo, one of the influences on Michelangelo di Lodovico Buonarroti Simoni. It's a bargain."

Carlo looked mystified. "Who?"

She smiled. "Michelangelo. You know, the Sistine Chapel."

"Oh yeah, him. Right."

She turned to Gabriel. "Have you brought the medallion?"

"Oh, yeah, it's here." He handed her the baggie. "Make sure you don't touch it. We'll need to dust it for prints and forensics."

"That's okay, all I need to do is put it under the microscope, and a few other tests that won't alter anything. Can you give us about thirty minutes? We just saw that customer out, and Faith is setting up the equipment. We'll be as quick as we can, so help yourselves to coffee."

They examined the artifacts on display. The gallery had been configured to resemble a small church with beams in the high roof, woodblock floors and walls clad in shaped stone. It was effective. There was almost a reverence to the place, as if there should be a high altar at one end, and a priest intoning the rites to the faithful. The place smelt of incense, too, a reminder to both men of their younger days when anxious parents had pushed them into church once every week.

"All this stuff, where does it come from?" Carlo asked

his partner.

"Just about everywhere. Collectors, churches who have storerooms stuffed with unused statues and pictures, estate auctions, you name it."

They both turned as Faith and Galina came out of a doorway marked 'Private'. Faith kissed her partner.

"We've done the preliminary examination. It's much as I thought, a Catholic piece, probably minted for some special purpose. Almost certainly a means of identification, something like that."

Galina handed it to Gabriel. "We'll draw up a report with the results of our investigation. It's genuine, of course. There are a few interesting details that we still have to look up. It carries a hidden message that is almost invisible, except with the use of special equipment. It'll all be in the report."

"A hidden message?" He looked at Carlo, then back to Galina. "What did it say?"

"We're not certain, but we're looking it up. We'll have a better idea later. We've got photos and scans to work from, so we won't need it again. The most interesting thing is its origin."

"Its origin?"

"Yes, that's odd. We need to look into it some more."

\* \* \*

"Seville! What the hell are you talking about? As in Spain?"

"Yeah, that's the way it looks, Captain."

Gabrielle stared at his Precinct captain. Kruger was dressed as normal, a dark-gray off the peg suit, one of five identical ones he kept in his closet, white shirt and dark-blue tie. Heavy, black, cop shoes polished to a mirror shine. He ruled the Precinct with a will of iron and a heart of gold. Fools didn't last long at the Ninth Precinct, but good men could always rely on him to back them to the hilt. No exceptions. As a result, their clear up rate was the best in the city.

"So where do you go next?"

"We're waiting on the ME's report, Cap'n. We need to identify at least some of those victims and then try and find the link between them. But if they were all whores, it'll be tough."

He wasn't sure whether to include the coincidences that pointed to a connection with Opus Dei but decided it was too early. They were wealthy and powerful, so the Captain would need some heavy artillery before he went looking into their affairs.

"But your thinking is that this is some kind of a religious nut? Save them from their life of sin, that kind of crap?"

Gabriel nodded. "That's about it, yes."

"Okay, keep at it. Carlo, pull out every arrest or complaint that has a religious angle. We need this guy stopped, and fast. Is the medallion down in forensics?"

"I just left it there, yes. They're doing the usual tests for prints and forensic residue."

"Right. I suggest you get out on the street and start talking to some of these sex workers. See if they've seen anything. Check with missing persons too, but I doubt you'll find anything there. These people are notorious for not reporting disappearances. Get to it, and remember, we need a result fast."

When he got home that evening, he was tired and depressed. Faith saw it at once.

"No progress with your case?"

He shook his head. "Nothing. It's as if they didn't exist, these women. No one knows anything, and no one saw anything. The ME has identified five of them so far, but their last known addresses are useless. All the landlords know is that they failed to get home several months ago, and they re-let the apartments. I confirmed they were all on the game, these five, anyway. But it's almost as if they just dropped off the face of the earth into a black void."

"So he hasn't struck again, not yet," Faith said quietly.

"Not yet, no. You think he will?"

"Darling, I know he will. The medallion, it belongs to your killer. When I was near it, I could feel him. A sick monster, a man who is waiting to stalk and kill his next prey."

"You make him sound like an animal."

"In a way, yes. But an animal kills for food. This one kills for his sick fantasies."

"Surely he thinks it's some kind of a religious crusade he's on?" Gabriel stared at her. "You think it's just an extreme perversion?"

"That is exactly what it is. He's found the perfect vehicle to explain away his sick mind."

The doorbell sounded to interrupt them. "That'll be Jonas and Galina," she continued. "Would you let them in? I invited them around for drinks. Jonas is going away tomorrow."

He let in his friends. Galina smiled at him and handed him a folder. "It's a report for you, Gabriel, about the medallion. It should make interesting reading."

He nodded his thanks and shook hands with Jonas. His friend was shorter than him by an inch or so. With his fit, slim body, blonde crew cut and clear blue eyes, he was the picture of an all-American college boy; a Mr. Average who now had his feet firmly on the corporate ladder. But looks in Jonas' case were deceiving. His neat clothing concealed a body that was a hard mass of solid muscle. They nicknamed him 'The Tank' in the field because he was unstoppable. When the shit hit the fan, there was one man you needed on your side. Jonas Savage.

"So this is a farewell drink," he greeted his friend.

Jonas nodded. "Something like that, I'm flying to Europe tomorrow. It's a rush job."

Gabriel knew better than to ask for details. Jonas worked as a consultant for a number of organizations, including the CIA. It was understood that what he sold included complete secrecy for his clients.

They sat down, and Gabriel poured the drinks while Faith prepared some snacks. Gabriel dragged four bottles of his favorite beer, the Schneider Kristall he always drank when he could get it. The Chinese grocery underneath his apartment building kept a small supply for him, and both him and Jonas were quiet as they savored the premium brew. They were introduced to it by ISAF peacekeepers in Afghanistan, and once tasted, there was nothing else for those men who had shared the almost heavenly beer, and a reminder of their post-mission drinking sessions. A reminder too, of the toasts to those comrades who hadn't made it back. Jonas grinned as he emptied the first bottle.

"It's still good, this stuff. Take me back a few years."

Gabriel nodded. "It always does."

They chatted and relaxed in each other's company. Four people with similar backgrounds that included periods of extreme violence, and four people who trusted each other implicitly with their lives, a trust that had been earned on more than one occasion.

"What's the deal with the medallion?" Gabriel asked Galina. "You said it was interesting."

The Russian girl gave Faith a nervous glance and looked back at Gabriel. "I'm not sure if interesting is the correct word to use. That message I mentioned, we managed to decipher it eventually. It translates as 'Only in her tomb will Faith look east to rest beneath Saint Mary of the See and the true believer will gain their rightful place in heaven'. I haven't a clue what it means. It was written in Spanish, but the writing was hidden in code that we had to break. Fortunately, it was one we'd seen before, so it wasn't too much trouble."

Gabriel excused himself and went into the spare room they used as an office. He booted his PC and Googled 'Tomb, Faith', Saint Mary of the See'. There was nothing for tomb of faith, but the cathedral got a hit. It was in Spain, sure enough. Seville. He went and rejoined the others.

"It's in Seville, Spain."

They gaped at him, and he got three different responses.

"Seville!" Galina exclaimed.

"Seville? What the hell?" Jonas looked astonished.

"Don't go there," Faith whispered. "Please!"

# CHAPTER TWO

Gabriel stared at his friends, unable to absorb what they said to him. He turned to Jonas. "What troubles you about Seville? It's just a Spanish city."

Jonas nodded. "True enough. I was reading about it only yesterday. Seville is the capital of the region of Andalusia. It's situated on the River Guadalquivir and was developed in Roman times, when it was known as Hispalis. A population of seven hundred thousand makes it the fourth largest city in Spain. I could tell you a whole lot more," he grinned. "But what's real strange is that I'm flying out there tomorrow, a flight from JFK to Madrid and then a local connection to Seville.

"Something secret?" Gabriel continued.

His friend shrugged. "Not especially, I can't name names, but it's essentially a diplomatic protection job.

"Right. Galina, why were you so surprised?"

The Russian girl was silent for a few moments as she got her thoughts together. Then she looked at him. "You know what synchronicity is, Gabriel?"

"Sure, it's a coincidence, that's all."

"It is that," she agreed. "But it's more than just a coincidence. It's a meaningful coincidence. I knew that Jonas was going to Seville. Now we know that the medallion is linked to something in Seville. Your investigation may take you to Seville, yes?"

"It's possible, yes," he admitted. "But by no means definite."

Faith was shaking her head, and they could hear her whispering. "No, no, no."

"And the hidden inscription mentions the Tomb of Faith." Galina stared at him.

"You mean as in Faith, right here? That's crazy! It refers to religious faith, something like that. It's obvious."

"Or it's synchronicity," Galina said. "Faith is obviously upset about it."

He looked at his frightened girlfriend. "What is it, what's worrying you?"

"That medallion is what worries me. It has been touched by evil, and wherever it leads, evil will follow. You're probably right about the meaning of the word 'faith'. I hope so, anyway. But there is nothing good to be found in Seville, I know it. Only what is bad."

He grinned. "Hey, relax, I'm a cop, you should be used to it by now. When folks go bad, it's my job to pick up the pieces, wherever they fall."

She gave him a weak smile. "I know that. I'm thinking which particular pieces are going to fall. I hope I'm wrong."

Later that night, Faith held him so tight that he had to work hard to breathe.

"Promise me you won't go to Seville," she breathed.

He pulled away from her. "Faith, I'm a cop. I know

you have these intuitions, but I have to follow the leads wherever they take me. Those dead women need justice. You should remember there's a killer running around these streets."

"I know that, and I know that it has to be done," she breathed. "But when I touched that medallion, I felt something dark, and something terrible that is about to happen."

"I understand what you're saying, and I know your premonitions have been right in the past. But just think about it. This time you could be wrong. And there's something you haven't considered."

She looked at him with a puzzled expression. "I hope you're right. What haven't I considered?"

"It's just this, Faith. There's no suggestion of me going to Seville at this stage. It's just an outside hint that may pan out to be nothing. I'm due to get the ME's full report tomorrow, and the chances are that there'll be enough there for us to find the killer here in New York City."

Her face fell. "I hope that proves to be true. But I saw you in Seville. And you were in trouble, and your life was in danger."

It was a troubled night. In the morning he had to leave early for the Precinct, and Faith was already up and about. He kissed her as she made breakfast in their kitchen.

"Feeling any better this morning?"

She gave him a wan smile. "I think so. I'm sorry about last night, darling. I hope it was just a stupid notion. Do you forgive me?"

He grinned. "Of course I do. Listen, I have to go to work. Let's go out tonight, maybe take in a show?"

"I'm sorry, I have to work. A client called yesterday just

before we left, and he wants to look at our stock with a view to a large order. Rain check?" she asked eagerly.

"You've got it. And I'll have to take a rain check on breakfast. I've got a lot to get through today. Maybe a late dinner would make up for it."

"As long as it's somewhere expensive," she grinned.

"It's a deal." He gave her another kiss, buttoned up his warm coat, picked up his briefcase, and went out into the chill morning. He called in to the Chinese grocery, and the owner, Lee Fat, sat behind the cash register as ever.

"Good morning, Detective. You are well?"

"All good, thanks, Lee. I could do with some beer for tonight. We emptied the ice box yesterday."

"Is no problem, I have two cases in stock room."

"Thanks, I'll see you tonight."

"Yes. Detective, are you Catholic?"

"Me?" What the hell was behind that question? "No, I'm not. Why do you ask?"

"What about your lady, Faith? She is Catholic?"

"Lee, what's this about? We're both Orthodox, as a matter of fact. Why do you ask?"

"Is strange. A priest came in early this morning. He say he look for policeman. I thought he mean you. Maybe I wrong."

So it was likely nothing. "Yeah, probably just a coincidence, Lee."

"Yes. He say something about faith."

"Faith?" Gabriel was instantly alerted. "What exactly did he say about faith?"

Lee looked worried. "I sorry, my English not so good. He say something about 'faith soon', or similar. I think he want you in his church."

"Tomb of Faith, was that it?"

The Chinese looked miserable. "It could be, but my English bad. I not know."

"Okay, Lee, thanks. I'll pick up the beer this evening."

"Have good day, Detective."

"You too, Lee."

Gabriel decided to walk to the Precinct, and as he strolled along the sidewalk, he chewed on his current case. A gritting truck narrowly missed him as he crossed the street without looking, but when he walked through the grey stone façade of the Precinct doors, his coat and pants were still cold from the shower of wet grit that had caught him in its backwash. He smiled as he remembered the abuse from the driver.

"If yer too stupid to know where yer walking buddy, I'd call a cop if I were you."

He started for the stairs, but Carlo was rushing down them. He shouted as he came towards Gabriel. "We got a lead on that case, the bodies in the basement!"

So that's what they were calling it. It was inevitable, he supposed.

"They've seen a guy go into the hole," Carlo continued. "The Crime Scene dudes were going in there a few minutes ago to look for forensics. They saw him going in and called it in."

"He could have been a street bum, looking for somewhere warm," Gabriel cautioned. "It's pretty cold out there this morning. Don't forget the last time."

Carlo looked at him, furious that he'd reminded him of the bad shoot. "In a long, black woolen coat? You know, the kind that Catholic priests wear. This was no bum, it's a possible."

Gabriel was dubious, to get such a strong lead so soon. But stranger things had happened.

"Right, so that's where we're headed?"

"Damn right, I've got an unmarked checked out in the garage. Say, you're soaking wet. You been swimming in the Hudson?"

"Something like that."

"Right." Carlo ignored the reply. "No time to change, we need to nail this bastard now. I've called for a couple of cruisers to close off the street. With any luck, we'll grab him before he gets away. Crime Scene are keeping an eye on the place, and they said he's still there as of five minutes ago."

Gabriel nodded when Carlo jumped behind the wheel and said he'd drive to the scene. The Latino detective drove through the wet, slippery streets as if he was chasing an escaping bank robber. He couldn't use the siren for fear of alerting the suspect, and twice he narrowly missed colliding with pedestrians, the second time a baby carriage that had almost reached the sidewalk on the 'Walk' signal. His blood was up, and there was no use in any attempt to rein him in. But when they arrived and stopped fifty feet from the tent, Gabriel spoke to his partner as Carlo snatched out his Glock and thumbed off the safety.

"Carlo, don't shoot anyone unless you're faced with no other choice. I'd keep that weapon on safe if I were you."

Without pausing, Carlo looked sideways at him. "Don't you trust me? You think I'd cap an innocent bystander again?"

That was exactly what worried him. But there was no way to say it without fueling his anger.

"No, of course not. I'm just being careful."

"Yeah, right. And I'm going to nail this sonofabitch before he butchers any more women."

They reached the tent, and Carlo led the way inside. On the ground, a dark hole lay exposed with the top of a ladder. He started down it still on the run, and Gabriel followed after a brief pause to check his weapon was on safe. Something was wrong about this bust, something very wrong.

"There's a narrow door here, and someone's opened it. I'm betting it's our guy," Carlo shouted. "Some kind of a metal hatch. I'm going through. You stay back, there's only room for one. Watch my back in case the perp's gone somewhere else in this damn labyrinth."

"I'm here. Watch yourself," Gabriel replied.

He heard the sound of Carlo slithering through the narrow entrance and along the tunnel that lay behind it. Then there was a shout.

"Hey, the motherfucker's here. Police! Don't move, fucker! I said stay there!"

Two shots hammered out, echoing around the dank, enclosed space. The flash ripped out of the entrance to the narrow tunnel, followed by the acrid stink of gunpowder.

"Carlo, are you okay?" he shouted.

After what seemed like an age, when he was considering going in to search for his partner, Carlo's voice came back.

"I'm okay, yeah."

"What happened?"

Another pause. "I shot someone. He's dead."

"Is it our guy?"

Another pause but this time it lasted a lot longer. "No, I don't think so. He's just a bum."

They waited for the paramedics and watched as the

corpse was manhandled out through the underground tunnel and up into the tent, then outside to be placed on a gurney. He wore a long, black coat that had once been of good quality. His clothes underneath were a blend of thrift shop necessities. The boots had once belonged to a workman. They were worn and well scuffed. On his hands he wore fingerless gloves. One hand clutched a tubular object, and de Sade leaned down to see. A length of German sausage; he'd been eating his breakfast. The paramedics covered him and loaded him into the bus.

"I'm sorry, I thought he had a gun." Carlo was white faced, stricken with the knowledge that he'd taken an innocent man's life.

Gabriel shrugged. "It was a mistake. No one will blame you."

"The hell they won't. Internal Affairs will crucify me for a second one. And how am I going to sleep at night, Gabriel? Oh shit, you warned me, and I didn't listen. Oh, God, I killed him, another one!"

He almost collapsed, and Gabriel helped his partner to stay standing. "Let's get in the car. Don't worry, it'll all be sorted out when we get back to the Precinct."

It wouldn't, and he knew that. IAD would be all over it, and Captain Kruger would have a coronary when he heard. At least Carlo was a practicing Catholic, so he could seek absolution. Maybe that would ease the hurt. But it wouldn't bring the victim back to life.

"I don't want to get in the car. I need some fresh air," Carlo objected. "We're no nearer finding this guy, so what are we going to do?"

"We've got a lead, that medallion we found down there. The girls took a look at it, you know, Faith and Galina.

They've got a small facility in the gallery. There was an inscription, something about Seville."

"Seville? That's in Ohio, what's it got to do with the case?"

"Seville in Spain. There's a religious connection, and we'll need to chase it down."

He didn't add what both of them knew. The bum that Carlo had killed may have seen the killer going in and out of his underground lair if it was a shelter he used regularly during the bad weather. Now they'd never know.

"We're going to Seville?"

"Not you, Carlo. You'll have to clear this up first. I expect you'll be behind a desk for a short time."

"If they let me stay on the job," he replied with bitterness.

"You're not the first cop to make a couple of mistakes. They know that."

But Kruger had other ideas. "I want your gun and your badge, Carlo. You're under suspension until further notice. Contact your union rep and have him meet you at Internal Affairs."

His face was stony, and Gabriel noticed a vein pulsing in his baldpate. Carlo handed over his gun and badge and left without another word.

"He'll need to talk to a psych, Captain. He took it real hard."

Kruger glared at Gabriel. "Not as hard as the poor guy he shot. Dear God, two of them. Now where are you with this serial killing? I'm starting to feel the pressure from the top floor."

De Sade explained about the medallion.

"So you think it could be linked to that Opus Dei

place? Jesus Christ, as if we haven't got enough trouble. And what's this Seville thing?"

Gabriel shrugged. "Just an inscription. It may mean nothing."

Kruger snorted. "Or everything. Get down to the Opus Dei building, and see who you can talk to. It overlooks the burial site, so someone may have seen something."

It was a huge building, and de Sade considered asking for help, but a look at the Captain's face told him he would be wasting his time.

"I'll get straight down there. And If I draw a blank?"

"Then follow up the other lead. Seville."

They were polite, exquisitely so. They even made a half-hearted attempt to convert him. But within minutes of talking to Opus Dei, he knew he was wasting his time. And something else was strange, he got the distinct feeling they were waiting for him.

"Of course, we'll do everything we can to help, Lieutenant."

"Detective."

"Yes, Detective."

The man was tall, lean and elegant. Two thousand dollar suit and a tan that he'd need to keep topped up, possibly at a tanning salon, but more than likely by regular trips to the Caribbean, or maybe Spain? When he'd arrived, the guy had bustled down to meet him. Why was that?

"I need to know if any of your people saw anything, Sir. They may have seen someone going in that place."

"I can assure you they have not, Detective."

"How would you know, Sir? I've only just asked you, so how could you have had time to ask all of your staff?"

The man smiled. It was intended to convey truth and

integrity, along with compassion. To Gabriel it looked as if it had been rehearsed many times.

"We are a religious organization, Detective. Dedicated to serving our fellow man. If any of our workers had seen something untoward, they would have come forward as soon as it was known a crime had been committed near to our headquarters."

Gabriel glanced around at the elegant décor, teakwood, soft lighting, and plenty of solid brass fittings. The two-inch pile carpet and paintings on the wall did not look like reproductions.

"The business of serving your fellow man looks pretty prosperous."

The man's smile didn't budge a fraction. "Many of our devotees come here, and we like to make them feel comfortable when they visit."

Their eyes met. Sure, the guy was pulling his chain, and Gabriel knew there was nothing he could do about it. Neither would he get a warrant for this place. It'd be easier applying to search the White House.

"Thanks for your help, Sir. I didn't catch the name."

"Amando, Federico Amando. I am the head of our historical archives, and currently I am the most senior person in the building."

"Spanish."

The man inclined his head. "I was born there, yes."

"Right, Mr. Amando."

"Monsignor Amando."

"Right."

He gave the man his card, and they briefly shook hands. "If you do find anything that will help us, please give me a ring, Monsignor."

"Of course. Good luck. Detective."

He returned to the Precinct, lost in thought. His years on the job had left him with an instinct for the good and the bad in people. He had no beef with Opus Dei, and as far as he knew, they were kosher. He smiled at the use of a Jewish expression for a Christian organization. But Opus Dei was just a bunch of Catholics who were more serious about their religion than the ordinary churchgoers. But that guy, he was hiding a big, dark secret. And like so many of the really bad ones, he was keen to show off his superior knowledge to lesser mortals, like a New York detective. It didn't make him a viable suspect, not by any means. But it sure put him on the list. So what next? He glanced at the tent, still there, but now surrounded by yellow crime scene tape that drooped into the wet street. The ME. That was next.

"Nothing, Detective. No idea at all. Whoever did this either knew what they were doing or was very lucky. The cause of death is anyone's guess." Dr. Margot Reese seemed cool. She lost interest in him and turned back to the corpse she was working on. It was not one of his, he noted. This one was in one piece. Then it struck him, the reason for her coolness.

"The street guy."

"Yes, de Sade, the street guy. Or more specifically, the one your partner shot. At least I can tell what killed him, if you're interested. Your partner is getting something of a reputation as a gunslinger."

"It was a genuine mistake."

She snorted. "How many more genuine mistakes will it take to stop him? Or maybe he's trying to keep us in employment."

He opened his mouth to protest but closed it. She had a point. Carlo had been stupid.

"Aside from the obvious, is there anything that connects the victims?"

"The obvious being that they were all prostitutes?"

He nodded.

"Nothing. They were just young women who'd fallen on hard times. About the only thing the killer left them was their jewelry, some of them anyway. Come to think of it, that did link them. The torsos, they all had something religious. The hands, the right ones, some held a crucifix on a chain, a gold cross. Some of them had a strange tattoo, looked pretty recent. It might be worth searching for the tattooist."

"What kind of a tattoo?"

"A crucifix again. Weird."

She opened a drawer and took out an arm, wielding it almost as if it was a tennis racket. She slapped it on the stainless steel examination bench. "See, the crucifix."

It looked recent and not very professional. "Could be the killer did this."

She nodded. "Very possible. The crucifixes we found are similar, just the bare cross."

"We were looking for a religious nut, and this confirms it."

"Make sure you stop him before he kills anymore."

He thanked her and left. He wasn't certain she was referring to the serial killer or Carlo. Knowing Doc Reese, it was probably both.

Kruger waved him in when he entered the long detectives' room that was home to him and a score of other detectives working at the Precinct on any one shift.

"Have you got anything?"

"A religious nut. That's about all."

He told him about the crucifixes, and Kruger grunted. "We already knew it was something like that, de Sade, but we need a name. I want this guy off the streets. What else have you got? For Christ's sake, I've got a raving lunatic walking the streets killing off prostitutes, a detective on suspension for a pair of bad shoots, and one of my best men comes in here and tells me we've got nothing. I want something, Detective. I need a result, and I need it fast. What else have you got?"

"Just the medallion, the link with Seville. But I don't see it as taking us any further forward."

"Unless the killer is over there, or a clue to his identity. I'll contact my opposite number in the Policia Nacional in Madrid and ask him for courtesy cooperation in Seville. Get yourself on a flight to Spain, and see what you can find out."

"But, Captain, it's…"

"Find the link, if there's anything to find, and bring me that bastard's head. You'd better take that medallion with you. The Spanish may have some ideas about it. I'll have Frank Willard take over things this end, at least until Carlo gets a clean bill of health. That's all, Detective."

That evening he watched TV with Faith. How could he break the news that after all she'd said, he would travel to Spain, to Seville to continue the hunt for the serial killer? But the number one news item was about Carlo Estevez. The presenter turned her five thousand dollar smile to the camera for a second, and then changed her expression to look solemn.

"A killer cop is on the loose in New York City. How

can any of us feel safe when New York's finest have such people in their ranks? So far, two kills have been attributed to this man, but who knows how many innocents this man has shot dead? Requests for an interview with the NYPD have so far fallen on deaf ears. We intend to pursue this investigation until we get answers, and we promise to keep you informed. In other news, a forty-four stone woman is fighting for her right to use the Subway system after she became jammed in a turnstile."

Gabriel turned it off, and they sat in silence for several minutes. He had to tell her, and yet he didn't know how. Finally, he made an effort.

"Faith, there's something I need to tell you."

"I know there is. When are you leaving?"

"You knew?"

"Yes, I told you. I saw you there when we were looking at the medallion. It was just going to be."

He grimaced. "I wish it didn't have to happen, but there's nothing I can do about it. I guess it's what Galina said, synchronicity."

She nodded. "Maybe. Your department's in a lot of trouble, isn't it? You've got this serial killer investigation and now Carlo. Will he lose his job?"

"Maybe. Chances are that he'll serve out a suspension, loss of seniority, something like that."

He got up to take another beer from the icebox.

"I'm coming with you."

He'd just taken a swig out of the bottle. He coughed, and it sprayed over the floor. "What!"

"You heard me. Galina has agreed to look after the gallery, so I'm joining you in Seville. You need someone with expertise of religious artifacts and their history."

Gabriel wiped the beer from his shirt and pants. "You said it was unsafe. I don't want you involved."

"I said there was evil attached to that medallion, something in the message, in its history. I'll be able to help you unravel it."

He sat next to he and put his arm around her. "Faith, it's a great offer, but I don't want you involved in this. Who knows what I could run into over there?"

"Exactly. You certainly won't know, but I will. It's our area of expertise, Galina and me. It's what we do."

"I'd sooner you didn't," he murmured. "This serial killer, it could be that he travels to Seville, and we don't know yet if he's doing the same thing over there."

"Yeah, so you'd prefer me to stay in New York, where there's a killer cop on the loose."

"Carlo isn't a killer cop," he objected.

"Maybe, but tell that to the families of those guys he shot. Anyway, I shall be on that flight, so you may as well get used to it."

He tried to think of some way of dissuading her, but he knew it was a forlorn hope. It was cop business, true, but to his knowledge, Faith Ward had never been dissuaded from doing anything. Even by her father, Raymond Glen, who happened to be the Director of the Central Intelligence Agency, so what hope did a mere NYPD detective have? And there was always the possibility that the lead to Seville was wrong. It could be a pleasant, expenses paid few days away from the Precinct.

# CHAPTER THREE

The flight was pleasant enough as far as Madrid. American Airlines were as courteous and comfortable as usual. His attractive partner seemed to smooth the way for an upgrade to business class, unless it was the unseen hand of her father, and not for the first time. Raymond Glen had a habit of interfering with his daughter's plans, and he always knew about those plans almost before she did; the perk of being the Director of Central Intelligence. Or it may have been a simple courtesy to a member of the NYPD. De Sade didn't want to ask. He felt uncomfortable without his sidearm. Even though he had no jurisdiction outside of New York City, he knew how bad the world could be, and he would be turning over a few rocks that some people would prefer were left alone. After Madrid, the going worsened. The connecting airline, Iberia, flew them down to Seville in an ageing Airbus. It was a short flight wedged into seats that were designed for midgets, and after less than an hour in the air, they needed time to stretch while the airline hunted for their baggage. Two hours later, they left behind a surly Spanish airline clerk and hailed a cab, to leave with their newly discovered bags for the city.

"I thought the Spanish had a reputation for manners and civility," Gabriel observed to his partner.

"They also have a reputation for laid-back inefficiency, so I guess that guy was halfway there. It's lucky you weren't carrying your gun. I could see you were ready to take out the Glock and shoot him. I could see the airport cops were starting to get interested."

He grunted. It was the same in most countries, lost baggage and rude staff, and the customer couldn't complain, which opened up accusations of abuse against staff. Thankfully, it wasn't the norm, not yet. Even though the PC Police kept on trying to turn customers into emasculated weaklings.

"This is a dump, it looks like Detroit!"

He was staring out of the cab window at the outskirts of Seville. Faith opened her mouth to tell him to keep quiet, but the driver overheard him and rushed to defend his city. "Seville is the most beautiful city in the world, Senor. This is just the industrial part, you wait until you see the city itself. It is beautiful, a paradise."

He didn't answer. They were both tired and jet-lagged, both on New York time so that they'd flown out at nine thirty from JFK, and it was now only lunchtime. Then they arrived in the city proper.

"Gabriel, it is beautiful, and he was right. Look, the river, the walkways, what a beautiful place."

They were driving alongside the River Guadalquivir, and on their right they saw the outline of the Alcazar, the famous palace fortress built by the Moors, and the stark, circular outline of the bullring.

"Yeah, it's not bad. What's that spire over there?"

The driver turned to glance around. "It is the Cathedral, Senor. The Cathedral of Saint Mary of the See."

"What's that on the top, driver?" Faith asked casually. "It looks like a weather vane from here, is that what it is?"

"Sure, it is a weather vane. It is built onto the Roman statue of a woman. Is very famous in Seville. People take Faith very seriously."

"I imagine they are very religious, and the Catholic tradition is very strong here."

He looked puzzled. "Religious? Some are, some aren't."

"I thought you said they take faith very seriously."

He laughed. "Ah, yes, Senora. Faith, it is the name of the statue on top of the Cathedral. She is called Faith."

They were both silent for a few moments. Then Faith asked, "Is there a tomb underneath that statue?"

"A tomb? I don't know. I guess there are many tombs underneath the Cathedral. You would have to ask the church authorities. They will know more."

Gabriel looked at Faith. She was staring at the statue that was backlit by the midday sun.

"What's up? The statue?"

Finally, she nodded. "Yes. That, and the link with the medallion." She turned to face him. "There's something bad going on here, something very bad."

"You mean like the killings in New York City?"

She closed her eyes, as if it would give her more understanding. "Worse."

They checked into their hotel, the Becquer on Calles Reyes Catolicos, Street of the Catholic Kings, just off the Triana Bridge. At least the suite was comfortable after the rigors of their flight, and Gabriel decided to it was time to eat. Then they could make a start.

"Room service? Can you bring up a plate of sandwiches and hot coffee? Thanks."

They sat on the couch and dived into the food and hot, fresh coffee. Replenished, he ran the shower and stood under the water jets, feeling the stress and tiredness ooze out of his body. He also felt something next to him. He opened his eyes, and Faith had joined him. Her naked flesh glistened with droplets of water that collected in her cleavage and ran down her pure, creamy skin to the cleft between her legs. He felt himself become aroused.

"Not yet," Faith admonished him. "I got in with you to freshen up, not the other thing."

"Maybe later?"

"Mm, they do say that Southern Spain had a reputation for fiery passion. All that flamenco and strong wine."

"I'll just take the passion, thanks."

"You've never been to a flamenco evening?"

He shook his head. "Not me. I'm not into that tourist stuff, wailing voices and women in flouncy dresses."

"We'll have to correct your education. This is where you come for the real thing. I'll book a show while we're here."

"Faith, it's not my bag?"

"I thought you were feeling passionate?"

It was a time to retreat. "If you put it that way, I'll go."

"Yeah, I thought you might."

He dressed in tan slacks, loafers, a cool, light-blue silk shirt and a lightweight coat. Even in Southern Spain, old habits die hard. A detective always wore a jacket. It was the only way to disguise the fact that you wore a gun, even though he didn't have one here on foreign soil. But he intended for that to change. Faith pulled on a pale lilac silk dress and low-heeled leather sandals. She'd performed the miracle that only women seem able to do, to transform from the shower to Parisenne chic almost as if by magic. Her hair was fastened up on her head and held by a plain but elegant ornament. Maybe it was something they were born with, in their genes.

They walked through the teeming streets of the fourth largest city in Spain. The place was a maze of noise and color, a combination of the old and the new. Horses pulling carts like the ones in Central Park for the tourists, and new, modern trams rushing almost noiselessly through the streets for the locals. Wide, tree-lined squares, where old and young alike enjoyed the sunshine while they read books, chatted or ate their lunch. And everywhere there were bicycles, yet it was strange, they were all identical. Strange until they reached a large square with racks and racks of the same cycles marked with the City of Seville logo. An inner city cycle hire scheme, and it explained the mass of two wheelers that made their lazy way across the city. And explained how they managed the main oddity of Seville. There were no cars. As a result, it was a city that vibrated with life, and both of them began to relax until they came to their destination, the Cathedral of Saint Mary of the See. It was a vast edifice, garish with rows of religious carvings etched into its ancient stone. They rounded the corner to the west side of the Cathedral and came upon the Alcazar. The wall of the palace stood gaunt and forbidding in front of them, and inside the gate of the Cathedral, a weathervane.

"Gabriel, I think it's a model of the one on top of the

tower. It's Faith."

He nodded. "Yes, I believe it is. The question now is how do we find the Tomb of Faith?"

"Maybe we should ask?" she said. But he noticed that the light had gone from her eyes. Was it because they'd gone straight to what appeared to be the source of the central part of their quest? Or was it something else, something she'd felt. Or seen.

"Can I help you?"

They both whirled, expecting some kind of trouble, even in this sacred place of worship. But the man who'd asked the question was entirely in keeping with his surroundings, a priest, or maybe some higher rank, and too high a rank to be a common guide. Gabriel felt the need to be alert. "What makes you think we need help?"

The man smiled. "Because you were looking at Faith and mentioned that it may be a model."

They both relaxed. "Yes, we were thinking exactly that," Faith replied. "Can you tell us anything about the statue?"

"I would be pleased to. You know that the tower upon which the statue stands is called the Giralda?"

They shook their heads.

"Indeed. It was originally a minaret and was converted into a bell tower after the Reconquista, the Christian re-conquest of Spain from the Moors. The statue is known as El Giraldillo, and it is the statue of Faith, or perhaps it represents faith. Who knows?" he smiled. "The tower's interior was built with ramps rather than stairs, to allow the Muezzin and others to ride on horseback to the top."

He seemed pleased to pass on his knowledge, and Gabriel felt obliged to introduce themselves. "I'm Gabriel de Sade, and this is my partner."

They shook hands. "Mr. de Sade, Ms Ward, I'm pleased to meet you and welcome you to our beautiful city. I am Bishop Raul Santiago."

He was a tall, elegant man, with iron gray hair, a thin, leathery face containing a pair of deep blue eyes, and a bearing that was straight and proud, like that of a soldier. He wore a long, black cassock, fastened at the waist with a dark red sash. On him, the well-cut garments made him look even more the soldier. A general possibly, like the old image of the Civil War generals who led their troops into Gettysburg.

"So you work here, Bishop Santiago, in the Cathedral?" Faith asked.

"No, I have other duties. But I come here occasionally to admire the beauty of this place. You know that the man who discovered America is buried here, Christopher Columbus?"

Gabriel was intrigued. "I'd no idea. I thought he died over there on a later voyage."

"Not at all, he returned a hero. This Cathedral is a veritable treasure trove of our history. And yours, I would imagine."

"How did you know we were American?" Faith asked him.

He smiled. "Come, your accents are known the world over. We are all admirers of American movies."

She nodded. "So the statue of Faith is on top of that tower, the Giralda, and this is a model."

"Not at all. The model is on top of the tower. This is the original statue, here in front of you."

They stood looking at Faith, the statue that had stood for so many hundreds of years in the Cathedral. Gabriel looked at Faith, and she raised her eyebrows. Was this the time to ask the obvious question, the one they'd come here to find out about, The Tomb of Faith? But Faith asked the priest to have a quiet word. He nodded, curious, and they walked over to a dark corner. De Sade followed. What was she up to?

"Bishop, there's something I need to know."

He gave her a kind smile. "I am happy to help with your questions. What troubles you, my child?"

"Why should anything trouble me? What makes you think that?"

He kept his smile intact. "I have served the church for many years, and I think I can judge people after all that time."

She nodded. "You're right. In fact, your ability to judge people is nothing short of miraculous."

Her voice had grown hard and cold.

"What's up?" Gabriel asked her. "What's the matter?"

She waved him to keep out of it and kept her gaze fixed on the priest. "So miraculous that you knew my name before either of us mentioned it."

He gave her a brief smile. "You are quite correct. I did know who you were. I was asked to look out for you."

"Who contacted you, Bishop?" Faith stared at him, and Gabriel was reminded of an animal that was trapped in the headlights of a car. But he checked his analysis, and Santiago was no frightened animal. He seemed no less relaxed than when he had first approached them. He looked around.

"There are things I need to discuss with you. Perhaps we could go somewhere less public than this, shall we take coffee?"

They looked at each other. This was unexpected, and they had to know what lay behind the literal ambush by the Bishop. Gabriel nodded.

"Okay, we'll do that. Do you have somewhere in mind?"

"There is a Starbucks not far away if you would prefer that."

They both laughed. Thousands of miles from the States, in the elegant, old capital of Seville, and there was no escaping America's most famous exports.

"That's fine, provided you don't suggest we eat in a MacDonald's."

"We have that too in Seville, if you wish."

Their voices replied in unison. "No."

Santiago smiled. "I understand. I suggest we go now, and I will try to answer all of your questions."

He led them through the ancient streets until they came to the familiar green and black logo. They sat in a small nook near the rear of the coffee shop and waited while the Bishop collected their coffees. Gabriel smiled at his partner.

"This is a first, being served coffee by a bishop."

She didn't return his smile. "My Dad always said to beware of Catholics. Too many secrets."

"I think this one is about to tell us some of his."

She nodded. "Maybe. Let's see what he has to say."

The elegant cleric returned with three coffees and sat down. He seemed relaxed and at ease. Gabriel reflected that if he was their enemy, he was hiding it well.

"Let me explain how I came to be involved in this. I work for the Congregation for the Doctrine of the Faith, and what used to be known as the Holy Office."

"I believe it was known by another name before then,

Bishop," Faith interrupted.

He acknowledged her with a nod. "Yes, I am sad to say that at one time we were known as the Inquisition. In fact, the Supreme Sacred Congregation of the Roman and Universal Inquisition. My organization is the oldest of the nine congregations of the Roman Curia. We work from the Palace of the Holy Office at the Vatican. I was on business in Madrid when I was contacted by a friend of mine who does similar work in the Eastern Orthodox Church."

"Galina. She spoke to them."

He inclined his head. "Miss Galina Polotsova, so I'm told, did contact them. I understand she worked for the Orthodox Church at one time."

"Yes, she did," Faith replied.

"Well, she asked them to get in touch with my office and request someone with knowledge of the Cathedral to meet you in Seville, so here I am."

His smile broadened, and he held out his hands wide, the shepherd welcoming his flock, or the spider to its web?

"Did they tell you why we're here?" Gabriel asked him.

"Yes, you're looking for clues to a serial killer connected to a medallion that was found at the crime scene."

"Right. So how can you help us?"

He hesitated for a moment, and his confidence appeared to drain away. "I'm not sure. Do you have the medallion?"

Gabriel took the medallion, still in its NYPD evidence baggie, out of his pocket and handed it to the priest. The man took it and examined it through the plastic.

"May I remove it from the bag?"

"Yeah, go ahead. They've done the forensics on it, and there's nothing there."

He examined the large coin and handed it back. He sat in silence, and they waited while he collected his thoughts.

"I'm afraid it is a story that does not reflect well on our Church. It began more than five hundred years ago, when one of Phillip the Second's galleons returned from the Americas with a cargo of treasure that exceeded the wildest expectations of those who had financed the expedition. A senior Spanish bishop took the opportunity to remove a substantial proportion of that treasure, and I imagine it was mostly gold, to store it in a hidden place. His purpose was to expand the Cathedral even though at the time it was the largest cathedral in Christendom. It was then a recent construction, built on the site of a mosque. There was at the time a kind of insane madness about such schemes. It is quoted that the local Sevillanos said 'Let a church so beautiful and so great that those who see it built will think we were mad'. This is all on record, as is their comment that 'The new church should be a work which like no other'. I believe if you look around the Cathedral, you will agree that they were successful in their endeavors. They began construction in 1402, and it was not until 1506 that the building was completed. They were so determined, so devout, that church workers gave half their salaries to pay for architects, builders and other expenses. That was not the end of the story, and five years after construction ended the dome collapsed, and work on the cathedral re-commenced. The dome again collapsed in 1888, and work continued on it until at least 1903. The most recent collapse was due to an earthquake and resulted in the destruction of a great number of precious objects that lay beneath the dome." He smiled depreciatingly. "But I digress. This gold that was stolen and stored in a hidden place, the secret of its whereabouts was lost when the man responsible, a priest by the name of Alfonso Diaz, died in an accident. Since then, men have hunted without success for the location of that treasure."

Gabriel interrupted. "Bishop, this is all very interesting, but I'm here to look for clues that link that medallion to a man who is killing and dismembering young women in New York City. This treasure hunt story, well, I wish you luck with it, but it's nothing to do with my investigation."

Santiago shook his head. "On the contrary, it has everything to do with it. Eight months ago, a hidden space was discovered beneath the Cathedral. Inside were the bodies of eight young women, dismembered. It is my belief that the man who killed them is the same one who is searching for the gold. During his search, he uncovered this space and decided it would be perfect to store his victims. It was only discovered by chance when a small earthquake necessitated a survey of the area. I believe if you find the gold, or find the man who is hunting for it, you will find your serial killer."

Santiago went on to explain about the fine traditions of the Cathedral of Saint Mary of the See, but neither of them was listening. Gabriel was dismayed. The search had widened now that there was evidence of similar crimes here in Seville, and that meant involving the local cops. It would make everything that much harder, more bureaucratic.

"I'll need to contact Captain Kruger in New York. He can fix me up an interview with the local police," he said absently. "There's no other way to play this now we know about these copycat crimes."

The Bishop nodded. "I imagined that would be the

case. Is there anything I can do to help?"

"We need to look at that Cathedral," Faith murmured.

They looked at her. "It would help to see the burial site," Gabriel agreed.

"No, not just that, the whole Cathedral."

"But they've searched for centuries, what's the point?"

"I haven't searched yet. I may see something they've missed."

"You have specialist knowledge of religious artifacts and history?" Santiago asked.

Gabriel replied for her. "Yeah, she does. Something like that."

"In that case, I will arrange for suitable credentials for you. Are either of you Catholic?"

They both shook their heads. "Eastern Orthodox," Gabriel told him.

"I see. But it makes no difference. I can arrange for you to have temporary accreditation within my office. The passes will allow you to go anywhere on Catholic property, or most places, anyway."

"You can do that, even though we don't belong to your church?" Faith exclaimed.

"Yes, I can do a great number of things."

"Who is your boss, Bishop? What we would call a line manager in the States."

He smiled. "I represent His Holiness, the Holy Father, Pope Benedict the 16th. I doubt that anyone will question his authority. I will obtain the passes for tomorrow morning. If you give me your details, I will send them to your hotel. I can also help bridge the gap between here and New York. A Vatican colleague of mine has taken up a post here, as the Honorary Curator of Cathedral Antiquities, and he is also an advisor to the Vatican Ambassador to the United Nations on matters of religious artifacts. I have no doubt that when he understands how serious this matter is, he will offer you his help. He flies in tomorrow, and I am to meet him here in Seville." He looked at his watch. "Now I have to leave. I have business to attend to here in Seville. I will contact you at your hotel when I know more, and I will leave a message for the Curator to ask him to offer you his assistance."

They thanked him as he stood up to leave.

"Bishop Santiago, there's just one more question I have for you," Gabriel stopped him.

"Yes?"

"Are you a member of Opus Dei?"

"Opus Dei? No, I am not. Would it make any difference?"

"Maybe not."

But Faith wasn't satisfied. "Which order do you belong to?"

"I am a member of the Society of Jesus."

"A Jesuit." Faith's voice was flat, but her suspicion evident.

"We're not all conspiracists, you know," he smiled. "I really am just a bureaucrat, despite our reputation."

"Of course, I didn't mean anything about your organization."

"No offence taken."

They went to sit down to finish their coffee, but he turned back as he was about to leave. "But my colleague may belong to that organization. I have no idea, so you will have to ask him. Does it make a difference?"

"No, not at all," Gabriel shrugged off the question.

"Very well. Perhaps we will meet tomorrow. I wish you luck with your investigation, and I hope you find this man before he kills any more poor souls."

\* \* \*

They had to know the whereabouts of the medallion. The lead detective was in Spain, so had he taken it with him? They had to know, and the answer would surely be in New York. The partner, Detective Estevez, he would know everything. He would be on suspension after that last killing, and that would make it all the easier. He wouldn't have his gun and so would be vulnerable. All he needed was to contact the right man for the job, someone who could subject him to a severe interrogation and then dispose of him. Yes, it would be easy. The detective was notorious in the city for his accidental shootings, and it would be assumed that a righteous citizen had killed him in revenge. He picked up the phone.

"I have a job for you. Carlo Estevez, New York cop. Yes, that's right, him. I have to know the whereabouts of medallion they found at the crime scene on East 34th Street. I need to know everything. Yes, when you're sure you've got it all, kill him, and make it look like a revenge by an angry citizen. He won't be armed, so you shouldn't have any problems. Call me when you know something. It has to be tonight."

# CHAPTER FOUR

That evening they found a restaurant and ate dinner while they discussed the case.

"I'm not sure about Bishop Santiago," Faith murmured.

Gabriel stared at her. "He seemed like a decent enough guy. What's your beef with him?"

She shrugged. "Call it a woman's intuition, but there's more to him that he's prepared to show us."

"He's a Jesuit, I believe they're the Vatican's spies, but that doesn't make him the enemy."

But she wasn't reassured. "Maybe, maybe not. All the same, I don't intend to trust him."

"Perhaps this UN guy will be someone you can trust, when he flies in tomorrow."

She pulled a face. "I told you, I was brought up a strict Presbyterian, and they said never to trust a Catholic. Old habits die hard."

"Right. I'll contact the Precinct in the morning and fix up the Spanish police side of things. There's something else, too. I need a gun."

She looked up at him. "What for?"

"The usual reason, to shoot back if anyone starts shooting at us."

She nodded. "Jonas is in the city, a pity we don't know where he is. He'd organize it for us. He can get anything."

"That's true, but Galina's pretty resourceful too. I've no doubt she can fix something up."

She brightened at the name of her best friend and business partner. "I'll give her a call on my cell as soon as we get back to our hotel room. I don't want to be overheard."

They finished their meal and ambled back through the still bustling streets of Seville. There was a fragrance in the air, almost like incense. Even in winter, some of the trees and bushes were in bloom, and it was a clear, balmy evening.

"It's a classy place to live," Faith murmured as she watched a pair of young Spaniards, a boy and a girl, cycle past, holding hands as they pedaled.

"It is that. But I looked up some of the history before we left. It was built on the proceeds of the Spanish Treasure galleons. They destroyed a South American culture to construct this place."

She nodded. "That's probably true, but it was a long time ago, and it's all in the past now."

"Is it? There's the link to our serial killer. It's not quite ancient history, not yet."

It was during the night that the dream came back to her. She was running through the tunnel, the footsteps pursued her, nearer and nearer. She heard the breathing, hoarse, labored as the man gulped in air. She ran for hours and hours, until she was so exhausted that she had to stop.

She realized she had a gun in her hand, but she was so tired. There was only one thing left to do. She crouched down in the shadows created by the dim lighting and held the gun ready to fire. The footsteps were loud, and he was almost on her, then the dark, evil shape was there, black and terrifying. She pointed the gun, emptied the magazine into his body, and it exploded in a shower of sparks and flames. She reeled back from the heat of the explosion, but when the smoke cleared the body had disappeared. She started to relax, and the images began to fade, but the nightmare wasn't over. The footsteps were still there. Another killer was stalking her. She heard his laughter, an echoing parody of a humor that chilled her very soul. The footsteps were still some distance away, but then they stopped. He must be looking at her, watching. She screwed up her eyes to see through the gloom. Yes, there he was, another dark shape, different. And there was something strange, very strange. He wore robes, ecclesiastical robes; religious robes, the robes of a monk or a priest. She saw his teeth as he leered at her through the gloom. Then he faded and disappeared.

She came awake suddenly, but she was in the hotel room in Seville with Gabriel asleep beside her. She wondered should she tell him about the dream. Perhaps not, he had enough to deal with. All she could do was watch. But she knew that the second man, the one in the robes, would present the greatest challenge. He was the alpha, the ringleader, and the man behind the ritual slaughters in New York City and now here in Seville. She instinctively knew that at some time in the future, she would meet this man, and that either she would kill him, or he would kill her.

In the morning, they woke to the sun streaming through the window. They took breakfast in the hotel, and halfway through Gabriel's cell rang. He went out into the lounge to answer it.

"De Sade."

"It's Kruger. How are you getting on?"

"Captain, I only just got here."

"Yeah, I know."

But there was something in his voice, something was badly wrong. "What's up?"

He heard Kruger's sigh across the line. "It's Carlo. He was killed last night."

"What! How did it happen?"

"He was stabbed to death. But before he died, he was tortured. His body is covered with burns and slashes. Our best guess is that they used a blowtorch."

Gabriel was numb, thinking of what his partner must have suffered, and how the suffering would go on now that he had left a wife and children.

"Any suspects?"

"None, but whoever did this was a pro, there's no doubt. How are things over there, have you made any progress?"

He brought the Captain up to date on his meeting with the Bishop, and the contact he'd had offered to make with the Curator.

"I need to speak to the locals, Captain. They've had a series of murders here that sound identical, so we'll have to swap notes. Can you put us in touch with them?"

"I'll get straight on it. We have good relations with the Policia Nacional, so I don't imagine there'll be a problem."

"I thought the cops here went by the name of Guardia Civil?"

Kruger chuckled. "It's complicated over there. They have the Guardia Civil who cover the rural beat, as well as smaller towns and traffic. Then there's the Policia Nacional, the National Police, who cover cities and larger towns. There is also the Policia Local, and they're everywhere. They cover stuff like parking, minor offences, and things like that. There is an element of turf wars between them sometimes, but it appears to work. You'll be in touch with the National Police as it's a city. I'll fix up an appointment and let you know when to go and see them. Keep me informed if you get anywhere."

"Yeah. Carlo's killing, you know it had to do with this case."

"The newspapers are putting it down to a vengeful citizen after those street people he shot."

"That's crap, Captain. Why would they torture him as well? They wanted information, period. The key to finding his killer will be with this case."

Kruger sighed. "You may be right, but I can't sell that to the Commissioner, not yet. He's trying to keep the serial investigation low-key. If it gets more publicity than it has already, the Mayor will bust his balls. Call me when you have anything, de Sade, and if there's anything that points to a suspect in New York, I'll set the dogs on him, believe me."

"What was that all about?"

Faith had come out of the dining room and stood nearby. He told her about Carlo.

"The poor man. He was a decent person, and he didn't deserve that. I overheard you say it was linked to this case?"

He nodded. "Without doubt. Before we go any further,

there's something we need to arrange."

"Yes, I know. I'll contact Galina, give me a few minutes."

She found a quiet corner and put the call through. Gabriel watched the whispered conversation to make certain there were no eavesdroppers. When she clicked off, she gave him a small smile.

"All arranged. We're to collect them from the Church of Saint Basil the Great."

He raised his eyebrows. "How did she manage to fix it up so quickly?"

"You know she used to carry out work for the Church that could be dangerous?"

He nodded. "Yes, I do."

"The department she worked for arranged for certain supplies to be kept for her in most of the major cities in Europe. They're still in place, and the parish priest is happy to help out. Like Galina, he was a member of the Russian Special Forces before he joined the priesthood. The killings in Chechnya were the end for him, and he turned his back on the military for good, but he is well aware of the nature of his fellow man, and so the request for guns will not come as anything of a surprise to him. She said he would call us later today."

"Good. I'll feel a lot happier with a gun under my coat."

"Me too," she grinned. "But I'll keep mine in my purse."

"Right."

She was a first class shot, and he had no concerns about her going armed. "I'll see if there's anything for us at reception, and I need to collect my cardigan from the room. It's still pretty cool outside."

She came out wearing a red cardigan over a white blouse and neat, short skirt. Gabriel admired her beauty and elegance for the thousandth time. Why on earth did she spend time with him? She could have her pick of the cream of society. Yet he'd asked her that question on more than one occasion. She'd simply replied that she loved him, and that was an end to it. They set out for the center of Seville.

The Bishop had been as good as his word. There were two small leather identification wallets waiting for them, bearing the gold seal of the Congregation for the Doctrine of the Faith. Inside were there two ID passes with a space for a photo. They were signed and stamped 'Vatican, Roma'.

"Impressive," Faith murmured. "With these, we can go anywhere."

"Yeah, if we track down the perp, we can even follow him into the Vatican itself."

"I wouldn't push our luck too far," she grinned. "Shall we make a start?"

"Good idea. Lets' go."

The Cathedral was vast, and almost a small town in its own right. They were both fascinated by the tomb of Christopher Columbus, and no less intrigued by the bell tower, the Giralda. They started towards it, but a security guard stopped them.

"Americans?"

"That's right," Gabriel replied.

"You cannot go this way. You must buy a ticket and follow the directions for tourists."

De Sade took out his ID pass. "We're not tourists."

The man looked at the pass, and his eyes widened. "The Vatican. I am sorry, please go ahead. Let me know if you need anything."

"Yeah, we'll do that, buddy. Thanks."

They started the long climb to the top of the Giralda.

"These ramps," Gabriel mentioned to Faith as they marched upwards. "Why not steps? It seems strange."

She had brought along a guidebook and read it as they climbed. "They're for horses."

"Horses?"

"That's right, the Bishop mentioned something about it. I guess those old Moorish architects knew what they were doing. It sure beats climbing up hundreds of steps."

"Provided you have a horse."

"There is that," she agreed.

The view at the top was spectacular with all of Seville laid out in front of them, bordered by the Guadalquivir River. When they looked up, they could see the statue of Faith.

"There she is," de Sade exclaimed. "All we need to do now is find out what that hidden inscription meant."

"Do you have the medallion with you?" she asked him.

"Sure."

He took it out of his coat pocket and handed it to her. She shuddered as she took it, closing her eyes.

"What's wrong?" he asked, concerned that it seemed to have had such a powerful effect on her.

For several long minutes she stood, her eyes shut tight. Then she opened them and focused on him.

"Here, take it. There is violence and death associated with this object."

"Yeah, it would have that kind of a history."

"Not in the past. I told you before we left that I knew you would come to Seville. There are men here who will cause you harm. I can't see their faces, but it will happen."

"So they'll be hunting for the gold, I guess. If it exists, and we don't know that yet."

"Oh, it exists. I don't know exactly where, but it's here. All we need do is find it."

"Faith, we're not here for the treasure. Remember, I'm on official NYPD business, looking for clues that will lead us to a serial killer."

"The man you're looking for is involved in the hunt for the gold, so if you find one, you find the other."

He nodded. "You're right. I guess the first question is where to start."

"Perhaps I can help you."

They turned to see the newcomer who'd stepped out onto the roof terrace. He was quite short and frail looking, and his face was slightly red from having completed the long climb up the Giralda ramps. It occurred to Gabriel that it might have been for men like this that they built it with ramps for horses. He stared at them with piercing blue eyes, his most striking feature, perhaps his only feature. He was prematurely bald, and what little hair he had left was on the sides. It was left long, so that the general effect was of a monk. On his upper lip he wore a thin mustache. Both of them assumed he was a Cathedral administrator, which was exactly what he looked like.

"That's okay, thanks. We're fine."

He showed the newcomer his Cathedral pass. The man nodded and drew out his own pass.

"Inspector Javier Garcia, National Police. They said I'd find you up here. I've been assigned to assist you with the enquiry into the serial killings that seem to parallel your case in America. Could you tell me how far your investigation has got?"

Gabriel was startled for a few moments. Then he started to explain the discovery of the bodies in New York City. Garcia took out a notebook and started to write, nodding his head as Gabriel continued. The Spaniard nodded to himself.

"Yes, it could well be the same person who commits these crimes. One thing I do not understand, what brought you here to Seville?"

Gabriel took out the medallion. "This. It was found at the burial site in New York, and we're fairly certain the perp dropped it. There is a hidden inscription that mentions the Tomb of Faith at this Cathedral."

"Perp? What is this?" Garcia asked.

The New York detective realized that he'd need to cut out the American police slang. "Yeah, sorry, it means perpetrator. They guy who did the crime."

"Ah, I see. So it's something to do with the treasure."

They looked at him open mouthed. "How did you know about the treasure?" Gabriel asked him.

The nondescript little man actually chuckled. "Everyone in Seville knows of the treasure, Phillip the Second's stolen treasure. Ever since I can remember, people have been looking through thousands of old manuscripts for clues about its whereabouts."

"Where are these documents?" Faith asked him. "Do they have them here in the Cathedral by any chance?"

"Almost. They are next door, in the building known as the Archive of the Indies. The archive is a repository of historical documents, such as maps and books, about the Conquistadors and the discovery of the Americas. You can see it from here."

They looked over the parapet to the building next door,

a vast structure that lay only feet away from the western side of the Cathedral.

"It's a big place," Gabriel noted. "There must be a lot of documents to cover in there."

Garcia nodded. "That is true. And of the tens of thousands of documents, I suspect that all have been examined at some time by those who have hunted for the treasure."

"Including the killer," Faith exclaimed. "If he's been in there many times, he will have shown up on CCTV camera."

"Yes, that's true. But sadly, there is no CCTV system in that building."

They stood for a moment lost for words. They'd come halfway around the world, yet now they were here they were faced with an impossible task.

"Inspector, the statue of Faith. We were told by Bishop Santiago that the statue above us is a copy, and that the real statue is the one outside the Cathedral building."

"Yes, that's true, in the Plaza de Triunfo. You think that can help us?"

Gabriel wondered by us did he mean the combined NYPD and Policia Nacional inquiry, or his own more local investigation. But it was almost certain that solving one would solve the other, and he decided to let Garcia handle things his way. It was his country, after all.

"The Tomb of Faith could well be hidden beneath it."

"Yes, but beneath which statue, the original or the replica that is at the top of the Giralda? What is the date of that medallion?"

"It's from the 1930s, or so our ME believes."

"In that case, it could be either. Hernán Ruiz added the

belfry with the statue of Faith in 1568."

Faith interrupted him. "It's the statue at ground level, the original one."

Garcia looked at her intently. "How could you possibly know this?"

"We looked at it yesterday when we first got here. I felt something, but I'm not sure what. Something evil is buried down below it, somewhere."

"I see." He was nodding slowly, trying to understand how she'd come by her information. "Well, you're right about one thing. There is something evil down there. Eight bodies were found last year."

"So I understand. But the bodies were removed when they were discovered, and what I'm referring to is now. There is something that you haven't uncovered."

He looked doubtful. "I assure you, we checked out that underground space thoroughly, and there is nothing else down there."

"It is there," Faith said in a voice that carried absolute conviction.

Garcia sighed. "Well, you have those Vatican passes, so there is nothing to stop you looking. But I can assure you, you're wrong. Is there anything I can do to help?"

Those documents you spoke of," Gabriel reminded him. "In the Archive of the Indies. Is there any way you can find out if anyone has spent an inordinate amount of time looking at them? There must be records of who has looked at particular documents, a visitor's register. It could give us a name."

Inspector Garcia smiled. "An excellent idea. I will check it out myself, and perhaps I can prepare a list of names."

"Maybe they'll let you have someone to help," Faith

suggested. "I mean, if there's a lot of ground to cover."

Garcia looked at her with a sad expression. "I am afraid there is no question of me asking for help."

Gabriel looked at him, and something about the man's tone suggested more than a simple staff shortage.

"Why not? What's the problem?"

The Spaniard looked away, his gaze taking in the whole of the City of Seville that lay spread beneath the tower on which they stood. Finally, he looked back at de Sade. "They are currently investigating me. I believe the expression is, I am under a cloud."

"Yeah, that's tough. What did you do?"

"Do? I did nothing. But the reason for the investigation is that someone suspected me of murder."

Faith looked at him with her eyebrows raised high. "The serial killings, the bodies buried beneath the Cathedral."

He inclined his head. "Yes. But I am innocent. I had nothing to do with it. I want to catch whoever was responsible for this crime. Violence against women is a foul crime, and it is one that here in Spain we are working to prevent. Spain overhauled the law in 2004 to make it easier for women to seek legal help for violence against them. We strengthened orders for abusers to stay away from victims, and aggressive behavior, like issuing death threats, became a criminal offense.

I can tell you that in the past six years, judges awarded special protection to almost 141,000 women, or 73 percent of the requests. And I have worked hard to support these new measures, so you can imagine how I feel about this accusation. I was pulled from active duty and now carry out administrative work only, until I am cleared."

They both stared at the short, pale man, lost for words.

So the Policia Nacional had assigned them a detective who himself was suspected of the crime they were investigating. Finally, Gabriel nodded. "Very well, thanks for telling us, Inspector. So we'll leave you with the document side in the Archive of the Indies. We'll start a search of the Cathedral basement as soon as we've met with the Curator. Perhaps we can meet up later and discuss progress."

He nodded. "That's good. There is a good coffee bar in the square, and it is called Cafe Cafe. Shall we meet there at four?"

"That's fine. Cafe Cafe?" Gabriel smiled. "A strange name. Cafe means coffee, right?"

"That is true. But here in Spain, Cafe Cafe means something more. Real coffee, the best, freshly brewed. And Cafe Cafe lives up to its name."

"That suits us, Inspector. Four o'clock, Cafe Cafe."

"And another thing, the Inspector continued. "My name is Javier."

"I'm Gabriel, and this is Faith, my partner."

"Faith?" He looked at her. "Like the statue on the Giralda?"

"Yes."

They shook hands, and Faith held onto the Spanish detective's hand. "Javier, I have one question before you go."

"Yes?"

"Did you murder those girls?"

He was shocked at first, but she held his eyes in a fierce stare while she waited for an answer. Then he shook his head. "No, of course not." He looked angry that she had even asked the question.

She gave him a small smile. "Thank you, Javier, I had

to know."

He shrugged. "It is no problem. But just because I denied it does not mean I am innocent."

"No, but I know you are innocent, and that is what matters."

"You know? How can you be so certain?"

Gabriel touched him on the shoulder, and the detective looked around. "What?"

"Javier, Faith just knows. It's not something I can explain."

"That's not good enough. How does she know?"

"The same way she'll help us find the solution to the Tomb of Faith clue on that medallion."

He smiled, not believing them entirely, but before she could speak, Faith went pale.

"The Curator, is he a German by any chance?"

"Yes, he is, a monk employed by the Vatican."

"Then he is here, and we have met him before. His name is Father Sebastian von Braun."

Gabriel felt as if he'd been kicked in the guts. "Not the same bastard we tangled with in Nogales?"

She nodded. "Yes, the same."

Javier look confused. "But, how did you know his name, and that he had arrived in the Cathedral?"

It was Gabriel's turn to sigh. "It's a long story, my friend. I told you, she just knows. But this job just got a whole heap more complicated. We'll see you tomorrow and explain. In the meantime, we'd better meet the 'Mad Monk' and get it over with."

They left the policeman and retraced their steps to the ground floor, a lot easier going down the ramps than going up. The door to the Curator's office was nearby. Gabriel knocked, and they went in. Sat behind the desk was the monk Faith had battled with in Nogales. He'd tried to hide his real mission on that occasion. This time none of them were in any doubt as to his loyalties. He was a Vatican specialist on religious artifacts and with a brief to recover those valuables he deemed should belong to Rome. Of more importance was the way he went about his work. He had no scruples whatsoever. None. He looked up from a document he was examining and stared at them through icy blue eyes framed by round, metal glass; his expression cold. Even sat in the chair, it was obvious he was a tall man. He was also very gaunt and thin, which made him look even taller. He had tonsured gray hair and had grown a matching gray beard that framed his lined, leathery face.

"Brother Sebastian," Faith greeted him. "I'm surprised to see you here in Spain. How are you?"

His expression didn't change. "What do you want?"

So he still bore a grudge. That was interesting, Gabriel thought to himself. He stepped up to the desk. "This is a police investigation into a serial killer. The person hid the bodies in this Cathedral, as you well know, in an underground space. What I want, and what the Cathedral authorities want, is for you to cooperate."

"Yes, I know that you have already deceived the Bishop into offering his help. But I know nothing of this. I can do nothing."

"That's not good enough, Sebastian. You can start by showing us the room where the bodies were found."

He reached inside his desk and took out a key. "The room is locked. Here, take the key. Is there anything else?"

"Yes. I want you to show us this place yourself. We need someone who can tell us about how things work in the Cathedral."

The monk glared at him. "I have no time for that kind of nonsense, and besides, there is nothing I can do."

"Did you kill these people, Brother Sebastian?"

He went bright red with anger. He looked away until finally his eyes settled back on de Sade. "Of course not. Now get out of my office!"

The monk stared at them for a few, long moments. Finally, Gabriel nodded to Faith. "Let's go, we're wasting our time here."

They started out through the door but stopped when his voice called to them.

"You won't find it, you know."

Gabriel and Faith turned. "Find what?" the detective asked.

"The gold."

So that was it, and it explained part of the reason for his hostility.

"We're not after any gold," Gabriel said quietly. "All I want is to find out the identity of the serial killer and put him behind bars."

"I don't believe you," he spat back. He turned to Faith. "After you stole the Church's property in Mexico, I have no doubt you are planning on no less a theft in this place. I shall make certain you don't get away with it again."

"We bought that property. The parish priest sold it to us," Faith tried to reason with him. "There was no theft on our part. You, however, did try to steal that artifact."

"The Catholic Church has control of Catholic property all over the world. It was not his to sell."

She smiled. "That is not Church law and never has been. But it is as my partner says, we are here only because of the serial killer. The gold, if there is any gold, has no interest for us."

He waved a hand of dismissal. "We shall see. Now leave my office."

They left and went to find the chamber where the bodies had been hidden. In the event, they had to ask a Cathedral security man the way. The basement room was accessed through a door off the north transept marked 'private'. A light switch showed a long, tunnel ahead of them. They followed it to the end where a heavy oak door fitted with iron hinges and bolts was securely fastened. Gabriel inserted the key, turned on the light, and they went in. Both of them gagged immediately as the room stank of strong disinfectant. And yet underneath, there was still the faint odor of rotting meat. Faith left the door open, and they inspected the death chamber.

\* \* \*

The sweet, sour stench of dead bodies. It reminded him that there'd been more than enough dead bodies during his service in Afghanistan, and most he came across were soldiers of one side or the other. But he vividly recalled a car bomb incident next to a coffee shop where they'd been enjoying some quiet down time. Some of the soldiers would go there for coffee in the mornings, and there were a lot of civilians in the area too. The car just drove up and exploded, indiscriminately killing more than thirty people, both soldiers and civilians. He clearly remembered the body parts flying into the air, punctuated by the screams of the wounded and terrified. Gabriel and Jonas had instinctively dived for cover when the initial blast occurred, but as the dust settled, they gripped their weapons and went looking for the enemy. When they saw the destroyed car and knew it was a car bomb, it became a search for survivors. Gabriel picked up a brightly colored object and recoiled when he saw it was a red shoe, a young woman's shoe. Her foot was still inside it. He never found the rest of her. She was just another innocent, like these victims of the serial killer, not guilty of anything other than being in the wrong place at the wrong time. On that occasion, the bomber had died in the blast. This time, the perp was still alive and still hunting, still killing. This time, he'd get him.

* * *

"I'll need a photo of how it looked when they discovered it," Gabriel muttered, almost to himself.

"They were stacked over there in the corner," Faith told him. "Just like the photos I saw of the New York crime scene."

"You're sure?"

She nodded. "Yes, I'm sure. Can't you feel it from over there? It's almost a scream."

"No, I can't. I'll leave that hocus pocus stuff to you. But if it's true, that ties it strongly to my case in New York."

"Except that you don't know who the killer is."

"I'll know that soon, and I already have some ideas."

"Who would that be?" she asked him.

"We're looking for the link to someone with a strong motive in finding the gold."

"Everyone wants to find a hoard of gold, that's not unique," Faith objected.

"But not everyone sees it as a command from God to locate it at all costs."

"Brother Sebastian? Surely not?"

"Why not? He has links to New York City through his advisory post with the UN, and he covets religious artifacts for the glory of his Church. He's a total nut job."

She smiled. "I can't imagine the prosecutor accepting 'nut job' to prove motive for a crime."

He shrugged. "Maybe not, but I'm keeping him at the top of my list."

They explored the room, but there was little to help Gabriel. Except that it bore uncanny similarities with the New York basement, lending support to the link between the killings in both countries.

"There's a problem I have with this, and something doesn't make sense. How did he get the bodies down here?"

"The same way we came, through the cathedral," Faith replied. "How else?"

"That's not what I meant. The only way in here is through the door in the transept, and in full view of one of the largest cathedrals in Christendom. How did he know he wouldn't be seen, dragging a corpse through the nave, which is incredibly public? Or he brought them across the bema, the space in the center of the transept."

"But, that's…"

"Exactly," he nodded. "That's only possible for members of staff. I'll have a chat with Inspector Garcia. We'll need an ultraviolet lamp to detect any blood residue."

"The place has been cleaned a thousand times since the bodies were dumped. They must do it every day."

"Maybe you're right, but I'd like to know the route

he took to bring them in here. That'll narrow down the suspect list."

They left the evil-smelling room and walked out into the nave of the Cathedral, then out into the fresh air of the Avenida de la Constitution in the main center of Seville. Both stood taking great gulps of fresh air to rid themselves of the rank stench of the death room."

"I need some coffee, somewhere outside would be good," Gabriel muttered.

Faith smiled. "We're in Seville, that's describes just about every coffee bar in the city. There's a square up ahead, let's go there."

They started walking to the nearby square. Gabriel turned to speak to Faith. "I guess we'll need a full list of the Cathedral employees with access at night. It's the only way he could have got the bodies in there."

"You're right, I can't see..."

Then she screamed as a pushcart loaded with heavy crates rammed into both of them. Gabriel managed to stay on his feet, but Faith was thrown to the ground. He looked at the cart, and a man was pushing it at speed away from them. He went to give chase but whipped around as Faith screamed again.

"Gabriel, the tram!"

He looked back. She had been thrown across the tram tracks, and a huge tram was bearing relentlessly down on her. He rushed to help her up and out of the way.

"I can't, my foot is jammed in the rails."

He looked down. Her foot had wedged with the force of her tumbling to the ground and wedged between the two narrow rails. The tram was nearer now and showed no sign of stopping. He waved to the driver, but the man was looking at a document, presumably his schedule for the day. Gabriel heaved and heaved again at the trapped foot, but it wouldn't ease out of the two iron rails that held it fast. The tram had to stop! He jumped to his feet and ran towards it, waving his arms. He was only a few yards from it, but there was no sign of it stopping, and in seconds it would run over Faith. He stood his ground, in the center of the tracks. The guy would have to stop, have to. The tram came nearer and nearer, and still the driver hadn't seen him. But he wasn't getting out of the way. People were shouting at the driver, but still he hadn't noticed. There were only feet left, maybe two seconds, before it ran into Gabriel. So be it, but he wouldn't desert Faith. He waited. Then the gunshots rang out. Three shots, fired in quick succession. The tram driver looked up, alarmed, saw Gabriel only four feet in front of his tram, and jammed on the brakes. At the last second, de Sade jumped out of the way as the tram slid to a stop several feet past where he'd been standing, but still six feet from where Faith lay trapped. Behind her was a man with a gun in his hand and a wisp of smoke spiraling out of the barrel. Inspector Javier Garcia, of the Spanish Policia Nacional. Gabriel carefully helped Faith to maneuver her foot from between the rails. They stood up and de Sade nodded at the policeman.

"You saved her life, Javier."

The Spaniard looked grave. "What happened? How did she fall between the tracks?"

"She didn't fall. She was pushed." Gabriel glanced around the square, but the cart and its owner were long gone. "It was a guy with a loaded pushcart. He rammed us to push us in front of the tram. Then he disappeared."

"Are you sure it wasn't just an accident? It seems unlikely

that someone would want to kill you."

Gabriel nodded. "Yeah, maybe you're right. Just an accident, but I'm glad you happened along at the right time."

"I was on my way to the Cathedral, a matter I have to follow up with Brother Sebastian. Are you hurt, Faith?"

She shook her head. "No, I'm fine, thanks. At least, I still have two legs, even if my hose are ripped. I think I lost a heel in that rail too, but I can replace those. The leg may have presented a problem. You saved my life."

"It was nothing," he shrugged. "I'm glad I was able to help. Is there anything you wish me to do?"

She smiled. "You've done enough. We won't keep you any longer, and I have to find a shoe shop."

"Very well, we will meet as planned for coffee?"

"That's fine," Gabriel replied. "And I'd watch Sebastian if I were you."

Javier met his eyes. "You think he is connected to the crime?"

"It's a possibility, yes."

"Very well, I will be careful in my dealings with him. I'll see you later, hasta luego."

"Yeah, adios."

Faith gave her partner an odd glance as they walked away. "You don't trust him, do you?"

Gabriel shook his head. "No."

"Because he was under suspicion for the killings?"

"Maybe."

They walked on. Faith understood that for the time being she'd have to be satisfied with his taut responses. What was on his mind?

# CHAPTER FIVE

He wondered if it was too soon to save another soul. The city had more than its share of fallen women. It was a righteous act to commend their souls to God, and to end the cycle of misery and despair that would consign them to hell. It would be a risk, now that the authorities had discovered where he stored the bodies. Both places. In fact, the coincidence was astonishing. Two cities, thousands of miles apart, and they had connected the crimes. All because of that damned medallion. Yes, the medallion. That was another piece of unfinished business. When Phillip the Second's gold had been stolen from the treasure ship returning from the Americas, it had been intended for the glorification of God. He needed to locate the gold himself, before the police uncovered it. They knew it existed, and of that there could be no doubt. They also knew there was an important clue hidden on the medallion. If he hadn't lost it when he was hiding that last body in New York, he could have deciphered it and uncovered its secrets. But there was no future in frustrating over what might or might not have been. He had to act, and act decisively. The medallion had to be recovered from Gabriel de Sade, and that witch who accompanied him had to die. She was too dangerous, much too dangerous. There was so much to do, and so little time to do it. What should he do first? Perhaps he would receive divine inspiration if he carried out the Lord's work to His satisfaction. Yes, tonight he would find another poor soul to save. He felt himself becoming hard as he always did when he began to plan these tasks. He slipped his hand down and massaged his penis, feeling the warm, thrilling sensations surge through his body. Then he withdrew his hand. There would be time for that later. It would be the reward for carrying out his work, as usual. But he could feel his heartbeat quicken as his brain sent certain signals to his nervous system. He knew he would float on a sea of heavenly anticipation until the job was done, and he carried out the final act of self-gratification.

In the meantime, there was still the matter of the two Americans. Perhaps he would find out exactly what they were up to and who they saw. It would make everything easier later on when they needed to deal with them. Where would they go first? They were both Eastern Orthodox blasphemers, so of course they would go to their cursed church here in Seville. He would wait in a café nearby. They were certain to arrive at sometime during the day. If he failed to find them there, he would have to return to the Cathedral, but it would be better to follow them from another location, and one where he wouldn't be recognized.

* * *

Gabriel and Faith found a pavement café and ordered coffee. When it came, it was fresh, strong and delicious.

"How are you feeling now?" Gabriel asked his partner.

"Better. But ask me when I've bought new shoes and pantyhose."

She'd contrived to slip off her shoes and hose, walking barefoot to the nearby café.

"It was a coincidence, Javier Garcia being there when it all happened," Gabriel mused.

"Come on, you don't think he set it up, and then prevented it from happening? It could even have been an accident, but Javier? No way."

"Maybe, maybe not. This is all very odd. There's another thing, if it wasn't an accident, then who were they trying to kill? Me, or you?"

She shrugged. "Or maybe both of us."

"No, not both. It was too clumsy. It was either one of us, or a setup to lead us in the wrong direction."

She raised her eyebrows. "That sounds too conspiracist. Either it was an accident or attempted murder, period."

He nodded. "I guess so. We need to look up that priest contact of Galina's, and then we should to head back to the Cathedral. I've got a few ideas I need to check out. Something about the whole setup just doesn't gel."

"I need to do some shopping first," she reminded him.

"Yeah, sorry. There are a hundred shoe shops around here, so let's take a few minutes out and get you fixed up."

It took an hour and a half before she decided she was satisfied with a pair of Gucci low-heeled sandals and several pairs of hose. He'd had to look twice at the price tag on the shoes, almost two week's salary for a New York cop, but for the wealthy daughter of the Director of

Central Intelligence, it was probably a budget purchase. They left the store and checked the map. It was time to rendezvous with the priest at the Church of Saint Basil the Great.

The priest opened the door of his house, a small, stone building situated next to the church. He was a short man wearing black, plastic rimmed eyeglasses on his pale skinned face. His hair was dark and unkempt, and he had a long beard. With the black cassock he wore to his ankles, he could only have been an Orthodox priest. Before he asked them in, he demanded to see their passports.

"I'm sorry, but I have a number of people who call here, and not everyone is happy about the presence of an Orthodox Church in a Catholic country."

They showed him the documents, and the man showed them through to his study. He introduced himself as Manuel Guzman. It was quite small, very dusty, dark and gloomy, except for a brass lamp that threw a spread of light over the many documents littering his desk. He gestured at them. "My hobby, I'm afraid. I am an avid historian, and I am working on a history of this city. Seville is such a fascinating place."

"Yeah, we're beginning to see that," Gabriel replied.

He looked up sharply, detecting the note of cynicism. "You've had trouble since you came? Is that why you wish to carry guns?"

"Something like that, but we're also expecting trouble."

"Yes, this is a turbulent city. I'd better show you what I have for you."

He unlocked a drawer in his desk and brought out a small, inlaid walnut box. He opened the lid and inside were two guns. They lay on a soft piece of dark red cloth.

He lifted out the first one and handed it to Gabriel.

"This is a Llama Max-1 pistol, Spanish made, similar to your Colt .45 automatic. It is chambered for a 9 mm Parabellum round, and the magazine carries nine rounds, I believe. There are also two spare magazines in the case, as well as a box of 9mm bullets."

Gabriel slid out the clip and pulled back the slide to check the action. It was satisfactory, and he stuffed it into his jacket pocket. "This looks fine, thanks."

The man nodded. "Good. The other pistol is a rather smaller Llama model, the model XVII, in a .22 caliber. It carries a six round magazine, and I also managed to acquire two spare magazines. I trust it will be satisfactory for you," he said to Faith.

She picked it up and expertly checked the action and the clip. "It's fine. I can fit this in my purse."

He smiled. "Your friend Galina told me the kind of weapon you would both prefer, so I tried to get as close as I could to what she said you wanted. I only hope you never have to use them."

Gabriel stared at him, thinking of the accident earlier. "If we do have to use them, the opposition will be the ones who hope we don't use them, believe me."

The priest read the anger in his eyes correctly. "So you have already had trouble."

He nodded and told him about the tram accident.

"You were lucky that policeman came when he did," the priest observed.

Gabriel didn't reply.

"Thank you for helping us, Father," Faith smiled at the priest. "We have to leave now as we have a meeting soon."

"You're more than welcome, and anything else you

need, please come and see me. There are not many places Orthodox Christians can seek help from in Seville, or Spain, for that matter. I understand you were once a nun."

"Only for short time, Father. But it was a wonderful experience."

"Yes, I'm sure. Don't forget, I am always available if you need help."

They left the priest's house, blinking in the sunshine. Gabriel felt fully dressed, now that he was armed. It was time to meet with Javier Garcia and devise a plan of action. One that the Spanish detective would be a part of, and another he would know nothing about.

\* \* \*

He'd already paid the bill and watched the Americans leave the priest's house, disappearing into the crowded Seville streets. He needed to know what they'd learned from the priest, and what could he have told them. The man was a well-known local historian, so could he have uncovered a location for the gold? Perhaps not, but he had to find out for sure. He got up, crossed the street, and knocked on the door. The priest answered.

"Yes?

"Father Guzman? I wonder if I could have a word with you.

"What about?"

"New information has come to light about the sixteenth century treasure that is supposedly hidden in the Cathedral. I wonder if I could ask your opinion."

"Phillip the Second's treasure? That's interesting, please come in."

The priest turned around and led the way into the house. He'd only taken three steps when he felt a massive pain to his head, and then he blacked out. When he recovered consciousness, he saw that he was in his study. He struggled to move his limbs, but the pain of his bonds was terrible. The visitor watched him from the chair behind the desk.

"You can struggle all you like, but you've been tied with thin bailing wire. All you'll manage to do is slice into your wrists and ankles."

Guzman slumped in defeat. "Alright, what do you want?"

"Tell me why the Americans came to see you. That is all I need to know, and then I will release you."

"The Americans? You mean the two people who just left here? They are merely Orthodox Christians. It was a courtesy visit, no more than that."

He looked at his captor. He didn't recognize him, but he'd seen the type before. Any man who had lived through the worst of the Franco years in Spain, when the Guardia Civil, the paramilitary police, could and did seize any suspect off the street and torture them into a confession, had seen men like this. And that was the real point. The man had let him see his face. He knew he would not survive this encounter. So be it, he'd had a good life, dying to save others in a just cause would be worthwhile. His reward would come in a later life. The man sneered.

"I asked you what they wanted. Why did they come to see you?"

Guzman shook his head. "I have nothing more to say to you."

His captor smiled, beginning to enjoy the encounter. And what was to come.

"Oh, I'm sure I can prove you wrong, Father. You'll tell me, I can assure you."

He drew out a long, razor sharp filleting knife and used it to slice down the front of the priest's cassock, not caring about the thin, red line of blood that started to ooze out as the knife cut through to the skin. The blade kept moving downwards, lower and lower, until the point was above the priest's pants, next to his genitals.

"Priests don't have any need of these, do they?"

"We have none of that Catholic celibacy nonsense," Guzman snarled at him. "Orthodox priests have relationships with women, and they do not bugger little boys in the darkness of the confessional. Arrgghhhhh!"

The man had stabbed down with the knife, angry at the man's description of men of God. The thin blade had gone straight in and through the scrotum, pinning it to the wooden chair.

"Because a few priests have erred does not make the rest of them sinners. You should watch your tongue."

He watched the priest struggle to fight the pain. He knew it must be terrible. And he had to work quickly, blood was pouring out of the cut onto the floor. He dragged out the knife, and another piercing scream resounded through the dusty old room.

"You must tell me, what did they want? What are they going to do?"

The priest stared into his eyes, and through the awful pain he managed a smile. "I forgive you, my son. You will surely go to hell for what you are doing, and what you have undoubtedly done already. I hope and trust you do not suffer unduly for the terrible crimes you have committed on earth."

His eyes closed, and his tormentor felt a terrible rage course through him. How dare this fool, this blasphemer, suggest that what he did was sinful? In a fit of rage, he slashed the blade through the man's neck, cutting his throat from ear to ear. When he realized what he'd done, he screamed in rage, "You fucking priest, you ruined everything!"

The blood spurted out of the terrible wound in his neck and splashed on the floor. A sigh of escaping breath came out of the priest's mouth. He was dead. Damn! Now he'd never know what they'd discussed. But at least he could send a message. It was time these people knew who they were dealing with. He released the wires holding the limbs of the corpse to the chair and began the gruesome task of dismembering the body. These people did not deserve for their bodies to pass into the next life intact, and it was important that he made it clear how undeserving they were. He could think of nothing more powerful than separating their body parts, so it was obvious to whoever received them that they were unworthy. Some would say he was mad. He knew that, but he was quite sane, and quite able to admit to himself that he enjoyed it. Enjoyed doing the Lord's work. What could be wrong with that? Finally, he stood back to examine his handiwork. Body parts lay stacked in a heap in the pool of blood that had collected in the center of the study. Yes, it was perfect. And tonight he would allow himself the relief of an orgasm; once he'd carried out the task he'd set himself.

\* \* \*

The café was filled with customers, enjoying the afternoon

sunshine and the chance for chatting with their friends over endless cups of fresh coffee. Inspector Javier Garcia had a surprise for Gabriel and Faith.

"My friends, I have arranged for a visit to a bull farm just outside the city. They breed and train toros bravos, fighting bulls for the ring, and I think you will find the color and the traditions very interesting. When you have finished your coffee, we can go there, if that is acceptable to you."

"A bull farm?" De Sade could hardly believe what he was suggesting. "Javier, if it's all the same to you, we'd sooner pursue the investigation here rather than waste any time. Maybe when our work is finished, we can go then."

"Ah, but this is not just a tourist visit. I know that you wish to proceed as fast as possible, as do I. It is why we are going. The owner of the farm, Diego Montalban, has put a lot of resources into uncovering the secret of the lost gold. It is possible he will be able to give us some clues that will help in our search for the killer."

"In that case we'll go, it could be useful." He looked at Faith. "Unless you have any other ideas. Or intuitions."

"Not really, no."

But he looked at her keenly. Her face was troubled, and her ability to perceive what others could not was a sense that he was learning to trust more and more.

"Is there any problem?"

She shook her head. "No, we should go."

Javier's car was parked nearby with a 'Policia Nacional' sign in the windscreen. It was a Range Rover SUV, a luxury four by four. They made no comment, but it was an expensive car for a humble Spanish police inspector. The journey was fast and comfortable, and from the cultured, ancient city center the road took them through a cluttered industrial belt that ringed the city. Then the countryside appeared, and within minutes, they entered the white columns marking the entrance to the farm. Javier parked near a corral in which several men were exercising a huge, black bull. One of them came over; a tall, powerfully built man, dressed in work jeans, hand tooled boots and a loose silk shirt. Most Spaniards were dark, a legacy of the mixed Mediterranean and Moorish ancestry, but this man was blonde, with pale skin and piercing blue eyes. He shook hands warmly with Garcia.

"Javier, good of you to come."

"Diego, my friend, nice to see you again. These are my friends and colleagues, Miss Faith Ward and Gabriel de Sade. They are both American."

He shook hands with them. "So, you are searching for treasure, are you?"

"No, we're looking for the sick pervert who's been murdering women and dumping their dismembered bodies in the Cathedral basement. But it may be someone who is hunting for the treasure too, and so we need to know more about what we're up against."

Montalban grimaced. "I will help you, of course. But I doubt I know much more than you, which is that it has never been found."

Gabriel nodded. "The question is, who is looking for it? That would give me a short list of possible suspects."

He stared at de Sade. "In that case, I would be on that list. I have done research amongst documents and plans held in the Archive of the Indies, and I have searched the Cathedral many times." His stare turned into a grin. "But I assure you I killed no one during my search, unless you include the odd bull, of course. Do you know anything about bullfighting?"

They both shook their heads, and Faith shuddered. "No, I do not, and I have no wish to."

He gave her a curious glance. "Many women are fascinated by the sport. You should be more open-minded. Whether they prefer the corrida itself or the magnificent men who fight, or even the smell of blood and death, I have no idea."

"Sport? How is it a sport, when the bull has no chance to survive the match? I'd call it butchery."

"Would you?" he murmured. "Perhaps I can persuade you otherwise. You see this bull my vaqueros have been putting through its paces in the corral, it has had a comfortable and pleasant life. It will die in the ring, there is no doubt, but surely it is better than the normal lot of cattle? Unless you are a vegetarian, naturally, that would be different."

"No, I'm not a vegetarian. I just don't like slaughtering these animals in such a cruel way."

He smiled. "It is no more cruel that what they normally endure. Come and see my prize bull. This one is due for the ring at Easter."

They went to the side of the corral. The bull was alone in the corral, and the vaqueros had disappeared.

"This is a Miura fighting bull, and they have been bred in Seville for hundreds of years. There are certain strains of bull that have a marked ability to learn quicker from what goes on in the arena. This is one such bull, and it will be a magnificent fight when he comes up against the matador."

"Have you ever fought a bull, Senor Montalban?" she

asked him.

"Indeed, many times." He tapped on his leg and his hand made a solid thud. "I lost this leg in one such fight. On that occasion the bull was too good for me."

"What happened to it?"

"Sometimes, the bull will be indultado, or 'pardoned', meaning his life its spared due to outstanding behavior in the bullring, leading the audience to petition the president of the ring with white handkerchiefs. The bullfighter joins the petition, as it is a great honor to have a bull one has fought pardoned. The bull is then returned to the ranch where it will live out its days in the fields, and in most cases will mate with the cows. This was the case with the bull that gored my leg that day."

"Senor Montalban," Gabriel interrupted. "This is all very interesting, but I need some help with this investigation. Could you draw up a list of people you know to be searching for the treasure?"

The man stared at him for a moment and smiled. "I will see to it now. Javier, come with me. There is another matter I would discuss with you. Senor de Sade, Senorita Ward, if you would wait here, you will be able to enjoy the sunshine and watch my magnificent bull at play during the last days of its life." He smiled again. "But I caution you, do not go into the corral. It would not be a good way to learn the art of bullfighting."

He laughed, patted Javier on the shoulder, and led him away.

"I don't trust him," Faith muttered. "Misogynistic macho bastard."

Gabriel smiled. "He did come on a bit strong, but that doesn't make him a killer."

"Except of bulls," she retorted. "Did you notice how friendly he is with Javier?"

"I did, yes. But they are old friends."

"Or maybe they're mixed up in something."

He shrugged. "It's possible, but I doubt it. I'll ask Javier to look into any visits Diego may have made to New York recently. That would help to keep him on the list or eliminate him."

"Unless there are two killers, one here and one in New York."

He nodded. "I have thought of that, but the medallion he dropped suggests to me that it's one man with a connection to both cities. That's the theory I'm working on."

"Gabriel," she whispered.

He looked at her. "What's up?"

"The bull. It's disappeared from the corral."

He stared, but she was right. It was no longer there. Where the hell was it?

"Gabriel," another whisper. "Look behind us. Slowly."

The bull was stood twenty feet away, its massive hoof pawing the ground. The eyes were fixated on them, and they both knew that when the head went down it would be about to charge them down. Gabriel glanced at Faith and saw her red cardigan.

"Your cardigan, take it off, slowly. Hand it to me."

She didn't argue, just undid the buttons with trembling hands, and shrugged out of the garment. The bull tossed its head several times and snorted as it noticed the movement, but the head was still up. Faith handed him the red cardigan.

"Now get behind me. I need to divert this monster," he

whispered. "As soon as it's gone past us, make a run for that nearby doorway."

She followed his glance; there was a stone built building thirty feet away. The door was open, and it looked to be made of solid timbers. If they could get in there, it would probably hold long enough for help to arrive. But the bull was ten feet nearer. Gabriel held up the cardigan and watched the bull's ears rise as the giant animal prepared to charge.

"What does it weigh, do you reckon?" Faith whispered.

"I'd guess a monster like that would go about two tons."

He felt her shiver.

"What about shooting it? Wouldn't that stop it?"

"I don't think so. A lucky shot to a vulnerable part of the brain would, but a miss would madden it even more. Unless the shooter was right on top of it and could aim a perfect shot at it."

That gave him an idea, and he drew the 9mm Llama from under his jacket. As he did so, the red cardigan moved, and the bull started to lower its head.

"Are you ready to run?"

"Oh, God, it's huge," she replied. "Yeah, I've slipped off my new Guccis. It's not my day is it?"

"Every day is your day if you live to the next one. Don't worry about it." Then the bull charged. "Here he comes. Stay right behind me!" He held the cardigan out to one side, but she was shaking even more. He tightened his grip on the gun, hidden behind the woolen garment like a matador's sword. If she knew what he planned, she'd go crazy and refuse to run.

The ground shook as the mammoth, almost prehistoric looking beast ran straight at them; two tons of solid bone and muscle intent on their total destruction.

"Move with me to the right!" he shouted, as he pivoted and let the bull charge into the red cardigan and continue to crash into the rail of the corral with a massive crash that resounded around the yard. With a bellow, it took the flimsy garment on its horns and kept on going.

"Run, Faith, run!" he shouted.

She began to head to the stone building, running fast and light on bare feet. Satisfied that she was safe, he turned to the bull. It had fallen over as it hit the corral rail and went down. He ran to the huge creature and leapt onto its head, using the horns to steady himself and hold on. The animal bellowed, again and again, like an angry elephant, enraged that this puny creature dared to challenge it directly. But Gabriel held on with one hand, and with the other he put the gun to the head, pointing the barrel straight down at the brain. Then he pulled the trigger, again and again, feeling the bull jerk in agony as each shot hit it. Then the gun clicked on an empty chamber, and he was out of bullets. He was also out of time. He leapt to the ground from the threshing animal and started to run. But there was no thunder of hooves pursuing him, and halfway to the stone building he looked back. The bull was almost dead, and it was staring at him with a mix of puzzlement and sorrow. How could such a small creature as this human kill such a massive beast? Then it twitched once and slumped to the ground, dead. Javier ran around from the back of the house, and Diego came out of the front door. Both men had red faces. Javier had a pistol drawn, and Diego carried a long hunting rifle. Javier ran up to de Sade, his breathing heavy, and his eyes wide with horror.

"Gabriel, what the hell happened? Why did you shoot

the bull?"

De Sade realized he was shaking as excess adrenaline started to bleed out of his system. He did his best to control it as he answered the Spanish detective.

"The question is who let it out to try and kill Faith? When I find who that bastard is, I'm going to tear him apart."

Faith ran from the stone house to join them. Gabriel knew that she hadn't even entered it. When she saw what he was doing, she stopped to see if she could help. In her hand she clutched the tiny Llama pistol.

"Are you okay?" she asked him. Her face was filled with terror.

He nodded, thinking what a woman she was. She'd been ready to help him armed with a .22 pistol against a rampaging two-ton bull. "I'm okay, how about you?"

"Yes, I'm fine. Who let it out?"

"That's what I'm about to find out," he replied grimly.

The three of them went to where Montalban was staring down at his dead Miura bull. The animal looked strange, and the red cardigan was still tangled in its horns. He looked up when they were close.

"This was one of the most magnificent animals I have bred in all my time here. And you just killed it."

"You'd prefer it killed us, would you, Montalban?" Gabriel spat out.

"Of course not, why would I do that?"

"That, my friend, is the question I am asking myself. Who let it out?"

"I have no idea," he replied. "But when I do find out, they will be lucky if they just lose their jobs. This is a disaster, a total disaster."

Despite the man's upset, Gabriel walked up to him and took him by the shirt collar. He brought him to his feet and thrust his head close to the other mans' head, staring into his eyes. The Spaniard tried to struggle, and he was obviously strong, but Gabriel was also very strong and very angry.

"Now listen to me, Buster. This is your spread and your bull. Someone tried to kill us, and I want to know who it was."

"But it was an accident, surely you can see that? I have lost…"

Javier tapped him on the shoulder. "Diego, forget your damned losses. Two people were almost killed. I need to know what happened. Fetch your people, all of them. I will question them now, and God help the man who did this."

Gabriel and Faith glanced at each other. The Spanish cop was red, so red with anger that he was almost incandescent. If it was an act, it was one that would have done Hollywood proud. Montalban went away to round up his staff. But after two hours questioning them, they were no nearer to finding out who let out the bull. Diego Montalban insisted it was an accident, and Javier was inclined to agree. Gabriel wasn't so sure, and he could see that Faith wasn't either. Even worse, the man turned out to be an amateur with little knowledge of the history and archaeology of the Cathedral. When they pressed him, he spread his hands. "Look, the costs of running this place are enormous. To be honest, I'd hoped to locate the gold and use it to help pay my debts."

Javier was scandalized. "Diego, if that treasure is found, it belongs to the church. What you planned for, it disgusts me."

Montalban glared at him. "As I recall, Javier, it belonged to King Philip the Second. I do not believe he has any use for it. The Church stole it from him, and what I intended was no worse than they did. But let us not argue. We are old friends. It is likely that the treasure does not exist anyway."

Javier nodded. "Yes, you're right. It would be ridiculous arguing over what may turn out to be nothing more than a myth."

He looked at Gabriel and Faith, and he could hardly meet their eyes. "I feel responsible for this. I understood Diego had a genuine interest in the Cathedral treasure, not that of a simple thief. It nearly cost you your lives."

Faith managed a small smile. "But it didn't, and it seems your friend is no more a thief than anyone else. It is not your fault."

As they walked out to the car, Gabriel shouted back to Diego. "Hey, there's an old bullfighting custom I heard of, Montalban. When a matador manages a good clean kill, he gets to keep one of the ears of the bull. Will you send me the ear?"

The Spaniard stared back at him. "You killed a prize bull worth tens of thousands of Euros, Mr. de Sade. If I send you anything, it will be a large bill."

The journey back into the city was quiet. It was obvious the Spanish cop felt responsible for them almost being killed at the bull farm. He stopped outside their hotel, the Becquer, and let them out.

"My apologies again for what happened. I intend to look into it further. If it was a deliberate attempt on your lives, I will find out. Could I ask you a question?"

Gabriel nodded. "Go ahead."

"Those guns you're both carrying. Do you have permits?"

"I'm a New York cop, Javier. And Faith is helping me investigate a series of brutal killings."

He inclined his head. "Yes, I know all that. I assume your answer is no. I should confiscate those guns and insist you apply for a permit. But I understand that I failed you today, and without them you may have been killed."

Would have been killed, Gabriel thought to himself. But he said nothing.

"Here in Spain, carrying unlicensed firearms is a serious offense." He smiled then. "And so tomorrow I will bring you both applications for permits, and I will advise you on how to fill them in. I have a suspicion that the applications will be lost in the drawer of my desk, but it will help if you are stopped by uniformed police. In the meantime, please keep them hidden away. Shall we meet in the Cathedral tomorrow morning, say at ten o'clock?"

"Make it nine, Javier, we have a lot of ground to cover," Gabriel replied. "And thanks."

"No problem. But the Cathedral does not open until eleven o'clock. This is Spain, not New York."

"It'll open for two accredited Vatican representatives, my friend. Nine o'clock."

Javier nodded. "Nine o'clock, as you say."

When he'd gone, they ordered coffee in the comfortable lounge. Faith held his hand tight, still recovering from the shock.

"He seems okay, Javier Garcia," she said quietly. "He didn't have to do that with the guns."

"No? I think he knew that he could have taken them off us, but we'd have acquired two more the same way we got these. And there's another thing. After I shot the bull, Montalban came out of the house. Javier was around the back. I saw him come running around the side of the house. What was he doing around there? I thought he said he had business with Montalban."

"There may be a simple explanation, you know. And the bull may have just got out, as they said, an accident."

He nodded. "Yeah, that's one explanation. But it's the other one that worries me. I suggest we watch him tomorrow. I don't want any more accidents while we're here."

"And if you think he's the one we're looking for? Can you arrest a Spanish cop?"

He looked at her with a grim expression. "Arrest him? Someone tried to kill you, Faith. When I find out who it was, who said anything about arresting the bastard? This is personal now, and it's about stopping him from trying again. And there's only one sure way to do that."

He felt her shiver again. But she didn't object.

# CHAPTER SIX

It was almost midnight, and the mild, balmy air of Seville had turned cold, almost as cold as the winters in New York City. He was tempted to put on some more clothing, but it would only add to the danger of forensic residue. No, this was the moment, his moment. He didn't want anything to go wrong now. It had been easy getting her here, especially when she discovered that he was an important person in Seville society. It was a simple matter to render her unconscious with a piece of cloth soaked in ether. She'd thought it was some kind of a sex game. He smiled, in a way she was right. Then he'd secured her to the base of the rails that ran around the platform they stood on. She begged. They all did.

"Please, Senor, don't kill, me, I'll do what you want." She'd worked the gag free with her tongue, and he felt a twinge of irritation as he refastened it. Even here, if she cried out, she could be overheard. He peered down at her face, satisfied at the terror in her huge, dark eyes.

"My dear, your agony and misery are about to end. You

are to go to a place where you will find redemption, a chance of a better life. First, I will hear your confession, and I have a gift for you. A Rosary, it will help you with your penance."

She shook her head from side to side, making piteous noises, but he knew what had to be done. It was for her own good, and besides, he could feel his own arousal flooding his nervous system with erotic sensations. He must be quick, before he ruined everything. It would be perverted if he came during the act of sanctification.

"In Nomine Patris et Filii Sancti…" he intoned, as he started to cut. She was so terrified that she swallowed her tongue, and the gag began to be drawn into her throat as well, choking off her cries. Her body struggled and heaved as she tried to suck in breath, tried to break free from her bonds. Tried to contain the terrible agony she must be feeling. It didn't last long, and she managed to a last sigh; a breath that filtered past the gag, and she was gone. Using every ounce of self-control, he kept on cutting. Finally, he stacked the parts in a neat pile. There was no need to abuse the dead by leaving her in an untidy heap. It was enough. The message would be understood when she reached the next life. He left his handiwork and hurried away to attend to his own needs. He had earned it. Would those Americans understand the significance of what he'd done? Perhaps, they were not stupid. It would be enough to throw their investigation off balance and send them in entirely the wrong direction. He smiled to himself. Tomorrow, he would need to give more thought to dealing with the threat they presented. And from where had they acquired those pistols. His plan had almost succeeded but for that unexpected development. No matter, it would work the next time. Perhaps Providence had been looking down on him. The two foreigners could well strike lucky and find the gold, in which case he would be saved from having to search for it himself. Yes, he would leave them for a day or two and see where they went and what they found. Then he would deal with them. Permanently.

* * *

He was dreaming of a night in a place far away. Afghanistan. It was shortly after the invasion, and Team Bravo had learned of a large force of Taliban who were rushing to defend a village that commanded a strategic route across a low range of hills. When darkness came, Team Bravo split into two, and each section patrolled around the village outskirts for a couple of hours. After joining back together, Gabriel set them up in an ambush site. On one side Jonas headed up a Minimi machine gun crew, and Gabriel waited on the other side. An hour later, the insurgents arrived but were forewarned of the ambush by an Afghan Army traitor. They attacked by throwing grenades into the Team Bravo positions. Immediately, Gabriel sent up the illumination round from his M-203 grenade launcher and placed a high explosive round into the launcher to prepare to meet the enemy. The next thing he knew, there was a huge flash, and he was flying through the air and slammed against the stone wall of a house. He was completely dazed, bleeding from his head, chest, arms, stomach and legs. There was a tremendous ringing in his ears, and his body was shaking from the shock of his wounds. At first he was bleeding so badly, he thought he was dying. All around him he could see and hear the violence of the attack as the Taliban insurgents rushed forward.

Then Jonas arrived, fighting his way out of the trap and through to Gabriel's unit to unite the two forces. His bleeding was quickly stopped by the unit medic who pumped him full of morphine to control the pain. He dragged himself up and looked around. The fight raged around him, yet the Team fought like devils. Even the machine gunner, also wounded from the bomb blast, kept firing magazine after magazine. Finally, they drove the terrorists from the village. When they investigated further, they found four American corpses thrown onto a dung heap behind one of the huts. They also found a high-ranking Taliban officer hiding amongst a group of women, disguised in a characteristic blue burqa. Shortly afterwards, the unit they'd been running recon for caught up with them. The Colonel heard from one of the men that they'd caught the Taliban prisoner and came looking for Gabriel.

"Where's the prisoner, Sergeant? They told me he was a senior officer, and our intelligence people will want to speak to him."

"We found four of our soldiers, Sir. They were slaughtered like stuck pigs, and their bodies were thrown on a trash heap."

"Yeah, they're bastards, I know that," the Colonel acknowledged. "I'll make sure our people know about it. That prisoner will have a lot to answer for. Where is he?"

"He's already answered, Sir. He was shot trying to escape."

The officer gave him a cold stare. "There are rules of war, Sergeant. You should know that."

Gabriel returned the stare. "Maybe you'd better tell the Taliban about your rules, Sir. They seem to have missed them somewhere down the line."

* * *

He dimly realized that something was trying to intrude into his subconscious. His eyes flicked open, and he saw the light on the telephone flashing in time with the ringer. Faith was starting to stir, so he picked the receiver up to try and stop her being disturbed.

"De Sade."

"It is Javier. Is it convenient to talk? I thought you would be here by now."

He looked at his luminous watch. It was nine fifteen. The hotel room blinds were impervious to sunshine, to allow residents to sleep during the afternoon siesta. He should have asked for an alarm call.

"Javier, I'm sorry, we overslept. We'll get down there right away."

Next to him in the bed, Faith was starting to stretch as she came awake after a long sleep. He smiled at her and was about to say something when he checked. It was Javier, his voice, something in the tone that sounded wrong.

"What is it? Has anything happened?"

"There's been another one, here at the Cathedral."

"Another body has been hidden there?"

"No, my friend, this one was not hidden. She was murdered and dismembered in the open air. At the top of the Giralda, beneath the statue of Faith."

They stared down at the gruesome pile of body parts. The balcony was crowded with scene of crime technicians, uniformed Policia Nacional cops and four detectives, as well as Javier. To one side of them, Bishop Raul Santiago looked on with a horrified expression.

"Any clues, anything we can use, Inspector?" he asked Javier, using his professional title in the presence of the other cops.

Garcia took him to one side, out of earshot of the group of cops around the body. Gabriel was glad he'd skipped the hotel breakfast. It was enough to make the strongest stomach revolt.

"They are telling me very little of the investigation. It is as I told you. I am still under a degree of suspicion. But it is without question the same man."

"It's a message," Faith interrupted. "You know that, don't you? Whether it was conscious or unconscious on his part, he was sending a message."

Javier gave her a curious look. "What possible message could he be sending, other than one to terrorize the local Sevillanos?"

"He has tortured, murdered and dismembered her under the statue of Faith. That is my name. Is it not too much of a coincidence?"

He shook his head. "No, I do not believe so. He has killed many women, which is what people like this do."

"Except that he always hides the body parts. This time he left them out in the open, and underneath Faith. It's a message."

Javier didn't look convinced. "Perhaps, perhaps not. What do you suggest is the message?"

Gabriel replied this time. "The message is for us to leave this case alone. To go back to the USA."

"And will you go back?"

Gabriel's expression was unwavering. "Would you, if someone had tried to murder your partner?"

Javier thought for a few moments. Then he shook his head. "No, I think not."

Bishop Santiago had left the Giralda, and Javier, Gabriel and Faith followed him down the long series of ramps. There was nothing to be gained from the balcony, not until the forensics technicians had cleared the scene. They found him in the Narthex of the Cathedral, the wide space between the entrance atrium and the nave. He was kneeling at an antique, heavily carved prie-dieu, his eyes closed and his lips moving as he prayed. They waited until he'd finished and approached him as his eyes opened.

"Bishop, we need to make a thorough search of the Cathedral," Gabriel stated. "If we're going to make any progress on this, we have to find the link between the gold and the murderer. We have to tread in the same steps as he has, and to do that we need your best and most experienced man to guide us."

He nodded slowly. "Yes, yes, I see that. Where are you going now? I will send him to you."

"We're starting back in that tunnel where the bodies were found. Where we go from there will depend on what your man tells us."

"Very well, leave it with me. I will send him to you."

They left him and went through the thick, oak door that led into the tunnel. This time they examined it minutely as they walked slowly forward towards the death room.

"There is something strange about this tunnel," Faith remarked. "Why would they build this tunnel only to lead to this single, underground room?"

"It is a storeroom, nothing more," Javier pointed out.

"Why would they not build a tunnel to it?"

"If all they wanted was a storeroom, they could have dug it much nearer to the entrance. So why was it built at the end of a long access tunnel?"

No one had an answer, but it was something to consider. A figure stepped through the door that led from the cathedral into the tunnel and then spoke with the familiar Germanic accent.

"Bishop Santiago has asked me to assist you. What do you want of me?"

They stared at the face of Brother Sebastian. He'd caught the light in a peculiar way so that his face was half illuminated with only the harsh, hard planes of his features visible on the other side. It was the face of an inquisitor, harsh, proud and cruel.

Gabriel was the first to recover. "Sebastian, there's a serial killer running loose, as you know. As well as killing women, he's obviously hunting for this fabled treasure. If we can get a lead to the treasure, it could lead us to our killer."

He thought for a few moments. "I do not agree with giving you free access to all parts of the Cathedral. And I do not believe that you will hand over the gold if it is found."

In a swift moment, Gabriel took him by the collar of his robe and rammed him against the wall.

"Listen to me, you bastard. I don't give a damn what you believe or not. And for your information, we don't have free access to the whole of the Cathedral. Our passes give us access to all Catholic property, even the Vatican. Do you want this killer stopped or not?"

Sebastian struggled to free himself until Gabriel

released him, and he stood shaking with anger.

"How dare you lay hands on me. I will call the police."

"Senor, I am the police," Javier informed him drily. "I saw nothing."

The monk shot him a murderous glance and looked back at Gabriel. "Very well. I will do as you wish. But I curse the day you ever set foot in this place."

"Curse all you want, monk. First of all, I want to see a set of plans for the Cathedral, the most complete set you have."

He waved contemptuously. "You did not need to disturb me for that. There is a guidebook with those plans in. You can buy it in the shop."

"He means original plans," Faith explained. "We need to see it the way it was when the Cathedral was built. I take it there is such a set of documents?"

"Of course, it was made into a leather bound volume and held in the Cathedral museum. But you cannot put your hands on it. The book is very valuable. I absolutely forbid it. I am the Curator of these relics, and they must be protected and preserved."

"Yeah, right. Take us to the plans, Sebastian."

"No, I will not."

Gabriel's hand shot out and gripped the man by the throat. The monk was strong, despite his age. Very strong for someone in such a sedentary occupation, which gave the New York detective pause for thought. Then he squeezed.

"No, you cannot have them, no, aarrgghh!"

De Sade had used his other hand to take the man's crotch in an iron grip and squeeze his balls, adding to his pain. He held the grip until he heard the words he wanted to hear.

"Yes, yes, alright. Let me go."

He released the pressure. "Lead on, Brother."

"But I will watch you as you look through them," the monk muttered. "There is no need for you to accompany me. I will bring them to you here."

Surprised by the man's change of heart, he let him go, and Sebastian scuttled back along the tunnel and out of the heavy oak door.

"Gabriel, no! He'll lock us in, stop him."

Almost without thinking, he whipped out his pistol, but before he could do anything, the door slammed shut. They heard the sound of the bolts sliding across, and the key being turned in the lock. A few minutes later, the monk found the trip switch that controlled the tunnel lighting. They were plunged into darkness.

Javier spoke first. "It's okay, he knows that he can't shut us down here forever. He's just being awkward."

"Unless he's the killer," Faith reminded him. "In which case, we could be down here for a long time."

They were silent as each of them ran through the likely end to their imprisonment in the tunnel.

"Javier," Gabriel said to the Spaniard. "Do you have a flashlight?"

"Only a small one," he replied. "The battery will not last for too long."

"Can I borrow it? While we're down here, why don't we take a look around?"

"Yes, I will pass it to you now."

A small beam flicked out and Gabriel took the flashlight from him. "I intend to take a look around and see if there isn't some other way out of here. Something may show up in the beam of the flashlight that isn't so obvious with the electric lights on."

He started inspecting the walls, stone by stone. Then he moved to the other side of the tunnel, the ceiling, and finally the floor. The other two watched him work. He had his gun in his hand now, using the butt to tap the stonework in the hunt for anything that suggested a hidden door. By the time he'd made a cursory inspection of the tunnel, he'd found nothing, and the beam was starting to dim as the battery faded.

"I'm going to take a look inside the store room where they found the bodies," he told them. "Be ready for the stench when I open the door."

"I'll come with you," Faith replied.

"I'll stay here in case I hear anyone coming," Javier added. "Believe me, if the monk returns, he'll wish he was never born. My father was an officer in the Guardia Civil during Franco's time, and he told me a few things about how to deal with people like him."

They left him guarding the Cathedral door and went to the end of the tunnel. Gabriel opened the door, and the pungent aroma of powerful cleaning fluids mixed with rotting human remains hit them like a thick soup. Gabriel was reminded that they hadn't taken breakfast, at least that much they'd done right. Inside the room, he started to examine the walls.

"I'm not sure how long the beam will last for. It's already very dim," he said to Faith. She didn't reply, and he looked around for her. She was stood near the center of the room, quite still. She seemed to have gone into some kind of a trance. He called to her.

"Faith, what's wrong?"

She didn't answer at first. He waited until she turned slowly to look at him.

"I'm sorry, I was distracted. There is no other way out of here. We need to find a way to break out through the door."

Javier had walked along the tunnel to join them. "How could you know that?"

She looked at Gabriel and back at the Spanish cop. "It is hard to explain, but I sense things. Messages, guidance, that kind of thing."

He stared at her and looked at Gabriel. "What is she talking about?"

"It's hard to explain," he replied. "She sometimes gets tuned into things that we don't hear or understand. All I can tell you is that we'd be sensible to listen to her."

Javier grunted. "If that is the case, where do we go from here?"

"To the door. If that's the only way out, let's take it."

"But how?"

"Wait, I have an idea."

In the end it was simple. The door was massively built from solid oak with heavy iron hinges, hinges that were visible on the inside. Javier flinched as Gabriel drew his 9mm Llama, fitted a new clip, and aimed at the huge, iron hinge.

"Are you sure? It could be dangerous."

"Yeah, I know, but so is staying trapped in here. Take Faith and go into the storeroom. I can stay below the angle for a ricochet, but anyone behind me can't. Do it, the flashlight is almost out."

He nodded and led Faith back to the storeroom, closing the door. Gabriel crouched low and pointed the pistol up at the hinge and fired. The boom was massive in the tiny, confined space, and he felt that his eardrums had been blown out. The bullet smashed into the iron and zinged away along the tunnel, bouncing of the stonework until it finally buried itself in the storeroom door. But the hinge held, although it had a deep gouge in the iron. He fired another shot, another massive explosion, and he wondered if his eardrums had been damaged. Another gouge in the iron, but still the hinge held. And the beam from the flashlight had almost gone. Without it, it would be almost impossible to aim accurately at the widening damage to the hinge. He decided to go for broke and fired off the remaining seven rounds in a continuous burst. The noise was astonishing, and he knew it would take some time for his eardrums to recover. But the hinge had broken, and the door sagged on the single remaining hinge. Even more important was that a faint light was entering the tunnel from the interior of the Cathedral, and they could see to finish off the business of opening the door. He could just make out shouts above, as security men headed towards the source of the explosions that wrecked the peace of such a holy place.

"Javier, Faith, I've stopped firing. You can come out now."

They hurried towards him, and they could see to move along the tunnel with the dim light that seeped in from above. Javier inspected the damage.

"Thank God, you have broken the hinge. We can open the door with a little more leverage."

"I don't think we need to worry, Javier. They know we're here. We'll be out soon." A voice shouted through the narrow opening. "Who is in there?"

Javier replied. "Inspector Garcia of the Policia Nacional. Someone trapped us down here. Find someone who has the key and release us."

"We have already called the police," the voice answered him. "They will be here soon."

"Good. Now find that key."

"We will await the police, and they will release you."

Gabriel grinned. "I can't blame them. They heard shots, and they don't know who's down here."

They waited a few minutes more, and then a new voice shouted down to them.

"This is the Policia Nacional. We will open the door, but be warned we have it covered with armed officers. Throw out your weapons, and come out with your hands up."

The key rattled in the lock, and the door opened a few inches, tilted at a crazy angle. Gabriel tossed out his gun, and Javier followed suit. He looked at Faith.

"Do you have a gun?"

She shook her head. "No."

He stared at her for a few moments and then nodded. "Very well. I shall lead the way out, as these are my colleagues.

They emerged into a cathedral that was as crowded as it would have been for Sunday morning Mass. Directly in front of them was a squad of armed officers, their submachine guns pointing directly at them. They were all dressed in dark blue paramilitary fatigues.

"I am an officer of the Policia Nacional," Javier shouted. "My identity card is in my wallet."

An officer in full uniform stepped forward. His epaulettes and cap were covered in gold braid. Evidently, he was the man in charge.

"My name is Colonel Velasquez." He looked at the detective. "Inspector Garcia, we know who you are, that is not in question. What I do want to know is why you are down in that tunnel, discharging your weapon? Or was it not your pistol that fired? I see two guns on the ground. Who was it who damaged Cathedral property?"

"It was me." Gabriel stared at him. "Detective Gabriel de Sade, NYPD. I'm here with the knowledge of your department to cooperate in a serial killing investigation."

"Yes, I know of your visit. But it did not include a license to shoot up our Cathedral. Nor to carry a gun, unless I'm mistaken."

"Dammit, the door was locked, we had no choice…"

"But you are wrong, Senor. I took the key from the Curator just now and inserted it into the door. It was unlocked."

Gabriel caught sight of Sebastian standing in the shadows at the side of the tomb of Christopher Columbus. The monk gave him a small sneer and disappeared behind the huge structure. So that was it, he'd unlocked the door when he heard the first shot so that they would appear to be vandalizing the building. He vowed to deal with the monk at a later time.

"Ask your detective. He'll tell you. It was locked, and someone has obviously unlocked it to hide trapping us down in the tunnel."

The senior cop gave him a steady gaze. "And who would do such a thing?"

"The Curator, Brother Sebastian."

The cop smiled. "Really. Perhaps you would come and explain all this at Police Headquarters."

He turned to a tough looking cop who stood right behind him. "Sergeant, arrest these men."

"Yes, Sir. And the woman?"

The Colonel turned to Javier. "What is her involvement in this?"

"She is just a civilian," he replied. "She has no official involvement."

"And was she armed?"

He didn't hesitate. "No, she did not carry a gun."

"Very well. Sergeant, you may release her, but make sure you take details of her passport before you do. Take the two men to Headquarters, and we'll find out what really happened here."

They handcuffed Gabriel and led him away. He nodded to Faith as they left. They brought Javier too, but out of deference to his rank left his hands free. The interview was conducted in a tiny, airless room inside the Policia Nacional Headquarters. Colonel Velasquez shouted and cajoled, while his sergeant wrote notes on a pad. But after two hours, he decided to let them go without charge.

"The Curator denies that he locked you in, and I see no point in him doing it. But you say he did. It's his word against yours, and I will not allow one of my officers to be called a liar. Even one such as yourself, Garcia."

Javier flushed, and it was evident there was bad blood between them.

"As for the gun you had in your possession, that is another matter. Who supplied it to you? Was it a priest here in Seville? We know about that Eastern Orthodox priest. His church was used to hide Republican prisoners on the run from Franco's men during the Civil War here in Spain. As a result, the activities of the incumbent priest are kept under observation. So it was him, was it?"

"I have no comment," Gabriel replied.

The Colonel nodded. "You do not wish to incriminate him. I understand that. But perhaps you would be more forthcoming if I told you that he was killed yesterday. Murdered in a similar manner to the killings you have under investigation. The man was dismembered, and his body parts left stacked in a near pile."

Gabriel stared at him, shocked that the old priest had been slaughtered, if it was true. He said nothing.

"I see." The Colonel stood up and nodded to the sergeant. "You can let them go, but this is not finished. A word of advice, Mr. de Sade, carrying unlicensed firearms is a serious offense in Spain. This is not the Wild West. Next time you are apprehended with a weapon, you will be placed in a cell, pending criminal charges. Inspector Garcia, you may continue working with this man, but I will require a full written report of your progress on my desk each day. That is all."

The Colonel and his sergeant walked out and left the door of the interrogation room open. Gabriel and Javier were able to walk out into the Seville sunshine. The first task for de Sade was to call Faith on his cell. She answered straight away.

"What happened?"

"We're fine, they let us go. No charges."

"So where do we go now?"

He told her about the Orthodox priest, Manuel Guzman.

"It must have happened soon after we left him," she murmured. "I imagine the killer followed us to his house."

"Yeah, that sounds about right. Are you at the hotel?"

"Yes, I was waiting to hear that you were okay."

"Right. I'll come there, grab some lunch, and we'll decide our next move."

He clicked off. Javier tapped him on the shoulder. "Gabriel, I have to go back inside. I need to retrieve my gun. I expect I will be busy writing up reports too, so shall we meet tomorrow?"

Gabriel nodded. "Sure. Café of the Indies, say about ten?"

"That's fine, I'll be there."

Gabriel hailed a cab that took him to the Hotel Becquer. Faith rushed into his arms when he walked into the room.

"I thought you were going to be held in a cell. They're not too happy about the damage to that door."

He smiled. "Too bad. I intend to find our friend Brother Sebastian after we've eaten. I'll persuade him to cover the damage, and then I'm really going to wring his neck, the bastard. He's involved in this, I just don't know how much."

"I know he's been acting strangely, but do you think he's capable of the actual killings?"

"It's possible. He's a religious fanatic, and we know what those kinds of people can do all over the world. The Middle East, Afghanistan, they're all religious madmen. Something about religion seems to drive these people crazy."

"Some people," she corrected him.

"Yeah, some people, not all." She was a believer, and he knew that. He also knew that she was incapable of doing harm to anyone, unless they threatened her or those she loved.

"Let's go eat, we'll talk some more over the food. Being

arrested makes me hungry."

She grimaced. "After what we've been through today, the last thing on my mind is food."

But she was wrong. They realized when the plates of tapas dishes was put in front of them that they were desperate for nourishment to replace the energy and adrenaline they'd burned. When they'd waded through the first two courses, Faith stopped eating and looked at him.

"What's next? The investigation doesn't appear to be going well so far. Back to the Cathedral?"

"Not quite, we have another problem. That Policia Nacional colonel took our guns, so somehow we need to locate replacements."

She smiled. "You know, I learned a little trick from my business partner, Galina. You remember how she seemed to make a little gun appear and disappear as if my magic?"

"You mean you held on to your .22 Llama?"

"I certainly did. When I heard the cops outside the tunnel, I tucked it in my underwear like she used to do. Actually, she wore suspenders and stockings, which made it easier. But I managed. I've transferred it to my purse now. You can have it if you like."

"Faith, I feel like giving you a hug and a kiss. Without a gun, we'd have been dead by now."

She pulled a face. "A hug and a kiss? I thought a pistol would be worth more than that."

She wore a pert, coquettish expression on her face, and he began to feel aroused.

"You're on," he smiled. "Let's see if we can push the room temperature up a few degrees tonight."

"Do you want me to wear something sexy?"

"You're sexy, and nothing could be better than pure,

unadulterated Faith Ward."

"I can arrange that."

She transferred the pistol to him under cover of the table, and he stashed it in his pocket. He felt better being armed once more, although he knew that if the local cops found him with another gun, they'd be pretty pissed. He paid the bill, and they got up to leave.

"We're off to the Cathedral?" Faith asked him.

"We are. It's time to have a word with Brother Sebastian, and maybe to wring his scrawny neck. I'd better speak to the Bishop first. It's only fair that he knows his Curator could be a killer."

They walked through the city streets. The shops were beginning to open after the afternoon siesta and people were milling everywhere. The sun shone; the day had become fine and warm, and they both felt their spirits lift after the problems they'd faced so far in Spain. They arrived at the Cathedral and went through to the Bishop's office. He stood up when they walked in and shook hands.

"I'm glad you were able to come. I wanted you to know that we have discussed the matter of the damage to the door. In view of your difficulties, we are not taking it any further."

Gabriel nodded. "Yeah, despite what you may have heard, that door was locked."

"You say it was our Curator, Brother Sebastian, who locked it?"

"There is no doubt. It was him."

"I see. I imagine you will wish to speak to him, but there is a problem."

"What kind of a problem? Has he gone into hiding? He knew damn well we'd be coming for him."

"Perhaps so. He has vanished from the Cathedral, but his personal effects are all in his office, so it does not seem that he went away permanently."

"Can we take a look at his office?"

He nodded. Of course, I will unlock it for you."

He showed them through the door of Sebastian's office. Gabriel and Faith both started a sweep of the room, looking for clues that might suggest where he'd gone. Faith called them over to the desk where she was examining a pile of documents and plans.

"Look, this stain on the desk. It looks like blood."

Gabriel stared at it, and touched it with his finger. It was blood. There was no doubt. The question in all their minds was whose was it?

"He's been making pencil marks on these plans," Faith pointed out. "It may give us a clue as to where he's gone."

"Or who's taken him," Gabriel added.

The Bishop looked troubled. "These are ancient documents, and he should not have been defacing them."

They examined the pencil marks that Sebastian had made.

"It looks as if he was altering the design," Santiago went on. "In very subtle ways, at least. Why would he do that?"

"Could he be looking for some kind of underground room, like the one the bodies were hidden in?" Faith asked him. "He may think he would find the treasure in a place that had been hidden for centuries."

"I don't think so," the Bishop replied, his brow furrowed in thought. They bent down and looked again at the plans. "Look, this marking here, it shows some kind of an entrance, but it's in the roof."

His voice shook as both of them looked at the man. It was as if he'd seen something totally unexpected, something that had shocked him.

"What is it? Is something wrong?"

The Bishop looked up at Gabriel. "I'm not sure what it is, but there is no entrance there. Yet one is marked on this plan?"

"What is up there in the roof, Bishop? Does the Cathedral store any valuables up there?"

He looked up as Faith put the question to him. "Valuables? No, no, of course not. The roof space is all empty, but as I said, there is no entrance where he has one marked."

Gabriel thought furiously about the markings on the plans. If the Curator wanted somewhere to hide, a place that no one knew about, it would be perfect. And what was true now would have been true five hundred years ago. Was it possible? But why would he then leave the plans open on his desk for others to find them? There was only one explanation. Someone had interrupted him and spirited him away after a struggle, and that left the bloodstain on the plan. Yet who? And did it make it more likely that Sebastian was the killer, or less so? They had to find him.

"What's the quickest way up to the roof, Bishop?"

"There are stairs either end of the building, in the Narthex and in the Bema."

"Are they locked?"

"Yes, always, but Brother Sebastian had keys. I will use his."

He went to the key cabinet on the wall and took down a key. "Come, I will show you the way to the foot of the stairs. Then I must leave you, but let me know what you find."

"Yeah, we'll do that," Gabriel replied.

They went through the Cathedral, and there were already a number of people sat in the pews ready for evening mass. The area around the damaged door had been sealed off with a roped enclosure. Near to it was the huge tomb of Columbus, with several very obvious Americans talking loudly as they stood next to it. The Bishop gave them an irritated glance and then carried on to a door. He inserted the key, opened it, and switched on the light.

"This will lead you to the roof. I will leave you with the key, just in case," he smiled.

Then he left them alone, and they started up the narrow flight of steep, stone steps that led upwards to the vaulted roof of the Cathedral. They started climbing, threading their way through the very inside of the structure of the building. Every few feet there were tiny openings, spyholes, where people could peer out at the nave. The climb went on forever, hundreds and hundreds of steep steps, until they reached the top. In front of them was a narrow walkway that ran all the way around the base of the vaulted ceiling. There were a number of pillars and irregular structures in the stonework, any of which could have concealed a secret room, or a body, or a murderer. Gabriel started forward until he came to part of the floor where pieces of stonework lay across it, probably fallen from the roof. He turned to Faith.

"Be careful, there's a pile of stones across the floor. You don't want to ruin another pair of shoes," he joked.

But there was no reply. He looked around, and the walkway was empty. Faith had gone. He started back. She hadn't just disappeared into thin air, so she couldn't be far away. Then he tripped and fell. It seemed like a long, long way, but he kept crashing into stone buttresses that stuck out from the wall. Then everything went black.

# CHAPTER SEVEN

He watched them step onto the walkway that circled the vast, open space of the inside of the roof. He felt angry that they'd come up here to the place he'd marked out to use for his next victims, but perhaps all wasn't lost. If they found nothing, he could continue to prepare it, and they'd think it was abandoned. But it was vital that the girl didn't make a sound. He looked down at her face, her eyes wide with pain and terror. As they should be, for someone who was about to sample the wrath of the Lord for their sins. She'd been here for two days, bound and gagged. He'd thought of her for almost every waking moment, and it had been hard not to pleasure himself prematurely. Soon, she would move on to the next life, a life that would see her cleansed and ready to live in a pure and devout manner. He smiled to himself. If only they knew, a brief period of pain and terror for an eternity of sacred bliss. He could see she was trying to work the gag free, so he took out his gun, an old Mauser 9mm automatic, and clubbed her over the head with the weapon. It was crude, but effective, and she slumped unconscious. It would soon be time to deal with her. He was in a small crawl space, barely four feet high, with a narrow viewing slot that looked out onto the open roof space. The American detective came nearer, and he smiled to himself. How would he feel if he knew that only feet away was an armed man, and a man who could blow out his brains with one shot if he chose. Perhaps he should do it, and put an end to any problems the interfering policeman could cause him. But where was the girl? One moment she was there, and then she was gone. Had she turned back down the stairs? He looked all around the roof space, but there was no sign of her. Yes, that's what must have happened, she'd gone down the stairs. What about the detective, should he finish him? He looked down. His victim was coming to. How close was the American? He looked around, but to his dismay, he'd gone also. Could he have got as far as the staircase and started back down? He looked again, but there was nothing. So be it, he'd gone. They'd both gone. It was time to deal with her, but he had to be careful. They were close. Yet somehow, it added to the excitement. He felt the arousal as usual, but the presence of danger increased it, and he felt ready to explode. Not yet, he had work to do first.

"My dear," he whispered. "Your time of trial if almost over. Do you wish to go to a better place?"

She understood all too well what he meant, and she shook her head with desperate intensity, trying to persuade him not to kill her. They all did, but he knew what was best for her. He took out his knife and stared down at her body. Her eyes goggled at him, and her terror now was absolute. Where should he start to cut?"

\* \* \*

When he came to, he was lying on a heap of rough stones. He felt around his body and found that nothing appeared to be broken. But he hurt where he'd landed and knew he'd be bruised for several days to come. Then his hand touched something soft. Faith! He crawled over to her. In the faint glow that came from overhead, he could see her face, scratched and bleeding, but her chest heaved in and out. She was alive, thank God. He put his face near to her head.

"Faith, can you hear me?"

She groaned, and her eyes opened. "Gabriel? Where am I, what happened?"

"We've fallen down some kind of a well or a chimney. I think a hatch covered it, and you knocked it aside by mistake. You fell into it. I was looking for you, and here I am."

Her eyes looked around the dark space they lay in. "Are you hurt? I remember now, it was a long drop."

"I'm okay, Faith. I kept hitting the stone outcrops that slowed my fall, and you must have done the same. It was damn painful, but without them we'd have fallen to our deaths."

"Yes. You're right, but I ache all over. I checked my cellphone, and there's no signal in here, which doesn't surprise me. What are we going to do?"

"Climb out, I guess."

"Are you sure? It was a long way down."

He stood up and looked around the gloomy chamber. The chimney they'd both fallen through stretched away in the gloom, but there was no way to see how far high it reached, or how far they'd fallen.

"I'll climb back up. It shouldn't be too hard. The stonework down here at least looks pretty rough. There should be enough handholds to hold on to."

"I'll take a look around while you're climbing. If it is impossible, maybe there's another way out of here."

He gripped an outcrop of stone and started to pull himself up. At first it was easy, if you were a professional mountaineer. He was very fit, but after the first twenty feet he was perspiring with the enormous effort required to grip the stone outcrops that were becoming smaller and smaller; until they disappeared altogether. He tried to edge his way up with his back to the chimney and his feet pressed against the other side, but it was just too wide to give him the purchase he needed. There had to be a way. He needed to work this one out. In the meantime, he carefully eased back down to the floor of the chamber. Faith watched him as he slid the last few feet.

"No go?"

"Not yet, no, but I'll work something out. Is there anything around here we could use? Any discarded lumber or even a length of rope?"

He saw her teeth as she grinned. "Or maybe an elevator in working order? No such luck, we're going to have to figure this out by ourselves. But there are a couple of passages leading off from this place, so it could be we'll find another way out. Do you know where we are?"

He took a deep breath. It wasn't good news, but there was no point in hiding the truth.

"We're inside the fabric of the building, I'd guess. The construction is complicated, and some of the curves and features are hollow. They left if open up in the roof space, or maybe it was covered by wooden planks that rotted, but we've fallen inside the actual stonework itself."

She was silent for a moment, thinking. Then she looked at him. "Do you think we can get out?"

What she was asking him was were they going to die here? He put his arm around her and kissed her gently.

"Have you ever known a situation we couldn't get out of?"

"No, but we haven't been trapped inside a cathedral before. And this is one of the biggest in the world."

"We'll make it. I've got a couple of ideas, but let's explore these passages first. It may be that we'll just find a door that opens into the nave."

She didn't reply. She didn't need to. The chances of finding a convenient exit were remote at best, and climbing the chimney presented almost an impossible challenge that despite his words, he hadn't a clue of how to begin to achieve it.

The first passage was low, no more than three feet. They started to crawl, feeling their way along. For some reason, there was a dim light that allowed them to pick out where they were going. Gabriel didn't comment on that, but he wondered where it could be coming from. The whole chamber should be in total darkness, as well as the passages that led off, but they weren't. The faint luminescence was their only ally as they groped their way along. He knew that without it they would almost certainly be doomed to die down in the dark bowels of the huge building. The floor was uneven, covered in pieces of stone and rubble, obviously discarded during the building process. Faith's voice came from behind him.

"Do you think we'll come across the treasure down

here?"

"Maybe. If we do come across it, we could find the way they brought it into the hiding place."

"Unless they bricked it up."

He kept crawling. There was no reply worth making to that statement. Then his hand touched a solid stone wall, and he knew they were at the end of the passage.

He called back to Faith. "Don't come any further, we need to turn back. It's a dead end."

"There's no way to turn around. I'll crawl out backwards."

"Yeah, okay."

He went backwards too, but it was painful as he kept hitting pieces of stone jutting out from the walls and roof of the passage. When they reached the chamber, he looked carefully at Faith, trying to make out in the dim illumination if she was hurt. He noticed several scratches on her face, but there was nothing that looked serious.

"If you're ready for it, we'll try the other passage. Were there only two that you found?"

"Yes, but I'm ready, and it's not as if we've got anything else to do. You know that this one is our last hope."

"Yeah, I guess. But there's always the chimney we slid down, and I haven't given up hope yet."

"Do you still think that Sebastian is the killer? I never figured him for someone who could do stuff like that," she asked him.

"They never do look capable of mass murder, these sickos. That's the only common factor. Let's try that other passage."

"Gabriel, wait."

"What for?"

She didn't reply. Once more, she'd gone into one of her trances. Her body was sat on the rough stone floor next to him, but he knew her mind was elsewhere. That was fine by him, better that she was in some better place. He knew that if this passage went nowhere, they'd have to face the reality of never getting out of here. It was obvious to him that they were the first human beings in six hundred years to reach this space that may become their tomb. No, dammit, he wouldn't allow it to happen. There wasn't a single piece of wood, metal, rope of anything else they could use to climb back up the chimney, but he'd find something. Somewhere, somehow, he'd get her out of here. There was no time like the present, so he left her and crawled along the second passage. Like the chamber he'd just left, there was a dim light that allowed him to see. Where the hell was it coming from? Could the answer to that question be the means of their escape, or was it just some natural phenomenon? He crawled on. This passage was longer than the other. But like the first one, it came to a dead end, and he was faced with a blank wall. He sat down with his back to blocked wall and thought about their options. He put his hand down, and it touched something metal. Metal! He looked down. It was a natural shelf in the stonework, and on it was a heavy, wooden handled hammer and three wide bladed stone chisels. He held them in his hands as if they were a miracle, which they were. The designs were very old, undoubtedly forgotten by some sixteenth century stonemason. He examined the tools one by one. The wooden handle of the hammer seemed okay, but who knew after all this time. The metal of the chisels was in perfect condition. He crawled back to Faith, clutching his finds.

"You'll never guess what I found back there?"

She had come out of her trance and peered at him hopefully. "A way out?"

"Not quite, no, but almost as good. Look!"

"Can we do anything with those? I mean, do you intend to hack an exit through the stonework?"

"If I knew where to start, it's a distinct possibility. But the best way is to hack handholds up through the chimney and climb out that way."

"Can we do that?"

"There's nothing else to do. I'll make a start."

"Gabriel, something's happened."

He stared at her face through the gloom. Her eyes were shut as if she was trying to remember something. He recalled her trance-like state only moments before.

"Is it bad?"

"It's Galina. She came here to see Jonas. You remember he had a some kind of a contract here in Seville?"

"I do, yes. But how do you know she came here too?"

"I know you don't always believe me, but I had a vision, Gabriel. You know how close Galina and I are. I saw, oh, God, it was awful."

"For Christ's sake, what happened?"

"Her plane crashed in the mountains. I saw flames and smoke, people screaming, and an aircraft skidding along the top of a snow covered mountain."

"Jesus Christ, is she alive?"

"That was all I saw, the crash. I don't know anything more than that."

He sat down on the rough floor and pulled her to him. "We're not having a good week, are we? We're trapped in this hole, and your best friend is, well, we don't know. But you have to face up to it, she could be…"

"Dead? Yes, but somehow I don't think so, I'd know."

"Listen, we'll get out of here. I'll get us out of here. There's no doubt that with those tools I can cut the handholds and pull ourselves up to the top."

"Gabriel, what if she's dead?"

"She's not dead, Faith. We'll get out of here and find her alive."

"How can you be so sure?"

\* \* \*

He thought back to a mission in Afghanistan that had gone wrong almost from the start. They had intel from a Taliban informer about a bombmaker. They were taking a period of R & R at Camp Phoenix in the capital, Kabul. When the informer came across, the brass were so excited that they called in the Delta Force Team Bravo specialists to stage an immediate raid and eliminate the bastard. They were tired; all of them, and the news that they were going back into the field was the first blow. The second blow fell on the morning they were due to depart, and the informer was found nearby with his throat slit. They boarded the Little Bird helicopters anyway and were airlifted to Ghazni, south of Kabul on the A1 road that bisected the country. The helos landed on the beaten earth of the village square. They clambered off the sides and deployed behind cover at the side of the stone huts surrounding the square. An automatic rifle started to fire, spraying them with bullets, and they dived further behind cover. Side by side with Jonas Savage, the man they called 'The Tank', and his best friend inside and outside the unit, they advanced from house to house, laying down fire to keep the rifleman's head down while other members of the team fought their way towards him. One of their Delta troopers, Specialist Ray Davis, broke cover and raced past the village well, heading for the shooter's position. He was new to the team, less experienced than the others. Probably he wanted to win his spurs on this one. But some instinct, honed from years of bitter fighting with the insurgents, sounded an alarm in Gabriel's head. It was wrong, all wrong, and nothing like their usual tactics. Jonas must have had the same idea, and they both said 'Suicide Bomber' at the same time. Gabriel stood up, emptied his clip and shouted, 'Ray, stop, it's a trap, get back!' The soldier didn't hear above the noise of battle, and he ran on. That was when the third blow hit them. The explosion, when it came was devastating. The house the shooter was firing from literally disappeared, as did three of the houses around it. The blast was massive, and it must have been caused by several tons of explosive. Perhaps more than they'd intended. It appeared to Gabriel and Jonas that the suicide bomb had ignited a much larger cache of explosives. Ray Davis had disappeared, along with the houses, the shooter and everything inside of a fifty-yard square. All that was left was piles of stone and rubble. It looked for all the world like the old black and white photographs of Berlin in 1945 after the Allied bombing. The surviving Team Bravo troopers walked to the edge of the rubble. Marty Abrams was the first to speak.

"He's gone, the poor bastard. You know he had a wife back at Bragg, Marla, couple of kids, too. Who the hell's going to tell them?"

No one answered him. There was no need for an

answer. The army had a set routine for these things. The wives of other serving team members would gather around the grieving widow and help would be offered. It was war, and war created a great number of grieving widows, it always had. But something wasn't right. Gabriel separated himself from the group and started measuring angles, trying to recall the way the village square looked before the explosion. He walked all around it, and Jonas joined him.

"What? What are you thinking, a problem?"

Gabriel shook his head absently. "No, no. The blast pattern, and the way it all happened. Do you remember where Ray was when it went off?"

"Yeah, of course. He was right there, about twenty feet away." He pointed to a huge pile of rubble.

"Right. And the blast would have knocked him back, yes?"

"Sure, it always does."

"Wasn't there a well by there?"

Jonas tried to picture it. "Yeah, I reckon so."

"It's not there now."

"Yeah, and?"

Then it came to him. "You think he may have been blown into the well?"

"It's a possibility. Call the men over. Let's start pulling the rubble away from the area where we saw the well."

They started ripping away at the broken masonry and rubble, using their hands and pieces of lumber to scrape and drag away the detritus of the blast. One of the posts that supported the winding rope appeared, and there was a sheet of rusted corrugated iron that lay across the well opening, covered in more rubble. They ripped it away.

"Ray! Are you down there?" someone shouted.

"I'm here. Get me out, it's freezing cold."

They went wild with joy. One of the men pulled out his rappelling rope and threw it down to the trapped soldier. Less than four minutes later, his head appeared out of the hole in the ground, and a grinning Ray Davis was pulled all the way out. He was covered in burns and abrasions from the explosion, but he would live to fight another day. And go home to his wife and kids.

*  *  *

"Believe me, I'm sure. I saw a lot of action in Afghanistan, and one lesson we learned from day one was never to give up on a buddy, and never to believe they're dead. Not until you see the body, and even then you can't be sure. She's alive."

Her eyes were wide, reflecting the faint luminosity that permeated the dark chamber that incarcerated them. He wondered again where it came from. Then he wrenched his mind back to the present. They needed to get out of here, so he picked up the hammer and the middle sized chisel and walked to the base of the chimney. The hammer came down on the chisel, again, and again, and again. He climbed up and tested the first handholds and footholds and discovered they were usable. That was good. It meant they could get out of here. It was just a question of time, a lot of time. As if reading his mind, Faith came and stood beneath where he worked and called up to him, "Have you any idea how long it will take?"

He climbed back down. It was useless lying to her, and she would see through the deception anyway. "I estimate the height of that chimney we fell down to be about three hundred feet. I guess I can cut out the niches for us to climb up with at the rate of about one hundred feet a day."

He felt, rather than saw, her disappointment. But she tried to cover it.

"That's marvelous, Gabriel. Can I help do the work?"

He climbed down to her and took her in his arms. "It's not marvelous at all, and you know it. Three days of sweaty work in this dark place, with no food or water, is going to be like a journey to hell."

"But at least we won't wind up in hell," she grinned. "Besides, even if we are a little hungry or thirsty, there are one or two things that we can sustain ourselves with." Her voice had gone sultry and husky. He was astonished that in this hellish dungeon she could manage to feel arousal. He was even more astonished that he felt just as horny. Was it the presence of imminent death that brought about a surge in human libido? He'd read somewhere that it did have that effect. Except that death was the last thing on his mind. Maybe that was it, and the sex act was a mechanism that allowed the human brain to forget the terrible realities they faced. Then again, it could just be that he was in a dark place with a very beautiful girl. As a soldier, he'd learned to take opportunities when they presented themselves. He pulled her tightly to him and their mouths met, their tongues intertwined, and they were a long, long way away.

He must have fallen asleep. He woke up with his lover in his arms, feeling a raging thirst in the back of his throat. He reached out to the bedside table for a glass of water, and his hand touched dusty, broken rubble. He felt the warmth of Faith, listened to her regular breathing as she slept after their lovemaking. It was time to get started and carve out the stone ladder that would take her out of this Kingdom of Hades and back into the warmth and sunshine of Seville. He shook her awake.

"Faith, I have to get started. Move to one side so that the chips of stone don't fall on you."

"Gabriel, what are you…" She returned to full consciousness and looked at him. "Of course, yes. I'd forgotten where we were. You have that effect on me, Gabriel de Sade. Or at least your body does."

He chuckled. "It sure took our minds of it for a while, but I have to begin cutting the handholds. Are you okay?"

"Sure, I'm not going anywhere."

He kissed her and picked up his tools. He used the niches he'd cut to climb up, and he estimated he was at about twenty feet. Only two hundred and eighty to go, provided he'd guess correctly. He didn't tell Faith that if he was wrong, they could have problems. He hammered at the chisel for hour after hour, and finally he had to stop when his arms were numb and unable to continue. He climbed down and found that Faith had stripped of her skirt, jacket and pantyhose and was twisting them into some kind of a rope.

"I thought it could be useful. You may be able to use it as a safety rope if there's anything to tie it on."

He took it from her and tested it. It was strong, very strong. "This'll hold either of us, and I can use it to work faster. Thanks, but what about your clothes?"

She grinned. "It's pretty warm in here, I'm fine. Take the rope and get us out of here."

"Sure thing. I just need another few minutes to catch my breath."

"It sounds like hard work."

"It's okay," he replied in a noncommittal voice. But she wasn't fooled.

"It's pretty bad, is it?"

"Yeah, it's not so good. But nothing I can't handle."

He managed another three hours, helped by the rope that supported him so that he could attack the stone. He checked his watch. He was all in, and he'd cut handholds up to about eighty feet, but it wasn't enough. He'd have to do better after he'd had some rest and a few hours sleep. His tongue was glued to the roof of his mouth, and he was desperate for nourishment.

The work was achingly hard, and he knew it would take the very last reserves of his strength to get to the top. When he climbed down, Faith could see he was in a bad way, and she pulled him to her, helping him lay down on the rough ground to rest. He fell asleep immediately, exhausted, hungry and filled with a raging thirst like none he'd ever known. He woke a couple of hours later to the sound of stone chippings falling around him. He could hear the chisel being used above him. Faith was cutting the handholds.

"Faith, you should be careful up there. It must be over a hundred feet up by now."

She stopped chiseling and called down to him. "I know, but I'm quite able to do this while you rest."

"How long have you been up there?"

"Not long, about an hour or so."

He knew that meant at least twice that. "Come on down for a break, and I'll take over while you rest."

She only hesitated for a moment. "It's a deal. I'm about all in."

When she reached the ground level, he was horrified at

the state of her. She was covered in dust, and the scratches on her face were much worse as chips of stone were spat out by the action of the chisel. He helped her down the last few feet.

"How do you feel? You had a bad fall when you fell down here. You should be more careful."

She picked up on his concern right away.

"I look that bad, do I? I feel okay, just sore and thirsty. A short rest, and I can go back up there."

"I'm heading up there now, so you can try and get some sleep."

She nodded. "That would help. I've never done anything so tiring in all my life. But if we spell each other, it'll get done a lot quicker, and we can get out of here."

He gave her a hug and kissed her with a passionate intensity. She looked like she'd just emerged from a collapsed building, battered, bruised, scratched and bleeding. But to him, she was still the most beautiful, brave girl he had ever known.

He knew she shouldn't be a hundred feet up the chimney, chiseling handholds into the rough stone. She'd taken a much harder knock than he had when she fell down here. But it was also true that the quicker they got out, the better it would be for her. That meant both of them taking turns with the work. He stared into her eyes.

"Faith, when we get out of this, when this job is done, I'm going to take you somewhere good. I mean really good, the vacation of a lifetime."

"Sounds good to me," she smiled wearily. "What did you have in mind?"

"A honeymoon."

"But we're…"

Then she got it. "Are you serious?"

"I am. Faith Ward, will you marry me?"

"Dammit, de Sade, this is not the kind of proposal a girl envisages when she's growing up, you know." Her eyes were dancing as she returned his gaze. "But I guess it's the only option we have right now. Okay, yes. Yes, of course. I love you more than anything in the world."

"Me too. I could change jobs, you know. This one is not exactly ideal for a married guy."

"Hey, one thing at a time. Get us out of here, then we'll locate Galina, nail that murdering bastard, and head back Stateside. Then we can make plans."

He laughed. "So all I have to do is escape from the Temple of Doom, search the mountaintops and…"

"What was that? What did you say?"

"Search the mountaintops. Why?"

"No, before that."

"Escape from the Temple of Doom?"

"Yes, of course. It meant temple, not tomb."

"What did?"

"The hidden inscription on the medallion. 'Only in her tomb will Faith look east to rest beneath Saint Mary of the See.' Don't you see?" she said excitedly. "In the old days, they sometimes called tombs temples, and vise-versa."

He wasn't entirely sure what she meant. "How does this help us get out of here?"

"It doesn't, but you'll do that, Gabriel. You always do. You're most capable man I've ever known. And when we do get out, it's a new clue to the location of the treasure, and that could lead us to the killer. One thing's for sure, he's a lot closer to it than we are. If we can get on the trail of the treasure, we'll find him."

"I still don't get it. This clue business, what does it point to?"

"Oh that, it's really quite simple. Inside the Cathedral, there is a marble statue, a miniature copy of the Statue of Faith outside. In her temple, you see, inside the Cathedral. It means that we need to take a line due east of the statue, and somewhere along that line will be some kind of an access to an underground room that houses the treasure."

"Do you think the murderer knows this?"

"I doubt it," she replied thoughtfully. "But I'm sure he'll know that the statuette of Faith has a special significance. There's more than one person hunting the treasure."

He didn't get it, but he had little doubt she was right. Her knowledge of the more arcane elements of religious history was incredible, and he wouldn't to argue with her. He got to his feet and started climbing up the hand and footholds. They'd reached well over a hundred feet, thanks to Faith's efforts. He'd secretly begun to doubt that he could complete the task before exhaustion and thirst killed them. Now he worked at twice the pace.

They could do it. They would do it. And he'd nail the pervert who was murdering women. And find Galina alive. And he'd marry Faith. He chuckled to himself. Maybe he should try and find a cure for world hunger. But no, those things he'd set himself to do, he would do. He knew he would, and he had not the slightest doubt. He had Faith. He almost fell from his precarious perch when a voice shouted from high above him.

"Hey, is there anyone down there?"

It was a voice he knew well. The one man in the entire world he'd trust with his life, and the one he'd come to rely on through so many battles and skirmishes that would have finished a lesser man. It was 'The Tank'. Jonas had come.

# CHAPTER EIGHT

They sat at a pavement café in the Seville sunshine. The hardwood tables were covered in lace cloths, the chairs thickly cushioned, and the umbrellas large enough to hide them from the sun that beat down on the city. Potted palm trees discreetly screened off the tables from each other, so they didn't notice the priest sitting at the next table who listened intently while they discussed the dual hunt, for the killer, and for the downed aircraft. A potted palm tree masked his table. Cyclists sped past them, sometimes only inches away, sometimes flanked by inline skaters. Once, a horse trotted past, pulling a beautiful and ornate black cart with two grinning lovers sat inside.

And yet only hours before, they'd teetered on the edge of a precipice that led all the way to hell. After Jonas helped them out of the chimney with professional climbing ropes borrowed from the local Proteccion Civil, the Spanish emergency rescues service, he'd helped them back to their hotel. It took a long, hot shower, several pints of fluid, and a few hours rest for them to recover from the shock of their ordeal. They'd come to eat Spanish tapas and relax in the fresh afternoon air after their entombment in the bowels of the Cathedral. But Gabriel was even more shocked at Jonas' appearance, now that he'd recovered enough to see his friend's face more clearly.

"How did you find out where we were?" he asked his former Team Bravo comrade.

Jonas shrugged. "It wasn't too hard. I asked that Bishop Santiago where you were last seen, and he said you were headed to the roof space. I took a flashlight the size of a small searchlight up there and saw the damaged timbers over the hole. That was when I called down."

Both of them had put off asking the question they were frightened of hearing the wrong answer to, but it had to be faced. Faith mentioned it first.

"It's Galina, isn't it? That's why you came looking for us?"

He nodded. "Yeah, that's right. I was finishing up an assignment here, and she was due to join me for a few days vacation. Her flight from Madrid never arrived."

"It crashed."

He nodded to her. "Yeah, I guess it did, but no one knows. It just disappeared off the radar. Crashed, probably. Maybe hijacked. But she's gone. I came to ask you to help. I have to try to find her, wherever she is."

"No, that wasn't a question," Faith corrected him. "I meant that it crashed, not did it crash?"

He stared at her. "How the hell could you know that? You can't know that."

She took his hand and held it tight. "Jonas, listen to me. You're aware that I sometimes get, for want of a better word, visions. I see things, hear things."

He shrugged. "Well, yeah, I suppose so."

"Her aircraft crashed in the mountains, in thick snow. That's all I know. I don't know if she survived. But the aircraft came down."

"Thick snow? But we're in Southern Spain. That's impossible. There is no snow in these parts."

Gabriel called over a waiter, a man who spoke good English. "Excuse me, is there anywhere around here with thick snow? A mountain, or mountain range, something like that?"

He nodded eagerly. "Of course there is. A range of high mountains called the Sierra Nevada. Very popular with tourists who go skiing there in winter."

"Is it a big place, possible for people to get lost in?"

"Sure, sure. But there are ski rescue organizations that track lost parties all the time. Is someone you know lost up there?"

"I don't know, maybe. Thanks."

"You're welcome, Senor."

Jonas was already on his feet. "I've got to get there, this Sierra Nevada place. Does anyone have a map? I'll call a cab. They'll know where to go."

Faith eased him back into his seat. "Jonas, we have to do this properly. You can't go up a mountain range in a cream linen suit, a pair of Docksiders, and a gun inside your jacket. Let's think about this. It won't help her if we go off in the wrong direction."

The wild look in his eyes faded. He inclined his head and gave her a small smile. "I guess you're right, Faith. Where do we start?"

It was a measure of his desperation that the normally methodical Jonas Savage was wrenched apart by the disappearance of the woman he loved. Faith pulled a notebook and a pen from her purse and began to make a list.

"First, we need maps of the area." She made a note. "Next, we could do with an overflight to try and locate the aircraft, unless it's hidden. I did see it come down in deep snow, and it skidded across the mountainside."

She looked across at Gabriel who was silent. "The serial killer, you're worried about abandoning the hunt?"

He nodded. "It's going to be difficult. The pace of the killings is increasing, and I don't know how I can justify leaving him to carry on his butchery."

Jonas gave him an irritated glance. "What the hell? This is Galina we're talking about! You don't even know the guy you're looking for is still in Spain. Maybe he's gone back to New York."

"Yeah, maybe. I'm not ducking out, my friend. But neither can I stand by and see a row of body parts lined up because I failed to do my job."

He felt uncomfortable. There could be an aircraft downed in the Sierra Nevada and people dying of shock, injuries and exposure. Or they could all be dead, and he could leave the killer free to continue with his spree. He realized that they were waiting for him to come to a decision.

"I'll call Javier and find out how things are going from his end."

He used his cell to call the Spanish detective. Javier sounded grim.

"Where are you?"

"In the coffee bar, the Café of the Indies."

"I need to see you. I'll be there in ten minutes."

He clicked off and turned to Faith and Jonas. "He's coming here. I don't know why. I guess something's happened."

Faith raised her eyebrows. She was about to speak when Jonas said "I can't sit here drinking coffee in the sun while she could be dying up in the snow. I have to go."

He made to stand up, but Faith put a hand on his arm.

"Jonas, please, a few more minutes. Let's see what this detective has to say. You know that if Gabriel can help with a clear conscience, he will. It will make the search much faster with all of us involved."

"Yeah, I know that, but…"

"And there's another thing. Do you have any contacts with the Spanish police or the Guardia Civil?"

He shook his head. "No, I don't. Can't even speak Spanish, except for stuff like 'manos arriba', and that's not going to help me up in the mountains."

"What does it mean?"

He looked blank, and then it clicked. "Oh, 'manos arriba', it means 'hands up'. We needed to know the basic phrases down in, well, somewhere in South America."

"Right. Maybe this detective can set up some kind of a liaison."

He thought about that for a few moments and then looked at his watch. "I'll give it twenty minutes, but then I have to start. The first thing I need to fix up is transportation to the Sierra Nevada. I'll contact a friend of mine. He can fix up a helicopter charter, that'll be the quickest way. As soon as we've talked to this cop, I intend to move out, whatever happens."

Faith and Gabriel tried to distract him, but all they could do was help him complete the list of the necessities for a mountain search and rescue. Suddenly, Jonas had an idea.

"I could contact the search and rescue people in that mountain range, tell them what you saw."

"Jonas, they'd ask for details, when and how I saw the aircraft crashing in the snow. You think they'd believe you when you told them it was a vision from someone you know?"

He looked downcast. "You're right. They'd tell me to go to hell. Politely, I guess, the Spanish seem to be very polite. But the effect would be the same, so I'm on my own."

"No," Faith objected. "We're with you, you know that."

They ordered more coffee, and as the waiter was putting it on the table, Javier Garcia arrived, his face gloomy. He ordered coffee for himself and sat down.

"There's been another one," he announced without introduction.

"Dear God, where was it?" de Sade asked him. "By the way, this is a friend of ours, Jonas Savage. Jonas, this is Javier Garcia."

The men shook hands. "The body parts were found in a roof space of the Cathedral. We believe that when you went searching for a hidden space, the girl was there already, tied and gagged. It was the same as the others, a ritual dismemberment."

Jonas looked at Gabriel. "So this is the same guy as the one who's doing the New York killings?"

"We think so, yes. He has to be stopped. The rate of killings is increasing. This guy is a real bad one, the worst. No, that doesn't even begin to describe him. He is the worst. The devil incarnate."

"That is an accurate description," the Spaniard agreed

with him. "It has become so serious that my colonel has taken over the inquiry, so it is now out of my hands. He has assigned ten detectives who will spend all of their time hunting this murderer until he is apprehended. He told me to inform you there is no need for your presence here in Seville, Detective de Sade. He also said if you wish to return to New York, you may pursue your investigation from there."

"Good of him," Gabriel replied, keeping his anger in check. "What about you?"

Javier spread his hands. "I have no duties, alas, and all I am required to do is make myself available if they need me, which is not likely to be anytime soon."

"What happened, why are you in trouble?" Faith asked him. "If that isn't too personal a question."

Javier froze for an instant. He looked around the café and then at the three of them. It was clear he couldn't decide whether to confide in them or not. Abruptly, his shoulders slumped. "The man at the bull farm, Diego Montalban. I told you he is a friend of mine, yes?"

They nodded. He seemed to gulp for air, for the strength to carry on. He is more than just a friend. You understand that although in Spain we have some of the most relaxed laws for minorities in Europe, not everyone agrees that it should be so. Here in Seville we have a strict hierarchy with a rigid set of social standards and morals. My colonel is from a family that can trace its ancestry back hundreds of years, to the Reconquista, when the Moors were driven out of Spain. He has a rigid and ruthless adherent to those standards."

He stopped speaking, unsure about how to continue. But Faith interrupted.

"Javier, you're gay, aren't you? So what, if Diego Montalban is your lover, that's your business?"

He shook his head. "Not in Seville, it isn't. I've not been pushed out of front line duties because of it, of course. My colonel found other reasons, supposed infractions of the code of conduct that had to be considered. But it was just an excuse. Besides, after what happened, I told him we were finished."

Jonas made to stand up. "Look, this is all very interesting, but…"

"Hold it," Faith stopped him. "Just a few more minutes. I have an idea, and it's worth waiting, Jonas. A few minutes, no more."

He slumped down and waited. She looked at Gabriel. "You know what I'm thinking?"

He nodded. "I do, but I'm not happy about dropping my investigation."

"It's been dropped for you," she pointed out.

He nodded. "I guess that's right. Maybe those detectives will strike lucky. Javier, how would you like an all-expenses paid trip to the Sierra Nevada?"

His mouth fell open, and he even forgot they were speaking in English. "Que?"

Gabriel turned to Jonas. "You'd better get that helicopter booked. It looks as if we're all going right away. There's nothing for us here."

He nodded. "I'll get right on it."

Jonas stood up to move out of earshot of the Spanish cop. It was a lifetime habit of being careful that strangers in strange lands didn't know too much about your business. His kinds of operations were often outside of the laws of the countries they took place in, and there was no sense in taking any chances where his lover was concerned.

Gabriel quickly explained where they needed to go, and why. Javier was staggered.

"You know that the Sierra Nevada is a mountain range? It is near Granada and contains the highest point in Spain, 11,411 feet above sea level. My friends, it is covered in snow at this time of year. It is a vast place, and there are literally hundreds of kilometers of mountains, so why would you wish to go there? Are you taking up skiing?"

Faith explained what had happened, the aircrash, and Jonas' lover on the Madrid to Seville flight. And her vision, her seeing the plane crash in the snow. He wasn't convinced.

"But, surely there will be a search for this missing aircraft. There cannot be anything you can add to what is being done."

She shook her head. "No, that's not correct. There will be a search, of course there will. But I can offer something they do not have."

"Your vision?"

Gabriel smiled at his obvious skepticism. "Javier, she's not some crazy psychic. Faith does have an ability to communicate..."

He stopped. Communicate with what? After spending so much time with her, he had sufficient knowledge of her powers to believe in them. But what they were, and where they came from, he still had no idea. No, that wasn't true. He had an idea, but to voice it would be more than he was prepared to do for fear of ridicule. The power had developed when she entered an Orthodox convent in Russia as a nun. It wasn't her intention to take the veil, at the time she was on the run and needed a hiding place.

But during her short time in the convent, something had happened to her, something that brought her uncanny ability to the surface, a sixth sense, the power of God or some long-forgotten part of her brain? Who knew? It was enough to know that she had the power, and it was real.

"Just accept it, okay? It's real."

Javier nodded, a little reluctantly. "Very well, for now, let us assume that she is correct. You intend to travel to the Sierra Nevada to search for this aircraft that may or may not…" He stopped and held up his hand. "I'm sorry, that you know has crash landed in the snow somewhere high up in the mountains. You intend to search for the wreckage and any survivors. Just the three of you."

Gabriel nodded. "That about sums it up. Except for one thing, Javier. We'd do much better with four of us, with you along. It's your country, and you're a cop. You could get us past the red tape and help us to conduct the search. It's an impossible enough task as it is, but with you along, we could pull it off. Besides, you're a member of the national police force, so that counts for something. What do you say?"

But it was Faith who spoke. "Listen, the Sierra Nevada. Doesn't it lie to the west of here?" She was thinking furiously. "And that statuette of Faith, the small one inside the Cathedral, doesn't it look to the east?"

Javier looked curious. "For the statuette I cannot say, but the Sierra Nevada is certainly to the east of Seville."

She looked with excitement at the three men. "The inscription read, 'Only in her tomb will Faith look east to rest beneath Saint Mary of the See and the true believer will gain their rightful place in heaven'. We assumed that Saint Mary of the See referred to the Cathedral here in

Seville."

Javier looked puzzled. "But that is its name. Saint Mary of the See."

"Yes, but we had a piece brought into our gallery in New York several months ago, a leather bound old bible. It was from before the days of the printing press, so it was hand copied, a beautiful piece, with ornate engravings on the edges of the…"

"Faith, you're not selling it to us," Gabriel reminded her.

She pulled a face. "I got carried away, sorry. But the thing is, it came originally from a tiny church, more of a chapel really, in the Sierra Nevada. It's there, the treasure, it has to be. Once we've located the air crash and called in help for the survivors, we can continue with the hunt. Javier, will you come with us?"

He stared at her. "You talk of a hunt. A hunt for treasure or for a serial killer?"

Gabriel answered him. "Nothing takes precedence over finding the killer once we've located the aircraft. And if we do find the treasure, believe me, Faith would insist that it is returned to the Church, to the Cathedral here in Seville."

He nodded. "In that case, I will come."

\* \* \*

How fickle chance was, he thought to himself. What made the priest, one of his acquaintances, to go to that particular café and sit at that particular table while he was taking his regular afternoon coffee? It was fate that had brought the man there at the exact time when the people were sat close by, surely it was meant to be. He listened as the man eagerly recounted the conversation.

"They talked of the Sierra Nevada, something about a connection with the treasure and the statue of Faith."

He scoffed at the man. "They must be crazy, thinking that anything could be hidden in the mountains."

"They seemed very certain."

"As do all fools, my friend. Forget about it. They've been sampling too many of our fine Sevillian wines."

When the man left, he thought how interesting the conversation had been. The Sierra Nevada, that was something entirely new. He booted his laptop and started a Google search. Yes, there had been a tiny church there, high in the mountains, several kilometers from Laguna de las Mares, a ski resort. The church was little more than a climber's chapel in a remote part of the mountains and well away from the established ski slopes. Apparently, it was now abandoned and had fallen into disrepair. According to the article, the chapel was something of a local joke because it possessed the same name as the mighty Cathedral in Seville. Was it possible that the treasure he sought was hidden in the ruins of some crumbling chapel in the snow-covered mountains? The more he thought about it, the more it seemed likely. It explained why the treasure had been searched for over so many hundreds of years and never found. His pulse raced, and he felt his breathing become shallow as excitement seized his body. It was there. It had to be there. The treasure was almost theirs. These Americans would find it. Then they would be killed, the men first. They were a danger, and then the woman. Soon, yes, it would be soon, and they wouldn't even see it coming.

* * *

They bought supplies for the journey. Fortunately, Seville was the kind of place that had stores catering to every need. Riding, hunting, and outdoor sports were well provided for, as was bullfighting. They managed to purchase tough, weatherproof clothing, leather climbing boots, and a range of supplies that would fit into four new canvas and leather rucksacks. Jonas approved of these.

"They're almost the same as the ones that Special Forces use," he smiled to Gabriel.

"Yeah, I remember. I can also remember carrying them over marathon courses that we were forced to jog in pouring rain."

"So?"

"Some bastard filled them with rocks, as I recall, someone by the name of Jonas Savage. It half killed most of us."

Jonas grinned. "I needed to get the guys fit and keep them that way."

"As I recall, I was fit before I started the course. It was afterwards I felt so bad."

"Okay, I'll make sure there are no rocks in these."

They filled the rucksacks with a range of supplies, flashlights, water bottles, high-energy foods, and spare warm clothing. While they were in the store, Jonas took a call from the air charter company he'd spoken to. They had a six-seat helicopter waiting on the tarmac at Seville Airport that would take them to Granada.

* * *

The sight of the helo took him back a long time. They were returning from a mission close to Laskar Gar, in Helmand province, when they got the call for their Chinook helicopter to detour and pick up several wounded Afghan Army troops. The pilot changed course and they headed to the LZ. When they came in to land, they suddenly came under mortar attack. It wasn't too serious as the LZ was secured by two hundred Afghan National Army troops. The attacking force included a Taliban mortar team that was dropping rounds at random into the area. The pilot held off while they surveyed the scene. To their astonishment, most of the Afghan troops had panicked. They began to run to the Chinook, hoping to be taken off. It was when they began pulling off the wounded to make room for themselves that Gabriel and Jonas had to act. They started knocking the Afghan regulars out of the cabin. A few were clutching at the landing gear, hoping to get away from a fight they considered lost.

Meanwhile the mortar team began to zero in the LZ. They started dropping rounds closer and closer. The rounds were hitting so close the Team could feel the impact of the explosions because they made the Chinook shake each time they went off. Time was critical. They had to get out of there or get out of the helicopter before a round hit it. Yet the wounded lay in disarray around the LZ, their dressings torn apart by the brutal handling they'd received at the hands of their comrades. The aircraft commander shouted at them to shoot the Afghans. They had to get the wounded aboard and get out from under the mortar fire. The pilots took the heavy helicopter off the ground, enough to prevent the Afghans climbing aboard. Beneath them, they watched the troops screaming and hitting and crying, trying to get close to the hovering Chinook. It was an ugly sight. They managed to push the remaining regulars off the helo. The pilot then landed the Chinook amidst the chaos of wounded and panicking men to make another attempt to reach the wounded. They took off and headed away from the LZ as rounds were exploding behind them and hitting where the helicopter had landed. When they returned to Kandahar Air Base, they discovered that the few wounded they'd recovered were already dead. Jonas tried to console him with the fact that they hadn't suffered any unit casualties, but for many nights Gabriel lay awake remembering that terrible panic as the unwounded tried to board the Chinook. And the wounded lay on the ground, like so much discarded trash.

\* \* \*

"What about getting up the mountain, do you think the guy will be okay with that?" Gabriel asked.

"Sure," Jonas nodded. "I'll offer him a few extra bucks. He'll play ball."

"Right, and if he doesn't want to play ball? As I recall, people get touchy about unauthorized flights into areas where there are skiers. They're worried it could set off an avalanche."

"If that does happen, I'll threaten to shoot him. Are you carrying?"

"The police took my 9mm Llama, so I had to borrow Faith's .22."

"That's no problem, I've got some spare guns in my bag. What about a Glock 17, is that still your weapon of choice?"

"Sure, that'll do the job. Faith, are you okay with the Llama?"

"I'm fine, thanks Jonas."

"Okay, then. My guy sold me a couple of Heckler and Koch MP5 submachine guns. They're useful tools. I'll keep them in my bag. There are plenty of spare magazines if we need them. I think that about covers it."

Behind them, Javier let out a low groan of despair.

A cab took them to Seville Airport, and they bypassed the passenger terminal and drove into the private aviation area. There was an assortment of light aircraft, a company jet, a Gulfstream, half a dozen single and twin prop air taxis, and the incongruous shape of an Antonov AN-2, a Soviet era passenger aircraft. It was a single engine biplane, looking out of date amidst the paraphernalia of a modern passenger terminal. Javier glanced at it, his face registering a mixture of fear and disbelief.

"Are we flying in that aircraft? It is too old, surely. It looks like a museum piece."

Jonas smiled. "It's okay, there should be a helicopter waiting for us somewhere."

A short, thin, wiry looking guy came out of an office at the side of one of the hangars and walked over to them. He wore canvas combat trousers tucked into jump boots, an A2 flight jacket, and mirrored aviator shades. He looked to be about sixty years old, his eyes heavily lined after a lifetime of squinting through aircraft windshields. They judged he was a former Spanish Airforce pilot.

"Mr. Savage?"

Jonas nodded, and they shook hands.

"My name is Miguel Rivera. I am your pilot for this charter. The aircraft is at the back of the hangar. If you'd like to come this way, we can take off straight away. They followed him around the building, and the helicopter waiting for them. It was a familiar sight, a Bell UH-1 Iroquois, painted in the livery of the charter company. Known more familiarly as the Huey, the helo was the icon of the war in Vietnam. It was painted silver and blue instead of the familiar green of the war in South East Asia. But it still managed to look warlike, despite the paintwork and the absence of a door gunner.

Miguel opened the rear door. "If you'd like to get aboard, I'll start up. I'm not clear on the destination, but I understand it is somewhere near the Sierra Nevada. Granada, I assume. It is a first class civilian airport, and you will find all the facilities you need there."

"Can we discuss it when we're on the way?" Jonas replied. "We have one or two details to finalize for our itinerary, and we'll discuss it then."

He nodded. "Very well. It is about a two hour journey, so there is plenty of time." They strapped in, and Miguel went through the pre-flight checks. The engine start was shattering, and they all reached for the communications headsets that were stowed in front of each seat. The pilot fed thrust to the engine, the rotors bit into the air, and they took off, climbing steeply away from the airport. At five thousand feet, his voice came through their headphones.

"I've given air traffic control at Federico García Lorca Airport, that's Granada, to advise them that we're en route. If you need to change anything, I'd appreciate your advising me as soon as possible."

"I'll come forward and talk to you about the options we have available," Jonas replied.

He unplugged his headset and went forward to sit in the

left hand seat, where normally the co-pilot would sit, and plugged back into the aircraft's communications system. He turned to stare at Rivera.

"Miguel, we've got a situation. You know about the aircraft that went down on a flight to Seville from Madrid?"

"Of course, I remember. I was on stand by for a search mission, but the aircraft simply disappeared, so they have so far failed to find a search area. It could be anywhere in Spain. Even elsewhere, if it was hijacked."

"Yeah, you've got it. We think we may have a lead on where the plane could have come down, and we want to go there and check it out. It is in an area high in the mountains, about ten miles from Laguna de las Mares."

"Where did you get this information? I understood that no one knew where the aircraft came down."

"It's a long story, and I prefer not to go into it now. We think there is a good chance this lead can help us find it."

"I hope that is true. But why do you not inform the search and rescue authorities? They will send hundreds of people into the area to conduct the search."

Jonas didn't reply at first. There was no easy way to answer him. "We can't do that, Miguel. The information came from an extrasensory source."

"I'm sorry, what is that, extrasensory?"

"It means outside the normal human sensory perception. Stuff like intuition, psychics, religious revelations, you know that sort of thing."

"I still don't understand. Are you saying you believe this?"

His voice was incredulous, which only to be expected.

"In this particular case, yes. The person who gave us

this information has always been reliable."

They could almost feel the pilot shrug and sense his smile of disbelief. "I see. In that case, the authorities will not be inclined to follow it up, but if you wish to do so, of course, that is your choice. The nearest airport for me to land is Granada. From there you will find transport to take you up to the slopes and ski lifts for the final part of the journey, at least to Laguna de las Mares. How you will reach this place ten miles away, I don't know, perhaps you can hire some skis?"

"We want you to take us, Miguel. All the way into the mountains and land ten miles north of Laguna de las Mares so that we can start the search without delay."

"You're not serious? I cannot land up there. There are no helipads. I doubt there is even a flat space for me to get the helicopter down even if Air Traffic Control allowed it, which they won't. No, it must be Granada."

Jonas kept talking to the man, his voice quiet and persuasive. "Miguel, my girlfriend, you understand, my partner, was on that flight. I have to get up there to find her. What would it take to persuade you? How about an extra ten thousand dollars on the charter?"

"Senor, I could do with the extra money, of course. Trade has been very quiet of late, but it is still impossible. You must land at Granada and arrange transport from there. My God, if they found out, they…"

The man stared at the huge pistol pressed into his ribs. He turned to stare at Jonas.

"You are a fool, Senor, to threaten the pilot. Who will fly this helicopter if you shoot me?"

"Part of my Delta Force training was on Hueys, Miguel. Would you like a demonstration? And my friend Gabriel in the back can also pilot one of these. I really want you to take us up the mountain. We can do this the hard way or the easy way. It's your choice, Amigo."

Rivera was indeed a former Spanish Airforce pilot. He'd been trained to assess a situation fast and then act the best possible outcome. In this case, there was only one.

"I will do as you say, Mr. Savage. But you should know that it is illegal and for good reason. An aircraft landing in those mountains could set off an avalanche. If Air Traffic Control finds out, and they are sure to, they are likely to arrest all of us."

"We'll have to take that chance," was Jonas' terse reply. "It's either that or we let those people die."

"If they are there, and if they are alive," Miguel pointed out.

"Yeah. We'll see. You need to get us down here," he took out the map he'd bought in Seville and pointed out a position. "It's called 'Montaña de la Muerte'."

"I will do my best. You know that means 'Mountain of Death'? I know of that peak, and it is named for good reason. Some of those areas are inaccessible, and there have been a number of fatalities from climbers and a few off-piste skiers that have tried to reach them. What do you plan to do if there is no place to land?"

Jonas smiled at him. "I'm relying on you, Miguel, and you'll find somewhere, I know you will, and one more thing, my friend. Don't try and use the radio. It really wouldn't be a healthy thing for you to do."

"I understand."

Jonas stayed next to him to keep an eye on him, and they flew on across clear blue skies. Then the heights of the Sierra Nevada appeared, closer and closer. Soon they were all able to see the kind of landscape they were heading for. Razor sharp peaks and narrow, snow filled valleys in between. As they drew nearer, Miguel pointed out one particularly steep peak, shaped almost like a church steeple. It stuck out higher than the other peaks that surrounded it, making it appear forbidding and ominous.

"That is our destination. The Mountain of Death."

# CHAPTER NINE

There was nowhere to land. No plateaus, no rocky shelves, nothing.

"It's hopeless," the pilot said to Jonas. "We'll have to turn back to the airport. You will need to travel up here using the ski lift."

Savage almost agreed, but just before Miguel moved his control stick to vector the helicopter back to Granada, he sighted a dark shadow inset into the mountainside.

"There. Can you see that? Go down and check it out. We may get in there."

Rivera stared at him. "You cannot be serious? You know what the crosswinds and updrafts are like on these mountainsides? We'll crash for sure if I try to land on that."

"Take her down. Let's take a look."

He shrugged and pushed the stick forward, nosing the helicopter downwards and towards the dark, threatening rock of the mountainside. As they got nearer, it was indeed a shelf that Jonas had seen.

"Yeah, that'll do it. Put her down there."

Miguel kept the Huey in the hover. "No, I cannot! If I try and land there, we will smash the rotors and destroy the aircraft. I will not do it."

Jonas put his hand on the control stick and felt for the collective, the Huey lurched slightly as he moved it. "That's okay, take your hands off the controls. I'll put it down there."

"Senor, you will kill us all. It is impossible."

"Impossible or not, we're going in there," Jonas replied implacably. "Take your hands off. I'm taking control."

Miguel shook his head. "There is no need. I have thousands of hours of experience flying this helicopter. I have the best chance of landing it. I will do it."

Jonas nodded. "Good. Take us in."

They were above the rocky shelf. He tilted the nose downwards and sideslipped towards the narrow strip of rock. As they veered nearer, the updraft caught them and swept the helicopter toward the mountainside. Miguel hauled on the collective, stamped on the rudder, and banked the helicopter over and away from the mountain.

"It is difficult, as I said. The updraft is sucking us towards the rocks."

"Yeah, you need to stand off. Come in slower, and let it pull us in for the last few feet."

The Spaniard glanced at Jonas. His expression was bitter and his voice cold. "As I said, I have thousands of hours experience flying this machine. I know how to counter the wind shear."

Jonas said nothing as they went in again. The aircraft bucked and tossed in the air. At one point, they all heard a scream from the rear when Javier thought the mountain was about to claim its latest victim. But Miguel steered the helicopter like the total professional he was, and it edged nearer and nearer to the narrow ledge. It was a brilliant piece of flying, and he seemed to become one with the rearing, bucking machine, soothing it past the worst of the vicious crosswinds and updrafts to edge; foot by foot, closer to the ledge. One landing ski touched, and another wind caught them, and they bounced back up in the air. He adjusted the collective, and they slammed down hard, but a further wind rushed in and caught the fuselage, tilting it over so that the rotor blade edged closer and closer to the rock.

"Quick, everyone move over to the port side of the aircraft. We need the weight to settle her," he shouted.

They scrambled to one side and felt the machine tip slightly, moving the rotors away from the rock. The wind blew forcefully, and still the blades tipped over nearer and nearer to disaster. Until there was an abrupt lessening of noise, and Miguel did the only thing he could do. He cut the engine power. It was risky, very risky. If a cross wind smashed into them, they had no power to correct. But as the power to the blades died away, the lift began to fall away, and the machine settled, or rather wobbled, to a precarious stop on the shelf.

In the back, Gabriel slid open the door, and an icy, gale force wind howled into the cabin. He slammed it shut again.

"We need to change into warm clothing before we go out there. Without it, we'll die of hypothermia."

They looked at each other grimly.

"If that aircraft came down somewhere in this vicinity," Javier observed, "there is no chance for any survivors.

They won't last have lasted long in this cold."

They dragged their thermal parkas out of their packs, zipped them on, and laced up the heavy mountaineering boots. Gabriel was ready first; fastening his thick, fur-lined hood on his head and pulling on thick, waterproof gloves. He turned to look at Javier.

"In that case we need to hurry." Faith finished zipping up her mountain clothing and prepared to go outside, but Gabriel stopped her.

"Before we do anything, we need some kind of a plan. Does any of this look familiar to you?"

"I'm afraid it does. Do you see that slope over there?" She pointed at a stretch of mountainside eight hundred yards away. "That looks like what I saw."

Miguel turned around to stare them, his expression incredulous. "You know there is a crevasse between us and that slope. It will be impossible to reach it. And don't ask me to fly over there."

"Why not?" Javier asked him. "You got us in here."

Rivera grimaced. "Indeed, and that was a miracle. But taking off is another matter. The moment the aircraft lifts off the ground, the crosswinds will smash the rotors against the side of them mountain. I cannot build up enough speed to get out of the ground effect to counter the winds. The Huey is trapped here. Forever."

They were all silent until Jonas spoke. "We can get her out. I've done it before in Afghanistan. You wait for the wind to change direction, and then give her full throttle in the opposite direction, and drift her away from the mountainside."

Miguel shook his head. "I think not. She will be smashed pieces if you try it."

Jonas fixed him with a stare. "That's okay, it's not my helicopter." His expression changed to a grin. "On the other hand, if you want to keep it in one piece, you'd better start thinking about how it's done. I think it's time we went and found those people."

"But the crevasse," Javier objected.

"That's why we brought climbing gear," Gabriel said, pulling a long rope out of his pack. "We should have enough rope, pitons, and karabiners to get us across. I suggest we make a start and find out."

"And me?" Miguel asked. "What do you wish me to do?"

Gabriel stared at him. "I suggest you start working out how to get this helo out of here."

He reached over and took the key out of the ignition switch. "Just in case you get any ideas about leaving us stranded."

They slid the door open again and forced their way out into the turbulent biting wind. It howled all around them, a massive wall of sound that made normal speech all but impossible. Javier was about to jump down when he shouted that he'd forgotten something. He went back inside the fuselage and emerged a few minutes later.

"Sorry, I dropped my ID badge. I didn't want to leave it in case we didn't come back this way."

"We need to rope up," Jonas shouted above the noise. "The snow is likely to have any number of hidden gullies we could fall into. I'll lead, Javier can come behind me, and then Faith and you bring up the rear."

It made sense as both of them were experienced in this kind of terrain. Faith wasn't, and Javier showed every sign of regretting that he'd agreed to come. They roped up, and Jonas led off into the teeth of the howling winds that seemed to be making every effort to blast them from the mountainside. The wide crevasse was five hundred yards away, yet it took them an hour to stumble and fight their way to the edge. They clustered around the side of the precipice, and below them was a drop of a thousand feet or more.

"Hold me," Gabriel shouted. "I need to lean over and see if there's a way across."

He leaned over while the others stood back, keeping a firm hold on the climbing rope in case he toppled. He finished his examination of the crevasse and shouted at them to haul him back in.

"We can do it. There's a less steep way to go down, and about two hundred feet below us there's a narrow spur that crosses over to the other side. It'll be tight, but I think I can do it. Jonas, it's almost directly below us. We need to fasten the rope and lower us down one by one, and then pull the rope through."

Javier was white with fear as he listened to them and peered at the crevasse. His lips moved, but his words were lost in the wind.

"What was that you said?" Gabriel shouted.

He cupped his hands. "I said we might as well take out a pistol each and shoot ourselves. It'll be a more comfortable way to die than this."

They all laughed at the Spaniard's pessimism. "No one's going to die," Faith reassured him. "Believe me, these two men will take you to hell and back."

"We're already there," he moaned. "Now I want to get back."

Gabriel fastened the rope around his body, and Jonas

found a rounded piece of rocky outcrop to loop it around. They lowered him down, his body twisting and turning, crashing against the mountainside as it swung in the fierce winds that lashed the rocks. His feet touched the spur, and he tugged the rope to let them know he'd arrived. He held the foot of the rope taut as Javier made his fearful descent. When he arrived on the spur next to Gabriel, his teeth were chattering so loud that it could be heard over the wind. Was he freezing cold or terrified? Maybe a bit of both, de Sade decided. Best not to ask. But the Spaniard helped him steady the rope to help Faith down the rocky slope, and when her feet touched bottom it seemed only seconds later that Jonas abseiled down. His feet touched, and he jerked on the rope to pull it through. De Sade looked across the narrow spur. It was only three feet at its widest point. Faith touched his arm.

"Can we do it? I mean, without someone getting killed."

He couldn't lie to her. Javier was staring at him, waiting for his reply.

"We can, but one at a time. We'll need every piece of rope we've got. Someone is bound to go over, but we can pull them back up. That spur is sure to be littered with broken rocks and hidden cracks. Untie all of your ropes. I'll use them all and go across first. We can make up a rope line for Javier and Faith, but you'll need to link your karabiners to it in case you fall."

"Are you sure you can do it?"

He looked at her. "Galina could be the other side, dying from exposure if they survived the crash."

She nodded. "Be safe, please, for all our sakes. But especially mine." She had to shout even louder as a renewed gust smashed into them, sending clouds of dusty snow that almost hid them in a dense cloud of white fog. "I shall pray for you."

"I'll be fine, don't worry. But if I do get thrown off, haul me back in."

She smiled, a small, weak smile. "We'll reel you in like a fish, but try not to fall."

Halfway across the narrow blade of snow-covered rock that stretched across the ravine, Gabriel knew he was in trouble. The first part was bad, but he was able to move slowly, testing each footstep to ensure he wasn't walking into a thinly covered crack in the spur. He made good progress, even if it was very slow. But after the halfway mark, the wind came howling around the side of the mountain, and it was all he could do to stop himself from being swept off. There was only one way to go ahead, and he dropped to the ground and started to inch his way forward on his stomach. Twice he almost fell where a thin layer of snow concealed a sheet of ice covering the rock below it, and there was nothing to hold on to. But at last he crawled off the spur and onto the mountainside the other side of the crevasse. He tied the rope to an outcrop of rock and tested it. The rope held. Now it was time to bring the others over. He waved to Jonas and saw him helping Javier out on to the spur. The Spaniard came across on his stomach. They'd seen the way he did it and followed his lead. It took precious time, almost half an hour for him to crawl across, but he made it, exhausted, blue with cold and almost unresponsive.

"Javier, you need to restore your circulation," he shouted at the detective. "Do you want to die up here? Jump around, wave your arms, do anything, but you have to move!"

The man made a feeble effort to wave his arms.

"Are you a girl?" de Sade shouted at him. "Is that it? Are you some homo's bum boy, nothing more than a little prostitute?"

Javier stared at him in shocked surprise, and his mouth open in astonishment. Then his face started to redden as it suffused with blood, and he became angry.

"You can't talk to me like that, you…"

"You're a fucking nancy boy, aren't you? Not fit to be a detective. You're nothing but a nasty little pervert!"

Javier lunged at him, and they struggled for several minutes as he tried to wrestle Gabriel to the ground.

"I'll fucking kill you, American scum! How dare you speak to me like that!"

De Sade locked his arms around him to stop him injuring himself. "Javier, calm down. I was trying to get you to move, to restore you circulation. It was all lies, for Christ's sake, calm down. Don't you feel warmer now?"

Comprehension came to the man's eyes, and he stopped struggling. He managed a weak smile. "Yes, you're right. I thought you were serious."

"Only about saving your life, Javier. Other than that, it was all lies. Now keep working at it, move your body, and keep your circulation moving. I'll help the others across."

He looked around to see that Faith was already halfway across, inching along on her stomach. She reached the end of the spur, and he helped her disconnect her harness from the rope.

"You need to move like Javier to get the blood circulating," he shouted at her over the howling of the wind.

She nodded. "I understand. Don't worry, I'll keep an

eye on him."

She started to move her arms and legs to restore warmth, and de Sade turned back to the rope to check on Jonas' progress, but he was almost across. He'd literally run along the narrow spur of rock, and Gabriel couldn't resist a smile.

"You're showing off, Mr. Savage."

Jonas smiled back. "I've done this a few times, and I didn't need to freeze to death crawling through that ice and snow. We need to move off. The cold will cause us problems if we stay still for more than a few minutes."

Gabriel nodded. "You're right, let's head for the slope that Faith recognized. If it isn't there, we're in trouble."

Jonas didn't reply. He just nodded and went to Javier and Faith, "It's time to get going. Are you sure that the place you saw in the vision was that one up ahead?"

"I'm sure."

"I can't see any possible place for an aircraft to have come down," Javier said doubtfully. It's too big to hide on this mountainside."

"I saw it," Faith insisted. "It was there."

"Yes, of course," he said. But his face conveyed his real feelings.

They had to be even more careful. Most of the ropes had been left tied across the narrow spur of rock so that they had a way back across the treacherous crevasse. Jonas led off again, Javier and Faith followed, and Gabriel brought up the rear. Jonas arrived first at the snow-covered shelf where Faith had seen the aircraft come down, and it was empty.

"What do we do now?" he asked, addressing the question to Faith.

She didn't reply at first. Her eyes were shut, and her arms clasped around her body as if in pain.

"Are you okay?" Gabriel asked, worried about frostbite.

Her eyes opened slowly. "I could feel their terror as the aircraft hit. The pilot was looking out at the crevasse we just crossed as the plane slid along the snow. It was heading in that direction."

She pointed up ahead where the shelf disappeared over the edge of the mountain.

"It looks like it went on off the mountain," Javier exclaimed in a bitter voice. "That means we've come up here for nothing."

"Let's go and check," Jonas replied. "We need to take a look over that edge."

The four of them trudged forwards and upwards across the snow. It took them ten minutes to reach the edge of the plateau. They looked over it, and four voices gasped with astonishment. There was a shallow, snow filled valley, only thirty feet below them. It was almost hidden from the air and the mountains that looked down upon it, due to the inhospitable nature of the peaks. The valley was almost half a mile across. In the center were the tiny ruins of a chapel, perhaps the work of some long-forgotten religious hermit who wished to live a life of seclusion. Lying next to the ruins, only feet away at one point, was the almost intact fuselage of a modern passenger airliner. Its wings had sheared off and lay in the snow some distance away. Close to the fuselage, a wisp of smoke reached up lazily into the air; a fire for cooking or to keep warm, maybe both. They'd found them.

"There's a way down there," Jonas shouted. "It's a kind of funnel in the rock where small boulders have stacked up to make it possible to walk down. We just need to be careful not to fall. I'll go first and check it out."

They hurried across to where he was standing, and it did look like a stairway or a crazed interpretation of one. He started down, moving nimbly from boulder to boulder until he reached the bottom.

"Javier, you next," de Sade ordered the detective. "Just go slow, and make sure you know where you're putting your feet. Those boulders could be icy."

The Spaniard made his careful way down to the foot of the valley. Faith followed him and then Gabriel. He had to hurry to catch up as they were almost running towards the wreckage. It was then that the miracle they'd been praying for occurred. A figure stepped out of the rear of the broken fuselage. There was a huge hole where the tailplane had been ripped away. They recognized her at once, Galina Polotsova. She stood still, staring in astonishment at the sight of Jonas running towards her. She started running too, and they met in a huge embrace that swept her off her feet. They kissed, and he finally set her feet back on the ground.

"What took you so long?" were the first words she spoke.

"I had a few things to finish off," Jonas grinned. Then his expression became serious. "What's the deal with the survivors?"

"It's bad. There were eighty-nine passengers and crew on board that flight. We had six who survived the crash, but four of them died of exposure and shock after the first night on the mountain. There's just me and Eduardo."

"Where is he?" Faith asked. "Why doesn't he come out, is he injured?"

"No. Eduardo is ten months old. He's asleep at the moment. I made him up a bed inside the fuselage after I got all of the bodies out."

"On your own? That must have been a hard task," Jonas exclaimed. "Where are they?"

"I put them in the ruins of the chapel next to the wreck. The snow has covered them now, and there's just a mound to show where I left them. It was all I could do. How did you find us? Was it the search and rescue services?"

"Faith had a vision," Gabriel told her. "They had no idea where the aircraft came down, and so the search was almost non-existent. They thought at one time you might have been hijacked. Probably the mountains obscured the radar trace, but whatever happened, your plane just disappeared. Do you know what caused it to crash?"

She shook her head. "The engines just died, but I've no idea why. Tell me, how do we get out of these mountains? Are the rescue services not coming?"

They explained to her about the Huey. "I doubt she'll ever fly off the mountain, but we can use the radio when we get back," Jonas told her.

She didn't reply. She was staring at Javier. He'd gone over to the ruins.

"Who is he?"

"A Seville detective," Faith explained. "He came along to help us."

"Do you know what he's doing?"

"Looking at the bodies, I expect. He's a cop from the Policia Nacional, so I expect he'll need to make a report about the fatalities."

"Yeah, of course. I need to go inside and check on Eduardo. Faith, come and take a look. He's little darling."

The women went away to check out the baby and left the two men to look around the wreck. "There could be something we can use inside the cockpit," Jonas suggested. "A working radio even, although it's a long shot. We need to alert the cops and get some people up here. If there's nothing we can use, I'll go back to the Huey and use the radio on board. I expect the pilot's getting cold by now. Once I've put the call through, he can come back here and shelter inside the aircraft until they come. They'll need to make the pick up here in any case."

They entered the fuselage through the forward door. A glance around the cockpit dashed any hopes of finding anything useable. There was no power. The crash had shorted out the plane's electrical systems and drained away any reserves of power onboard, even if the communications equipment worked, which seemed unlikely.

"I'll go back to the Huey," Jonas said. "It shouldn't take long."

"First rule of the mountains," Gabriel informed him. "You never go alone. I'll go with you. We'll leave Javier here. There's nothing he can do to help us. I expect he'll need to get his act together. He'll have a lot of explaining to do when he gets back."

"Yeah, hey, look at that!"

Galina and Faith came forward to the cockpit, carrying a small bundle. The baby was wrapped in layers of airline blankets to keep him warm. He was sleeping peacefully.

"How did you feed him?" Gabriel asked her. "He must have been starving."

"The mother has several packets of formula in her hand luggage, and I've been using it up. But he's very cold, and he needs to go to hospital for a checkup as soon as possible."

"Right, we're going back to the Huey to call for help. We'll find Javier and let him know. He can stay here with you. I think he's over in the ruins looking at the bodies."

Galina looked puzzled. "I just saw him at the rear of the fuselage. What could he be doing?"

Both men shrugged. "No idea," de Sade replied. "But we'll find him and let him know what we're doing."

* * *

It was the culmination of a lifetime's dream. He found a statue, a miniature version of Faith, the stonework slightly eroded by the passage of time but still in good condition. It stood on a stone plinth, staring due east where there was a stone tomb. It had a single word carved into the stonework, 'Faith'. He went to lift the stone slab, and at first it refused to move. He cast around and found a long piece of strong aircraft alloy. It looked like some kind of a hydraulic leg. With trembling fingers, he inserted the edge under the slab and used every ounce of his strength to lever it up. The slab came away from the ground enough for him to get his hands underneath, force it upright, and then tip it over. Inset in the ground were several rotting planks of wood. He tossed them to one side and exposed a narrow compartment. Inside was an old, leather bag. He felt a surge of disappointment that after a lifetime spent searching, the treasure he sought had gone, and there were just a few old scraps of leather left by some long forgotten tomb raider. That was when he saw a glint of dull gold under the leather. He reached down with his hands and touched something solid, something heavy. When he pulled it up, it was an exquisite, solid gold statuette, and a representation of an Aztec deity, without a doubt. He examined it carefully. The statuette must have weighed as much as ten pounds and was inset with precious stones. Diamonds, he was sure of that, huge gems, worth millions, and each one unique and priceless. The value of the piece was incalculable, but it would be fifty million dollars at least, maybe more. His head spun with the realization that at last he was wealthy, wealthy beyond his wildest dreams. Now he had to get it home, but first he needed to deal with these people. It would be a pleasure. And perhaps he could take more of that pleasure away with him. Yes, why not? He deserved it.

\* \* \*

They went outside the aircraft, but there was no sign of him.

"Javier," de Sade shouted. "We need to get back to the Huey and call for help."

There was no sign of him at first, but they turned around as they heard a footstep. Javier Garcia stood behind them, but this was not the man they remembered. His eyes blazed with a fanatic intensity, and his lips were curled in a sadistic snarl.

"Javier, what's the matter?" Faith asked him.

One hand was inside his coat. When he removed it, he held a gun but no ordinary gun. They all recognized it as a MAC-10; gangsters and Special Forces favored the tiny submachine gun for its lightweight and ease of concealment. Chambered for either .45 rounds or 9mm

Parabellum, it was devastating at close quarters, such as the situation now.

"You will all put up your hands if you wish to live. I warn you. I am no stranger to using one of these," the Spanish cop shouted.

He slipped a hand into his other pocket and drew out a knife, a huge, long, Spanish hunting knife, a Navaja almost a foot long. He flicked his wrist, and the blade swung out and locked, a narrow, thin, filleting blade. It came to them in a flash. The killer had been under their noses all along. No wonder it had been so difficult to track him, he was a cop. They realized that the Navaja was the blade that had been used to slice the victims apart. Jonas, Gabriel and Faith all carried guns, but they were deep inside their thick coats, and they couldn't reach one before they were gunned down. Galina had been on a commercial flight, so she would not have carried a gun. They put up their hands.

"What's going on, Javier?" de Sade asked. But of course, they all knew. How could they have been so blind?

Javier ignored him. "Throw down your guns. I know all three of you are armed. You first, Jonas, then Gabriel, and then the delightful Miss Ward."

"But Javier, don't you think…"

A single shot spat out of the barrel of the MAC-10 and kicked up snow at the feet of de Sade.

"No, Detective, don't try to delay. If I do not see your weapons on the ground in three seconds, I will kill this woman and the baby she holds as well. I'm counting, one, two…"

They threw down their guns. He smiled as he picked them up, putting them inside the pockets of his anorak. He gave his Navaja a flick, and the long blade swung back into the handle. He put it away too.

"Good. Now, Faith, you are coming with me while I find a way off this mountain. The rest of you, well, you'll just have to wait for someone to rescue you."

"You can't go back," Gabriel shouted. "They'll come after you with everything they've got when they know who you are."

His face contorted into his manic grin. "Who said anything about going back? A man can achieve much with the prize I found in the Tomb of Faith in the chapel ruins." He pulled it out and held it up so that they could see his prize. "Why would I return to Seville? I shall vanish out of sight and live out the life I was always destined to live."

"So it was all about greed?" de Sade asked him. "Was that all, the reason you killed those women?"

"Not at all," he mocked. "It was much more than that. I have vowed to use a small proportion of the treasure to build a church. It will be dedicated to the glory of God, as were the women we killed. They were useless souls, and I merely committed them to God to save them from further misery. So you see, it wasn't just greed. I have done a great number of good things and will do many more. It just takes money, and now I have it."

"What about Faith?"

"She is a hostage to your good behavior. If you try to follow, she will be killed. Otherwise, I will release her unharmed after, let us say, two days. Her life is in your hands. Now, I have what I want. I have to leave. I will release Faith in the town of Monachil, so when you do descend the mountain, you may look for her there. Come, we must leave."

"You're forgetting a few things," de Sade called out to

him as he pushed Faith in front of him, hurrying away. He looked back. "Really? And what would that be?"

"First off, my friend, there's no way off this mountain. You'll get lost before you've gone more than a mile."

He smiled. "I think not. I gave a good impression of being terrified back there, did I not? In fact, before I joined the police, I spent three years in this area as a mountain rescue guide. There is a way down, but if you wish to follow me, remember to wait forty-eight hours before you do, that is, if you wish to see your woman alive."

So it had all been an act. De Sade felt guilt sear through him, a terrible guilt that he hadn't seen it coming. No sooner had they managed to reach Galina and been able to help her escape from the snow-covered mountain, than he'd lost Faith. He watched Javier start to walk away again, his MAC-10 pointing at Faith's back.

"The other thing," he shouted out to the Spanish cop, "is the helicopter. We'll radio for the police to meet you before you've gone more than a mile. You may as well give it up now, Garcia."

He grinned back at them. "The helicopter? No, I don't think there is anything there that will help you. Stay back. Forty-eight hours, or she dies!"

They watched as he disappeared behind a snow-covered mound, and there was little doubt that it marked the start of a track that led down and off the mountain. Galina was silently cursing to herself in Russian.

"So that's the way out of here. I saw there might be a possible path out that way, but it was impossible to risk it with Eduardo. But you know we have to go after them? He'll kill her, there's no doubt. You heard his comment about the helicopter? He will have killed the pilot for sure, that's what he was doing when he went back inside. I guess he smashed the radio too," said Gabriel.

"I wonder was he telling the truth about Monachil," Jonas mused. "It may be possible to get there before him."

"I checked the maps and charts in the cockpit while I was stranded here," Galina told him. "I think it's probably true he's heading there. There isn't any other town in this area, and he'll need to find transport to get away."

"In that case, I'll head him off," Jonas snarled. "And when I find that bastard, I'm going to rip his fucking throat out."

"But how can you get past him?" Gabriel stared at him, his expression white with anxiety over Faith.

"I'll take the Huey. I can fly through the mountains. He won't know I'm in the area."

"But it won't take off, you know that! It's impossible in these mountains. The second it lifts off, the rotors will be smashed against the mountainside."

Jonas stared at him. "In that case, we'll be no worse off than we are now," Jonas muttered.

"But you'll be dead!" Galina cried.

"No. I won't be dead. I've done it before, in Afghanistan. Remember?"

Gabriel nodded. "I remember."

\* \* \*

It had been a routine patrol into the mountains, chasing a gang of insurgents who'd ambushed a supply convoy and made off with supplies of food, fuel and ammunition. It was fortunate that they were so heavily loaded. They'd put their haul onto donkeys and were leading them through a high mountain pass when Team Bravo intercepted them. On that occasion, it was in mid-summer. The mountain air was crisp and cold, and the sky a harsh shade of blue. The sun shone, but not enough to dispel the chill of the post-dawn air. The insurgents were not inexperienced, and they'd prepared an ambush that despite all the precautions taken by the Team, they stumbled into. The first indication was the sniper's bullets that hit Josh Welland, who'd only been in the Team for two weeks, in the stomach. While one of the men desperately plugged the wound with dressings, the rest of them started forward, rushing from cover to cover to flush them out. They got within twenty yards of the enemy when someone shouted 'grenade', and they all ducked as he fired a round from his M203 that sailed overhead and landed in the middle of the enemy position. Jonas was first up, hurtling towards them and jumping into their position before they could recover. When Gabriel reached the defensive bunker they'd prepared, he was standing on his own, clutching a still-smoking Heckler & Koch HK416, the Delta Force submachine gun of choice. He looked up and grinned.

"They've gone to paradise, my friend. I reckon we should catch up with the donkeys and retrieve that ammo they stole."

Gabriel had nodded. "Yeah, there was enough ordnance on that convoy to start another war. We need to…"

"Sergeant, quick, he doesn't look good!"

They ran back to where Josh Welland lay on the ground, deathly pale.

"I'll call in a Medevac helicopter, Jonas. Find somewhere near where he can land."

"Got it."

The helicopter came in fifteen minutes later, and there was almost another disaster. The shelf of rock that Jonas had indicated with a smoke flare was sufficient for it to land, but as it dropped lower a storm came up. A furious blast of wind smashed into it, sending the helo off the designated area to land precariously on one skid and with the other mangled on a rock. The rotors tilted down dangerously, and the whole machine rocked and vibrated as the full force of the storm hit. The pilot switched off, jumped down, and ran over to them.

"I can't take off from here. We'll need to get the engineers in to fix the damage and wait for the wind to ease before I can try it. Sorry, but you'll need to stretcher your guy out. There's no chance of another flight in this storm."

"The guy's dying," Jonas pointed out. "You have to get him out of here."

The pilot shook his head. "Sorry, Buddy, but it's impossible. I'll have the paramedic take a look at him. Maybe we can make him more comfortable."

He went over to Josh's body. He took one look and stood up. "Yeah, it's not good. Sorry, there ain't nothing I can do about it."

"Maybe not, but I can. Gabriel, get them to load him onto the aircraft. I'll fly it out of here."

The pilot stared at him. "You're crazy. It'll never get off the ground, not in this storm and with the landing gear damaged."

"Sure. But I'm not standing doing nothing while Josh dies."

"I'd come with you," Gabriel said. "But we need to nail these guys that took the guns. Are you going to be okay?"

"I'll be fine. See you at Camp Phoenix."

Gabriel nodded. "Yeah, you will."

They watched the troopers carry Josh on board the aircraft. The paramedic shouted that he'd stay with him.

"I'm not in this business to abandon my patients. You sure you can fly this thing?" he asked Jonas.

The Tank grinned at him. "If I can't, this is going to be a mighty short trip."

They watched him crank up the engine of the modified Sikorsky UH-60 Blackhawk. The rotors whirled dangerously close to the rocks, so close that they almost seemed to be touching when the wind caught the machine and tilted it over at an even more severe angle. Jonas waited, and waited some more. He'd watched the wind carefully, observing all of the signs that indicated its strength and direction. There was no fixed direction for the howling winds, but he'd seen that at one time the wind blew in a certain way that would give the helicopter lift in the opposite direction to the rocks. He waited longer, five minutes went by, and still he sat in the cockpit, watching the sparse foliage move, the tiny flutter of the small clumps of grass, and even the rustle of the Team's uniforms. Abruptly, he fed maximum power to the engine, twisted the collective over hard, and the aircraft leapt into the air. He climbed for a few hundred feet then leveled out for Kabul. They all breathed a sigh of relief. No one got left behind in Team Bravo, no one. The pilot uttered the final comment on his take off.

"Holy shit, that was fucking incredible. Who is that guy?"

Gabriel nodded to him. "You're right, it was incredible, but to him it's nothing unusual. His name's Jonas Savage.

We call him 'The Tank'."
    The pilot nodded. "Fuckin' A!"

# CHAPTER TEN

The going down the mountainside was more difficult than he'd remembered. It was made more difficult with the woman, but he needed her for two purposes. As a hostage, she would stop them coming after him until it was too late. And afterwards, well, he felt himself becoming hard as he thought about afterwards. She would be a real prize, one to savor, one to treasure. She may not be a whore, and perhaps she would did not need saving the way the others did, but he was entitled to some recreation and reward after all the effort he'd put in. Was she deliberately trying to slow him up, he wondered, as she stumbled for the tenth time? Probably. He smashed the barrel over her face, slashing the perfect, creamy skin and leaving a cut where her blood ran down and dripped onto the snow.

"Stop that, I know what you're doing. Either you keep up or I'll do this again, and again, until you get the message. Understand?"

She nodded. "Yeah, I get it. What are you going to do when we get down to Monachil?

"Do? I already told you and your friends. I'll leave you in Monachil for them to find you."

"Sure. How can I believe you?"

He grinned. "I think you do not have any choice but to believe me."

Her eyes widened, and she suddenly looked over his shoulder. "Gabriel!"

He whirled around, she located the spot she needed, and pivoted on one foot while the other made contact with her target. Javier spun to the snow covered ground, and his scream echoing around the hills, but he kept his grip on the gun.

Faith ran. There was only one way to go. She was already downhill of the Spaniard, and she kept on running. She heard him shout at her to stop but ignored him and kept on going. He fired three single shots in her direction, but the MAC-10 was a weapon designed to shower bursts of bullets at targets, not a precision rifle. The shots went wild, and she kept on going. She ran for what seemed like hours, stumbling down the slippery path, sometimes losing sight of it altogether and having to retrace her steps. She fell often and knew that her hands and knees would be bloody and raw by the time she reached the foot of the mountain, but she was determined to escape. She knew what lay in store for her if Javier Garcia managed to get away. They way he got his kicks was no secret from any of them. She reached a fork in the path and hesitated, which way? Then she ducked as a shot rang out, and the bullet hissed past her head. She went to the right, and the path seemed more defined, or perhaps less undefined than the other. She rounded a hairpin bend on the rocky track and halted. She was on the edge of a precipice. She'd come the wrong way. Movement made her look down. It was Javier. He'd gone the other way and now stood fifty feet below her on the correct path.

"I think you made a poor choice, Faith. A pity, and I had such plans for you. Now you have ruined them all."

She saw him raise the barrel of the tiny submachine gun. A shot cracked out, and then she was falling with a terrible pain to her head, but it was cut off as she blacked out.

\* \* \*

Gabriel looked around in the wrecked aircraft. He needed something to use as a weapon, in the event that he caught up with Javier. Behind the pilot's seat he found what he sought, a small, locked cabinet. He knew that most aircraft carried a pistol on board for emergencies, locked away in a small gun safe. The problem was how to open it. The key would have been with the pilot, and his body was frozen with the others that Galina had laid out in the chapel ruins. The door had been damaged and bent during the crash, leaving enough room to fit a lever to prize it open, if he had a lever. He had an idea and lifted a hatch in the cockpit floor. Beneath was the electronics and hydraulics that operated the control surfaces and the nosewheel. He climbed down amidst the pipes and cables and found what he needed; the six-foot long lever that cranked the undercarriage when the power failed. It was immensely strong, and more importantly, had a wedge-shape on one end. He unclipped it and climbed back up into the cockpit. The wedge fitted perfectly in the lip of the door of the gun safe, and he was able to wrench it open. Inside was a box marked Colt. A minute later, he was checking the Colt M1911. It carried a full clip as well as a spare clip in the box. He stuffed them in his pocket, picked up the lever, and went back outside where Jonas was saying goodbye to Galina. He showed him the pistol.

"If I can catch up with him, this should even up the odds."

Jonas nodded and eyed the lever. "I'd sooner bust his head in with that bar."

"I'll keep it in mind. You're sure about getting the helo out?"

"No question. I've done it before, and I'll do it again. It's just a question of waiting for the right wind."

"You shouldn't do this," Galina shouted bitterly. "If the rotor touches the mountain, you're dead. Isn't one aircraft crash enough?"

He put his arm around her, holding her with difficulty as she clutched the baby.

"Here's a promise, my love. I know what I'm doing. That helo will take off, and I'll get to Monachil and call in the cavalry. We'll nail Javier too, with Gabriel behind him and me in front. We'll box him in and roast his ass. Remember, he's got Faith. We have to reach her before he reaches the bottom of the mountain. Once he gets there, he could disappear, and we'll never see him or Faith ever again. You know what he'll do to Faith, don't you?

She nodded. "You're right. I just don't want to lose you, especially now that you've come this far and found me."

"You're not going to lose me. I have to get going, take care."

"And you."

They kissed and hugged each other warmly. Jonas

214

broke off the embrace and went towards the crevasse that he had to cross to reach the helicopter. She gave Gabriel a hopeless glance.

"I can't change anything, can I?"

He shook his head. "Nothing. I have to go to. I'll need to move fast if I'm going to have a chance of catching up with him. You'll be okay?"

"Sure. I wish it was just me, and I'd come with you. But Eduardo needs looking after, so I'll just have to wait."

"I'll be back soon, believe me," he murmured. "That's a promise. And I'll have Faith with me."

Gabriel ran off in the direction that Javier had taken Faith. They had a head start, but he knew Faith would do everything possible to slow him down. The descent down the mountainside was narrow and precarious, and in places he almost went over the edge. He found that the undercarriage lever he'd brought with him served as a hiking pole, allowing him to move faster and test the unknown surfaces for cracks and potholes. The trail was easy to follow at first where Javier and Faith had kicked it up. At one point, he almost went the wrong way but noticed they'd made the same mistake. But he retraced his steps and picked up the downward trail again. After a few hundred yards, he re-examined the tracks he was following. There was something wrong. At first it seemed that only one person was using the path, but then he found a second set of footprints that petered out again after another few hundred yards. There were specks of blood that had spilled onto the snow; bright and ominous under the harsh and cold blue sky. It meant Faith was injured. The question was how badly? The specks of blood continued down the mountain. Every few yards another red dot showed bright on the surface of the snow, and then they disappeared completely. He looked around carefully, but there was no sign of a body. He had to assume Javier had bandaged her wound and was still dragging his hostage downhill towards Monachil. His mind was alive with possibilities. Was she badly wounded, would he be able to free Faith when he caught up with them, or would Javier see him coming and kill her, as he'd promised? But he had to keep going, had to know in his heart that he would destroy the beast that had caused so much death and misery and now threatened to kill the woman he loved. He squeezed through a narrow gap between two rocks. It was the only way down. The path threaded along a dark, narrow cleft and emerged into daylight again. Hundreds of feet below lay the town of Monachil, about two miles away. Immediately in front of him were the ruins of an old farmhouse, surrounded by small hills of jagged rocks. The path led around to the right of the ruins. He started towards them when a shot rang out.

"De Sade, I warned you. Come any nearer and I'll blow your head off."

He examined the ground that lay between him and the ruins. It was flat, thick snow, bearing the imprint of footsteps that had recently crossed it. Javier and Faith. The open ground was less than two hundred feet across, but there was no cover, and no way to go around it. Either side was sheer mountainside. If he was to reach Faith, he had to cross it. Yet the second he started to move, the Spaniard would open fire, and even with just a pistol, he would be an easy target. He had to somehow get the man to reveal himself. De Sade had one huge advantage. The man sheltering in the ruins did not know he was armed. He had to use that to enable him to get close. Close enough to tear him to pieces.

"Javier, it's all over, you know that. Let the girl go, and you can keep the gold statue. It's of no use to me."

"No. Go back up the mountain or I kill her."

"She's wounded, isn't she? Did you shoot her, Javier?"

"It's just a scratch, she's fine. She was trying to escape."

The bastard. Gabriel felt his anger grow into the white heat of rage.

"I want to see her. I have to ask if she is all right. Let her show herself, Javier."

There was a brief silence, and he shouted an answer. "No. You have to go back. Otherwise I kill her."

It came to de Sade in a blinding moment of clarity, that he didn't have Faith, and that could only mean one thing, he'd killed her. There was no other explanation. If he still had her alive, he would have used her to force him to back off. He lost all reason, every ounce of control, and every fiber that had guided him through hundreds of firefights was stretched and broken. He only had one thought in his mind, to kill. He could feel his hands around the man's neck, squeezing, seeing his skin turn a mottled shade of purple, and his last breath as death overtook him. And de Sade would be the instrument of that death. He dropped the six-foot lever and charged forward, drawing his gun as he ran, nearer and nearer to the ruined building. Then the first of Javier's shots cracked out. Snow kicked up around him, and he dived to one side, rolling out of the fuselage of bullets that came much too close. There was a pause, and he instinctively knew the man was changing magazines or changing pistols. It was a brief window. He leapt to his feet and ran on, more precious yards that took him closer and closer. Another shot whistled passed his head. He swerved and dived to the ground yet again.

He estimated he was halfway across. More shots zipped into the snow around him and then the pause again. He ran forward and got within twenty feet of the ruin and threw himself to the side, but this time the Spaniard had anticipated him, and a bullet took him low in the side. He gasped in agony as he went down. Waves of pain rolled through him, but he had to keep going, had to. He slid forward, slowly and carefully. Just in front of him was the house where his target sheltered, and where the man who had killed Faith lay in wait. Gabriel's brain was filled with one thought, one motivation. That man must die! He was almost there, and despite the terrible pain in his body, he pressed forward, driven by his overwhelming determination. He was almost there, just a few feet. He leapt up, wincing in agony, and dived for the cover of the first of the tumbled stones that lay in front of him. He lifted his pistol, searching for Javier Garcia, for the chance of a shot that would deliver judgment on the cruel killer. Then he heard a click behind him. He started to turn, but it was too late, the barrel of a gun pressed into his back.

"Drop it, de Sade."

He dropped his Colt automatic. There was still a chance, and he waited for an opening that would allow him to twist and disarm the Spanish detective. But Javier had backed away, wary of his opponent.

"You can turn around now, de Sade. I'm sure you'd like to see what awaits you."

He turned. Garcia stood pointing a pistol at him; his own pistol, the Glock.

"Yes, I can see you recognize it. Fitting, isn't it? That

you're about to meet your end with your own gun."

"Where is she, Garcia? What did you do with her?"

The man smiled, an awful, terrible rictus that twisted his lips into an obscene shape. "You'll never know, will you? Did she die quickly, a merciful shot to the head? Or was it a long, screaming, agonizing death? Yes, you know that's my style, don't you? I'm afraid you'll have to wait until you join her in death to find out the answer. Get down on your knees."

"No. If you're man enough to shoot me, go ahead. But you can face me, this isn't going to be one of your sadistic executions."

Garcia shrugged. "It doesn't matter how I do it. What matters is that you die."

He cocked the pistol and brought it up to aim. "Goodbye, de Sade."

As his finger tightened on the trigger, an extraordinary shape leapt out of the snow, holding a long, metal lever. It fell on him like a tiger. At first Gabriel thought it was some awful, mountain creature, covered in blood and snow. Then the truth dawned. Faith! She'd approached in the snow, undetected, crawling forward, and probably with the intention of killing Garcia as well. She must have followed him, found the undercarriage lever he'd dropped in the snow and picked it up to use as a weapon. She smashed it over his head, again and again, and he dropped the pistol, screaming in pain. She hit him again, and he started to run. At first she made to give chase, but she stopped and went back.

"Gabriel, you're hurt."

"It's not serious. Faith, I thought you were dead," he replied.

She grinned. "Not quite yet. He tried. The bastard shot me, but the bullet just grazed my head. I'm okay, really. It looks a lot worse than it is. Show me your wound."

He protested, but she lifted up his thermal coat and shirt to inspect the wound. Her eyes narrowed as she saw the blood welling out of his side.

"It's bad, and I need to dress it, otherwise you'll bleed to death. You'll have to lie still until the emergency services get here."

"No! I'm not letting that piece of scum get away, not again. If it needs it, put on a dressing to stop the blood flow, but that's all. I'm not stopping now."

She looked grim. "You're crazy, it could kill you, if Javier doesn't. He could be waiting in ambush for you."

"I don't think so. His main pre-occupation will be to escape. It's not going to happen, not after all this. Put the dressing on, and I'll go after him."

"Okay, I'll find something to make a pad to put over it."

She unzipped her coat and removed it, then her woolen sweater and the undershirt. Wearing only a bra on her upper body, she folded them into a pad and pushed it hard against the wound. Gabriel flinched as the pressure caused more waves of intense pain to surge through his body. He closed his eyes and clenched his teeth, forcing himself to put up with the pain.

"I need something to tie it off with," she said to him, discreetly pretending not to notice his agony. "Do you have any string, or twine, anything like that?"

"Yeah, in the pocket of my coat, there's some emergency twine. You can use that, and there's a knife in the other pocket to cut it. Hurry up, the bastard's getting away!"

She found the twine and the knife, cut off a long length,

and fastened the makeshift dressing. Then she started to put on her sweater and coat as she was already shivering badly with the cold.

"That's it, it's the best I can do."

"Thanks, it's time to get after him."

He got to his feet, stumbling as the agony knifed through him.

"I'm coming with you," Faith said. She reached down into the snow and picked up the Colt he'd dropped. She slid out the clip, checked the barrel and action, and reassembled the gun. "This looks fine. Are you ready?"

He nodded. "I guess. So you're riding shotgun for me?"

"Yeah, someone has to look after you. Let's go get him."

\* \* \*

Jonas skipped over the narrow land bridge that crossed the crevasse, not even stopping to grip the rope. The one thing he didn't have to waste now was time. The Huey rocked in the violent gusts of wind that lashed this side of the mountain, but it looked to be intact. He climbed into the cockpit. The pilot was in his seat, his head leaning over at an unnatural angle. He bent to look down at his neck. His throat was slit. Javier had murdered him when he went back into the aircraft, and the front of the radio was smashed too. He pulled the pilot out of the seat and laid the body gently in the rear of the cabin. He was about to leave it when he had a sudden thought and looked inside his coat. Sure enough, the man had a shoulder holster with a small automatic, an old French Ruby. The 7.65mm pistol was light and small, but good enough to take down Javier in a close quarter fight. He put it in his pocket, returned to the seat, put the starter key into the socket and twisted. For the first few seconds nothing happened, but then the starter began to whine as the engine started to spool up. The rotor blades spun slowly at first, and only feet away from the rock face, but he ignored it. When the time came, he was relying on the gale force winds at this altitude to sweep the aircraft away from the rocks and into the air. The engine settled to a steady hum, and he strapped in, changed his mind, and unstrapped. If something went wrong, he needed the freedom to move fast. He checked the gages, the engine temperature and oil pressure were coming up well, and the gas tank showed plenty of fuel. Enough to get him down the mountain if he got off this rock. Then he increased power and waited for the wind. It started to blow hard, then eased away, and then came at him in a howling fury; as if the Gods of the mountain were angry that he would dare to defy them by trying to release the helicopter from the deadly embrace in which it was held. He looked at a small bush several hundred yards away. He would use it as his weather gage. It was all he had. The bush bent in the wind and eased back. Then the wind changed, and the helicopter was thrown towards the rocks. He prepared to switch off, but the wind direction changed again. He saw the bush bend over, almost flattened by the fury that blew across the mountain range. It was what he'd been waiting for. He increased power to full, feeling the machine already starting to lift away from the mountainside. At exactly the right moment, he wrenched on the collective, kicked on the torque pedal that controlled the rear rotor, and the machine leapt into the sky; away from the mountain.

Dear God, he'd made it. Again. He climbed away from

the rocky shelf and saw the wreck of the aircraft below him next to the chapel. Galina was there. He could see her clearly, standing next to the fuselage clutching a small bundle that had to be Eduardo. Of course, it was an easy landing. He could take her off the mountain, and it would only cost seconds to land and pick her up. He hovered near to the wreckage and put the Huey down. Galina rushed over to the door.

"You made it, Jonas. What's happening?"

"I'm still heading down to Monachil to try and head off Javier Garcia. I thought you may have had enough of this mountain and would like a ride down with me."

She was already climbing in. "Thank God, I couldn't last much longer in this desolate place. Can you land somewhere near a hotel that has a vacant room with a hot shower?" Then she winced as she saw the body. "The pilot?"

"Yeah."

"Another of his victims. He doesn't deserve an easy death, Jonas."

"No, he doesn't. Strap in, I don't want to miss the bastard."

He slid the door shut and climbed back into the pilot's seat. The helicopter shot up into the sky and he headed for the nearby town of Monachil. Galina put on the headset but found it was dead. She unstrapped, and still clutching Eduardo, went forward to shout into Jonas' ear.

"The communications system doesn't work."

"No. Javier wrecked it when he killed the pilot."

"Right. Make sure he goes down hard, Jonas. No easy end for this guy."

"I've already come to that decision, don't worry. The

only concern I have is missing him. You'd better strap in, we're almost over the town. I'll put her down between the town and the foot of the mountain and go after him. With any luck, Gabriel will be on his tail, and we'll squeeze him between us. You'd better wait in the helicopter with the baby."

She nodded and went away to prepare for the landing.

\* \* \*

They were almost running downhill, stumbling over the steep, rough, slippery path. Javier's tracks were easy to follow in the virgin snow. They knew that if they kept going fast, they had to catch up unless he was moving even faster than they were. They had some advantages. The Spaniard had been hit hard when Faith hit him with the undercarriage lever, and it was evident from his tracks that he was staggering rather than walking or running. He was also having to find his way past the increasing number of trails that branched off the main track, and several times they saw where he'd retraced his steps. Then they saw blood in the snow.

"He must have fallen here," de Sade pointed out to Faith. "You hit him hard with that lever, and he's bleeding badly. The blood is where his head hit the snow."

"Good. Let's keep going."

"Make sure you have that gun ready. He could easily bushwhack us if we're not careful."

"I'm ready," she said grimly. "Believe me, this sucker is going down."

On the outskirts of the town was a lone church. It was big, very big for such an isolated structure. The building was constructed of white stone with stained glass windows and hundreds of intricate carvings set into the facade. Faith read the sign and translated the Spanish.

"It's built on a site where a shepherd discovered a statue of the Virgin Mary. It's some kind of a shrine, so they get a lot of pilgrims. It says here the church is only open in the summer months, so I guess it's deserted now."

"Not quite deserted, I wouldn't think," Gabriel pointed out. The footsteps led to a set of steps in front of the main door. They sighted Jonas, running up the narrow track toward them. He came up to them with a broad grin.

"Thank Christ you made it. Galina's fine too. I brought her down in the Huey. Where is he, in there?"

"We think so, yes."

"We'll need to box him in. I'll take the back. You two take the front."

"You haven't got a gun," Gabriel noted.

Jonas produced the small pistol. "I took this from the pilot's body. It'll be enough for our Spanish friend."

"Let's finish this," de Sade replied, his voice cold. "Whatever happens, he doesn't get out of here."

"Gabriel, it's a church," Faith objected.

"That's good, he's in the right place for funeral."

While Jonas went to the rear, Gabriel and Faith opened the heavy, oak front door.

* * *

His mind flashbacked to a time they were on R and R in the center of Kabul after serving eight long, straight months out in the boonies. The Star of the East Hotel had been taken over by the military, and Team Bravo was relaxing over a few beers, some of them taking a shower ready for the night's entertainment. That's when the first bomb went off. Gabriel made a grab for his pistol. At that time he was trialing an Israeli Military Industries .50 caliber Desert Eagle, and he only had time to pick up the heavy belt as he ran through the door. He buckled it on as the second explosion came, and he realized that Jonas was beside him, holding a Colt .45

"I reckon down in the basement," he said to his comrade."

"Yeah, that'd be my guess. You could have worn some shoes."

He looked down. He hadn't realized he was only wearing his shorts and green vest. No shoes. He was barefoot. That could be a problem if he had to fight over ground littered with bomb debris. But it was too late to worry. They took the stairs side by side, three at a time. When they reached the first floor, the reception area was a swirling chaos of smoke and dust. Bodies lay strewn on the ground, but there was no time to check them out. The door to the basement yawned open, and they both heard voices coming from down there at the same instant.

"They could have it covered with an assault rifle," Jonas cautioned. "I've got a frag grenade on my belt, I'll toss it down there, and we can go in and take them."

"They could be friendlies," de Sade pointed out. "There've been enough casualties here, and we sure don't want to add to them."

Jonas shook his head. "The friendlies are all down. They hit them hard with those first two bombs. Anyone still on their feet is definitely unfriendly."

Gabriel nodded. "Let them have it, and we'll follow the

blast down."

His partner pulled out the pin and tossed the grenade. The excited voices rose to a terrified series of shrieks and shouts, and the grenade went off. They hurtled down the steps. The insurgents lay broken and dying on the floor of the basement where they'd been assembling a rocket launcher. The hotel was on a hill, and to the side of the basement room there was a clear view of Kabul International Airport. Then an Afghan fighter stood up near the window, and in his hands he was clutching a satchel charge. He started to shout, "Allahu Ak…"

It was all the chance he got. Both men fired, but it was the Desert Eagle that did the damage, its .50 caliber bullets smashed the man back and out the window. His bomb exploded as he dropped below the sill, and part of the wall collapsed and blew in. The two men ducked as small pieces of brick and rock slashed at them. When the cloud cleared, Gabriel was a bloody mess of fine cuts, many of them weeping blood. But he was alive. The bomber was dead, as were his men, and their bodies a testament to the failed operation. Three days later, Team Bravo was back in the field. Whenever he had to go into a basement, he never forgot that operation, or how close they'd come to destruction if the heavy .50 caliber slugs had not punched the bomber outside the room.

* * *

He forced himself to concentrate on the threat that faced them now. Inside, the church was surprisingly light. The huge stained glass windows faced south, catching all of the available sunlight, flooding the interior and providing warmth and illumination as its designers must have intended. It also meant they would be totally exposed when they went in. Gabriel picked up a nearby rock, tossed it through the door and stepped back. He watched it hit the floor with a loud noise, but no shots rang out. He turned to Faith.

"He's not covering the door. We'll go inside and search the building room by room until we find him."

"Room by room?" she replied, puzzled at his description of the church.

"Yeah, it's not one big church inside. It's one of these mountain places that serves the local community, you know, as well as the religious side, they use the church as a school, a social center, whatever."

She nodded in understanding. "Do you think there are any children in there?"

"No. The place is empty, almost empty. Garcia is in there, that's all. Let's get inside. The area to the left of the door is furthest from the windows, so we'll go that way. Ready?"

"I'll lead the way. I have the gun," she reminded him. "Let's go."

They darted through the door and started to work their way through the classrooms that lined the church on one side. They checked everywhere, under the pews, behind the altar, and the priest's robing room. Finally, they went up a long, stone staircase to the bell tower. Nothing. They started down when they heard a slight noise on the stairs, but it was Jonas. He joined them, his gun held at his side.

"There's no sign of him. He can't have vanished into thin air, but somehow he has. The question is what to do now?"

"We need to start again at the bottom," de Sade murmured. "He's hiding somewhere. It's just a question of where? Maybe there's a basement."

Something stirred in Faith's mind. A memory of something, an event, a dream, even a vision, but she couldn't quite work it out.

"I'll see if there's a door to any kind of an underground room if you two check back through the rooms on the first floor."

"Are you sure?" Gabriel asked, his face showing the concern he felt for her.

"You can hardly walk," she explained. "You should be in the emergency room, not chasing around the Sierra Nevada. Besides, I have the gun. Of course, I'm sure. Jonas, he's in no state for any Cowboy and Indian stuff."

"I'll watch him, don't worry. We'd better get back downstairs. We don't want this guy slipping out while we're up here."

They went back down the steps to the main floor of the church. Faith started a search for an entrance to the basement, but there was nothing inside the church. She had an idea, why should it be inside the church? Houses in rural and mountain regions often had storerooms that were accessed from the outside for storing winter supplies. She went back out through the main door, down the steps, and found it almost straight away. A door set into the side of the steps that could only be the basement. She walked up to it, put her hand on the handle, and felt a ripple of fear; some kind of déjà vu, a feeling that she'd been here before. And something terrible had happened, but what was it? She looked up, and Gabriel stood there watching. She didn't say anything, but he was holding the rail at the top of the steps for support. Her eyes met his, and his message was obvious. Be careful. She nodded to him and turned the handle of the door. A flight of stone steps led away from the entrance. She put her foot on the top step and started down. Despite the chill mountain air outside, it was even colder as she walked down the stairs. The fear that she'd felt as she touched the handle started to grow inside her, and she made an effort to put it into a compartment. There was no room here for fear. She was hunting an armed killer. But still the fear still nagged at her as she reached the bottom of the stairs and looked around. It was a labyrinth. There could be no other description for the dark maze that stretched ahead of her. The stone tunnel led off to right and left, and in the dim light of the caged bulbs set into the stonework, she could see that there were openings that led off the main tunnel. She made another effort to control her fear and set out on the tunnel to the left. She kept her gun held ready to use, knowing that the man she hunted was down here. She could feel him, smell him, and hear his breathing; the thud of his pulse as his heartbeat sent blood coursing around his body. She crept carefully forward silently but knew her own heartbeat was thudding so loud it must have announced her presence as loudly as a trumpet call.

"Faith."

She whirled. Someone had called her name.

"You shouldn't have come. Now I will have to kill you."

Javier! He was behind her.

"You always were going to kill me, you bastard."

"Perhaps."

Where was he? She searched the dim tunnel. There, at the end, where she'd come in at the foot of the steps, stood a dark shape. He must have come out of the other tunnel. Then he started towards her, and she ran. The lights went out, and she crept forward, feeling her way along the wall. Her hand touched a door, iron and hardwood. She found the handle and opened it. Should she go in? She could be trapped in there, so maybe she should continue along the tunnel and away from Javier. Then she remembered the dream. Gabriel! He was in danger. She pushed the door open and went into the dark room. Across the other side was the peephole, just as she'd remembered in her dream. She looked through. Sure enough, there was Javier, and his gun pointed at Gabriel as he reached the bottom of the stone steps. He lifted his gun, and there was a loud explosion, the muzzle flash as the pistol fired, and the Spaniard fell. The bullet that had entered his brain killed him instantly.

She was still shaking when she emerged back into the open air. Even wounded, de Sade managed to help her up to the top of the steps. Jonas hurried out of the church entrance.

"I heard a shot. What happened?"

"He'd dead," Faith explained. "I got him. He was waiting in ambush down there, but I managed to get behind him."

"How the hell did you manage that?"

She shrugged. "I remembered being there before, once. A long time ago."

"Here? In this church, in the Sierra Nevada?" He looked incredulous. "I thought you hadn't been here before?"

"No, I haven't, not in the way you mean. But there are other ways to see things than with your eyes, Jonas."

"Yeah, I guess so."

He shook his head, not sure what she meant. But

Gabriel did. She'd talked to him once about that dream. He stared at her. "Was it that dream, the one you saw that night?"

"Yes, it was."

"So you knew he'd be there?"

She nodded. "I did, yes. I'd seen it all before. It was very clear."

"And you knew I'd come down the steps?"

"Yes."

He shook his head. "Jesus Christ, that was a close one. I never told you that I doubted you when you told me."

She smiled. "I realized that, Gabriel. But it doesn't matter. He's dead, and you're alive."

"So it's all over?" Jonas asked.

De Sade turned to look at him. "It is, yes. We'd better go and tell Galina."

"How would you like a lift into town? The Huey's still has gas in the tank, and it'll save walking through the snow."

But de Sade didn't answer. The wound in his side had opened up, and blood poured on to the snow in a steady trickle, turning the pure white into a macabre pattern of red splotches. He dimly heard Faith shout "Jonas" before he pitched forward and fell.

# CHAPTER ELEVEN

When he came to, he was lying in a hospital bed. He looked out of the window and saw it was dark. The clock on the wall said it was three o'clock, and he assumed that meant it was the early hours of the morning. He went to move his left arm, but it was handcuffed to the bed. He shouted out, the door to the hospital room opened, and a uniformed cop came into the room. He looked at de Sade, said something in Spanish and left. Gabriel waited for a half hour until the door opened again and another cop entered. This one wore the dark blue uniform of the Policia Nacional stretched over his obese body. The amount of braid on his cap made it clear he was no humble constable. The man was of medium height, dark haired, with small, dark, suspicious eyes. He looked down at de Sade, his eyes cold, but the effect was ruined by the amount of surplus flesh he carried, making him look slightly comical.

"You are Gabriel de Sade, of the New York Police Department?"

He nodded. "Yeah, that's right. What's going on?"

"I am Colonel Pesaro of the Policia Nacional. You are under arrest, Detective de Sade. We found the body of our man, so the charge is murder. It may be that the charge will be reduced to complicity in the killing of my officer, Javier Garcia, but we shall see where the evidence leads us."

"You're crazy. Garcia was a serial killer."

"Rubbish. It is you who are suspicion for the serial killings, you and your friends. They too are in custody, by the way."

"Ask them, they'll tell you the same thing."

"I already have," the cop countered in an exasperated voice. "And they do say the same thing. The problem for you is that I do not believe it. Javier Garcia had his problems, it is true, but he was not a serial killer."

De Sade wracked his brains. He knew they were in trouble, very serious trouble. No police force worldwide would want to believe one of their own was a sick serial killer, and their instinct would be to blame anyone but a cop. He needed something, anything that could prove what their man had done. The Navaja!

"Did you find a knife on Garcia's body?"

The man hesitated for a moment. "How could you know that?"

"Check out the knife. You'll find it matches the forensic evidence for at least the recent killings in Seville."

The man gave him a hard stare. "And why should I do that when we already have the killers in our custody?"

"Because you'll look damn stupid when it gets to court, and they find out you've been holding the wrong people."

The Colonel smiled, and it was not a pleasant expression. "If we have the wrong people, and I'm not certain that is true, but we will find out eventually. There is plenty of time. Spanish justice moves slowly. I doubt your trial will take place for at least two years, and it could take as long as five years before there is a hearing."

De Sade laughed. He could rot in a Spanish jail, as could Jonas, until someone decided that they were innocent. But Faith was the daughter of a VIP, and no ordinary VIP. There was no way her father would let it happen, no way at all.

"That's where you're wrong, buddy. You're trying to cover your ass because it's one of your own officers who did the killing. But I'll make you a promise. You'll hear from the State Department inside of twenty-four hours, and soon after that, you'll have the choice of releasing us from this trumped up nonsense, or you'll spend the rest of your career policing the frontier high up in the Pyrenees Mountains."

The man gave him a furious stare. "We shall see. When you are fit, you will be transferred to the local prison where your accomplices are being held. I suggest you think about the wording of your confession."

He stormed out, and de Sade lay back in the hospital bed, trying to maneuver himself into a comfortable position. He must have been given a strong painkiller, for the pain in his side from the gunshot wound came searing back to remind him of the events on the mountain. Then he realized that he didn't even know where he was. He determined to find out when a nurse came in to see him. But the next visitor was someone more familiar. Galina Polotsova, complete with babe in arms.

"Gabriel, how are you feeling?"

"I've been worse," he grinned, nodding at the handcuff

that held him to the bed. "They didn't arrest you, then?"

"No, I got out of the helicopter and stayed clear when the cops arrived. I thought I could do better from the outside than if they ran me in to the local jail. You know about Faith and Jonas?"

"Yeah, they're being held on a possible murder rap. I told that colonel to check out Javier Garcia's knife. The forensics on that alone will clear us all, if they do their job properly."

"I called Raymond Glen, Faith's father."

He grinned. "Yeah, I reckon the Director of CIA will clear it up a lot quicker than any forensics. What about the baby, does he have family coming to collect him?"

"I've tried to contact all of his last know addresses, but there's nothing. I believe that the parents were loners and without any family. Eduardo was in process of being adopted from an orphanage in Ecuador. That's where their flight originated. I've been able to determine that much from the paperwork I found on the parents bodies and in their personal effects."

"It's going to be complicated," de Sade acknowledged. "I guess the poor kid will have to go back to the orphanage in Ecuador."

"Maybe," Galina replied, her voice flat.

He stared at her. "Maybe? What does that mean?" Then it dawned on him. "Oh, Christ, you're thinking about keeping him? Galina, it won't work, there's no way."

She shook her head. "You misunderstand. I know that it wouldn't work, but neither can I send him back after all he's been through. What I mean is that I want to supervise the process of finding him a new set of adoptive parents, that's all. And maybe I could visit him sometimes. After all, we share something important. We were the only survivors of that plane crash."

He nodded. "Yeah, I see that. It's a strong tie. I'm just worried about the legalities."

"That's a first for you, Gabriel de Sade. I thought you were in the habit of strong-arming the legalities."

He grinned. "I guess that's true. Yeah, if you hit any problems, let me know, and I'll invoke the family reputation for torture."

"I may just do that. Listen, I'm going to visit the local cops and demand to see Jonas and Faith. Is there any message?"

"Just tell them to watch out for that cop, the Colonel. He's trying to get a reputation by clearing up this case, and I don't think he cares too much about who goes down for it."

She nodded. "I'll tell them, but I think Raymond Glen's influence will sort things out there. You take care." She leaned down and embraced him, kissed his cheek, and left.

It took three more hours, and by eight-thirty in the morning a disheveled, tired looking Colonel Pesaro entered the hospital room, his face wreathed in smiles.

"I have good news for you, Senor de Sade. It is all cleared up. We have spent the whole night examining the forensic evidence on that Navaja, and it proves the link between Detective Garcia and the murders. I personally supervised the process, to make certain that justice would be done. Your friends have been released, and you are free to go. It's all over."

"No, it's not over."

They both looked up as Faith came into the room, the wound on her head covered with a prominent dressing.

"Miss Ward, you have come to visit. I wish to say that…"

"I said it's not over, Colonel. Gabriel, you look terrible, how do you feel?" She smiled at him, ignoring the Spanish cop. "Jonas and Galina checked into a hotel, by the way. They're shopping for new clothes and hiring a car to take us all back to Seville."

"Miss Ward, what exactly do you mean? We caught him, Javier Garcia is dead."

"YOU caught Detective Garcia?" she asked him, her eyebrows arched. "I would think you were taking your morning coffee in the town when we were fighting for our lives on the mountain."

He reddened. "A slip of the tongue, that is all. Of course, you caught and killed him, for which we are all grateful. Surely that is an end to it?"

"No, it is not. Are you certain that there was only one person responsible for these killings?"

"What do you mean?" Then comprehension dawned. "Madre de Dios, you are saying there is another, that he had an accomplice? My God, I called off the investigation. I'll be sacked, or demoted. I have to get to a phone."

They smiled at the fat man's panic as he ran for the door and then back into the hospital room, dragged out his cellphone and back towards the door. Then he stopped.

"How do you know there are two men involved?"

"Because of the timescale," de Sade explained. "There were murders that took place in Seville and in New York at similar times. It couldn't have been the same man, and also Garcia mentioned 'we'."

"My God, I'm ruined."

They smiled as he plunged out of the room to try and

undo the damage. Then Gabriel suddenly realized. "Faith, grab him. The handcuffs."

She chased after him and brought the sweating colonel back to unlock the cuffs. He went back out, still wailing about his career prospects.

"Serve him right, the stupid fool," Gabriel muttered. "He didn't give a damn about who he fitted up for this one, provided it wasn't one of their own."

"Is the NYPD any different?"

He thought for a few moments. "Sometimes, but not always, I guess. Look, I need to get out of here."

"They said you would be discharged tomorrow if there were no complications with the wound."

"That's not good enough. I'm leaving now. Help me up, I need to get dressed."

She protested that he'd kill himself if he caught an infection that could spread.

"You could even get gangrene, you could lose a leg or something."

"If we don't get the other guy, some other girl is going to lose her life."

She was silent for a moment. "Yes, I know. You're right. Gabriel, but before you do, I have something to tell you. You know that solid gold statuette that all the fuss was about?"

He smiled. "Yeah, I do, an ugly little thing. He showed it to us up on the mountain. Worth a lot of money, though, so I guess the Spanish will be glad to have it back."

"Well, that's the thing. They don't know it was ever recovered."

"What! Oh no, what have you done? Does Jonas know about this?"

She nodded. "He does, and Galina knows. It was her idea. It's to do with the orphanage in Ecuador where Eduardo came from. When we knew about the statuette, and that Javier was stealing it, she said how much good it could do for those children. They're desperate for funds, even the most basic things like food and medical supplies. To us, it's a simple equation. The gold was stolen from somewhere in South America, but we'll never know where. We intend to get a good price for the statuette, enough to pay for whatever they need. Probably a new hospital, and maybe even a whole new building."

"Jesus, they could have several new buildings for what you'll get for that statuette. Where is it?"

"After you passed out, I remembered what we'd discussed. I retrieved it from his pack and buried it close to that church. When it's all died down, we can go back there and recover it. The way I see it, it's only going back to its rightful owners. Galina was thrilled when I told her."

"Yeah, I can believe that. It sounds fine to me, but God help us all if they find out what we're doing. That Colonel Pesaro will lock us up and throw away the key."

"I'm glad you said 'we'," she smiled. "We'll be careful. Remember, no one knows what it looks like. Galina and I are accredited dealers and researchers into religious artifacts, so we can prepare documentation to make it all legal. Or at least, give it the appearance of being legal."

"You've thought it all out, haven't you?"

She chuckled. "I suppose so, yes. Except for one thing."

"Yeah, what's that?"

"How we can make love without you opening that wound and starting the bleeding again."

He smiled. "Maybe we can experiment a little, find a

solution? I'm sure there's a simple answer if we work at it."

"Good. I still don't agree with you discharging yourself, but you're right, lives are at stake if we don't stop this bastard. I'll help you get dressed, and you can sign their discharge forms. We're staying here overnight, and tomorrow we start back for Seville."

"Where is here?"

"We're still in the town of Monachil, in the Sierra Nevada. The hotel is about half a mile away, in the center of town. I'll call a cab when you're ready to go."

The hotel was busy with skiers, enjoying the nearby slopes of the Sierra Nevada. They were fortunate to find an empty table in the hotel restaurant amid a raucous hubbub of shouted conversations that enabled them to talk without fear of being overheard. Galina fussed around with Eduardo. It was obvious she was growing very attached to the cute little kid. It was Jonas who finally said what they were all thinking.

"Okay, who is he? Does anyone have any ideas?"

"I've given it a lot of thought," Gabriel replied. "I'm certain that it's someone we've met, someone who knows Javier Garcia, obviously. I did consider his former lover, Montalban."

"It's not him," Faith interrupted. "The man we're looking for is some kind of a priest or a monk. I've seen him, well, you know…" She smiled. "Anyway, he wore robes, or something like that."

"Yeah, we understand," Gabriel nodded. "If we're looking for a priest or a monk, some kind of crazed lunatic, and someone single minded enough to pursue his beliefs no matter how psychotic they are, there's one name comes to mind."

She nodded. "Brother Sebastian."

"Right. It has to be him. He had the opportunity, the motive, and we know he's fanatically driven enough to go to any lengths to achieve his ends."

Galina leaned forward. "But surely that's not enough. Certainly, we know he's all of those things, but this guy is something more, a sick psychopath. There's nothing to suggest that Sebastian is like that."

"But surely these people are so clever and manipulative, there's no way we'd ever know what they're like until they're caught. A psychopath is by definition someone with a personality disorder characterized by a pervasive pattern of disregard for the rights of others and the rules of society. That fits Sebastian perfectly," Faith argued.

"That's true," Gabriel added. "Psychopaths have a total lack of empathy and remorse, and have shallow emotions. I guess you could say that about this particular monk. Last time you crossed swords with him, he never showed any sign of giving a damn about anything except his mission."

"So you're sure?" Jonas pressed him.

He hesitated and looked at Faith. "I don't know. It's a strong maybe, but something doesn't feel quite right. There's something we're missing here."

"Surely we can check and see if he was in New York at the time of the other killings. It will help us decide one way or the other," she said thoughtfully.

"Yeah, I'll send an email from the hotel computer center and see what they say. Then we need to get back to Seville and have a word with our friend the monk."

She nodded. "I agree, but there's still something we're missing, Gabriel."

"We'll find that out when we speak to him. I reckon the killer will be panicking now that Javier Garcia is dead. If it is Sebastian, I'd guess we'd be able to work it out from his reactions."

"Maybe."

"Yeah, maybe. Don't worry, if it's him, I'll get it out of him."

Jonas grinned. "Yeah, that'll be something to see. Give him the old 'de Sade' third degree. I'd like to help you there. I've got some suggestions for getting reluctant suspects to talk."

"Jonas!" Galina exclaimed. "He's a monk, a holy man. You should show him some respect."

"If he's the guy who knocked off these women, I'll show him the barrel of my Colt .45, and that's all he'll get from me."

"And if he isn't?" Faith asked him.

He shrugged. "Then we'll find out who it is, and he'll get the same treatment. One way or the other, this guy is going down. Him and Javier Garcia tried several times to get us killed, and that's enough for me." He looked at Gabriel. "What about you?"

"I agree. We'll drive back in the morning, go see him, and find out what he has to say. I'd better get that email sent. It may clear it up one way or the other."

But by the evening, he still hadn't had a reply. They walked around the town, avoiding crowds of skiers. The scenery was incredible. They could look up to the surrounding snow covered slopes that surrounded the whole town nestled in a valley. When they returned to the hotel, there was a message waiting for Gabriel in reception. The NYPD had sent a fax with details of Sebastian's visits to the US. On each occasion that an abduction and murder had occurred, he'd been in the city, in his capacity as religious artifacts advisor for the Vatican representative to the United Nations. He passed them the fax, and they all read it.

"I guess that's it. It's all we need to deal with Brother Sebastian. We'll leave in the morning. When we get to Seville, I intend to go straight to the Cathedral and deal with him. He's our man, no question."

They all nodded. "Thank God for that," Jonas grinned. "We can all pack up and go home." He looked at Faith. "Does that satisfy you? Surely you must be satisfied now every piece of the jigsaw fits together."

She stared at him. "Not quite every piece. There are one or two things I need to know. I'm going out to find a priest. I'll be back soon."

They stared at her. "A priest? There won't be an Orthodox priest in a place like this," Galina pointed out.

"I'm not looking for an Orthodox priest. I want a Catholic priest."

"You're not thinking of joining them?" she asked, in a worried voice.

"No, not at all. I just have some questions I need to resolve. Don't worry, I won't be long."

She left the hotel, and they watched her in astonishment.

"Is she okay?" Galina remarked. "It's not like her to seek out a priest."

Gabriel shook his head. "I don't know. I just don't know. Maybe it was the wound to the head. I'll talk to her later."

"Yeah, I'd do that, buddy," Jonas muttered. "Something's not right."

She didn't return until late in the night. Gabriel was still waiting in reception. She came up to him and kissed him. "Thanks for staying up for me."

He nodded. "Did you find what you were looking for?"

She gave him a small smile. "Actually, I did. The parish priest was very helpful. He even gave me a gift." She held out her hand. "These are rosary beads. They use them to help remember and count the prayers of penance after confession."

"You've been to confession? In a Catholic church?"

She smiled. "Yes and no, really. I went to find answers, and the priest took me through the whole process, but don't worry, I'm not turning Roman. It's just some information that may come in useful later."

They went to bed, but neither of them slept for a long time. Faith's ardor had cooled.

"Gabriel, just hold me. I feel that we're up against someone who is determined to kill us all. He's evil beyond belief, and I know he won't ever stop until we're dead."

"Why? Surely he'll move on and lie low after we uncovered his accomplice, Javier Garcia. The last thing he'll want to do is hang around and wait to be arrested."

"No, it isn't like that. I can feel it, almost feel HIM. It's like a dark shadow hanging over us, can't you see? We've done him a great deal of damage, killed his friend, and wrecked his murderous scheme. As well as that, he may not believe that we never found the treasure he was seeking. I know he'll come after us, and he's a bigger danger than he ever was before."

"I understand," he soothed her. "I won't let it happen. I assure you that we will get this guy. I'll phone Colonel Velasquez in the morning and fill him in on everything we've found out. I've no doubt he'll want to question

Brother Sebastian himself. With any luck, this could be all over by the end of tomorrow."

She lifted her head and looked into his eyes. "Gabriel, there are two things that I'm certain of. One is that that it won't be over tomorrow."

"We'll see about that. What's the second thing?"

She shook her head. "I'll save that for later."

In the morning, he awoke to find that she'd gone. He dressed quickly and found her downstairs in the restaurant, drinking coffee. She gave him a pale smile.

"Sorry, I just couldn't sleep. I'll catch up on the way to Seville. It's a long journey."

He wanted to ask her more as she wore her anxiety like a badge, but he decided to leave it.

"I'll go and phone Colonel Velasquez and see what he has to say."

She nodded as he left her and went to use the hotel phone. It took him ten minutes to get through to Policia Nacional in Seville. Velasquez picked up the phone.

"Digame!"

"This is Detective de Sade, Colonel. I'm still in Monachil, but we're coming back to Seville today. I'd like to call in on you to discuss the progress of the case."

There was a long pause, and for a moment de Sade thought he'd hung up.

"The case? But you killed my detective. It is over."

"No, Sir, it isn't. There were two killers and two crime scenes, both in Seville and in New York City."

"Then I suggest you go back there and make your inquiries, Detective."

"Sir, you don't understand, the man we're…"

"No, it is you who do not understand. The case is closed

246

as far as we're concerned. I have enough problems to sort out as it is, following the murder of one of my men."

De Sade didn't understand at first, but then he realized with growing astonishment that the Colonel was still trying to cover for his rogue detective.

"I therefore suggest you get on the first flight back to the USA. You are not welcome in Seville. Good day, Detective de Sade."

When he returned to the restaurant, Jonas, and Galina who was holding Eduardo, were sat with Faith eating breakfast. He told them about his conversation with Velasquez.

"That could make it awkward if we do return to Seville," Galina pointed out.

"Maybe, but I came over here to track down a serial killer. That investigation is still ongoing, and I reckon the killer is in Seville. Colonel or no colonel, I'm going back."

"Hey, we're going back," Jonas reminded him. "You're not on your own here."

"Right, thanks. Did you get a car?"

"I sure did. She's a Mercedes-Benz C63 AMG, and I hired it from the local Hertz. It's big, fast and comfortable, so it'll get us there in no time."

"Good. What about Eduardo?"

"I've arranged for a private nurse to take care of him. We're meeting her here, and she'll look after him until we leave Spain. This fight is no place for a child, and I feel that we're all going to be needed to finish this."

"It's still a police investigation," he reminded her. "It's not just us involved."

"Really?" she snorted. "And who else is trying to stop this killer before he murders yet more women?"

He could only shrug. The Spanish nurse came into the restaurant and introduced herself. She immediately fell in love with Eduardo and promised to take care of him until their business was complete. She left with him in her arms and a fistful of dollars in her purse to buy everything she needed. Galina saw them to the door and watched them go with a wistful expression, then returned to the table. She stared at them.

"I'm ready. Let's take this bastard down and finish this."

# CHAPTER TWELVE

As Jonas had promised, it was a fast journey to Seville, and they arrived back in the city by early afternoon. They still had their rooms at the Hotel Becquer, and he persuaded them to find space to park the car. As usual, it was amazing the effect a ten-dollar bill had on finding additional space when there was none to be had.

"I guess we're going to the Cathedral?" Jonas asked. "We know who we're looking for."

"Brother Sebastian, yes." Gabriel replied. "Let's see what the monk has to say for himself. I'm pretty sure it's him."

For some reason, he looked at Faith who he knew still had doubts.

"If he's innocent, we'll find out and get after the real killer. But I think it's him."

They walked quickly through the streets that were mainly empty during the afternoon siesta. Inside the Cathedral, they went first to talk to the Bishop, Raul Santiago. When they reached his office, the door was slightly ajar, and they walked straight in. His jaw dropped open when he saw them, and he rose to his feet. He was wearing a lightweight black raincoat and had been fastening a bulging briefcase.

"Why have you returned? Colonel Velasquez called in this morning to tell me that the detective Javier Garcia was the man who murdered all those poor women. Is the investigation not all over?"

Gabriel stared at the Bishop. His face was red and flushed, and he obviously had something on his mind. He told him why they were back in Seville, and Santiago's eyes widened in astonishment.

"So you think there's yet another killer on the loose in the city. This is terrible. How may I help?"

"We need to speak to Brother Sebastian, Bishop. If we may have your permission, we'll have a word with him. We think he may be able to help us."

"Sebastian? He's not here, I'm afraid. I wanted to speak to him myself, but he's not in his office, in fact, not even in the Cathedral. I asked security to find him, and they said he's vanished."

De Sade swallowed his anger. They'd missed him.

"We'll look around, Sir. He may be hiding somewhere close. May we search the Cathedral?"

The Bishop spread his hands. "Of course, you still have you passes, so you may go where you wish. I find it hard to believe that Sebastian is mixed up in this, though. I'm sorry I can't help you more, but I shall be away for the next week. I have affairs to deal with elsewhere, but I will leave word that you are to be offered every assistance."

"Thank you, Bishop Santiago, you've been very helpful," Gabriel replied.

Santiago nodded. He noticed Galina for the first time.

"I don't believe we've met."

"Polotsova, Galina Polotsova."

"A Russian? An Orthodox Christian, I imagine."

She nodded. "Yes, I am. I was a nun."

"An Orthodox nun, I see." He looked at Gabriel again. "As for Brother Sebastian, I have no way of knowing where he is. There is probably a reasonable explanation for his absence."

"And what would that be, Bishop?"

He looked away from her, and up to the crucifix on the wall. "I have no idea," he muttered.

De Sade nodded at the others. "Let's take a look around and see if we can find the monk. He could be hiding in here somewhere. It's a huge building, as we know. Let's start up in the attic, just stay clear of those funnels."

Faith grimaced. "If he's in there, he isn't getting out. We know that much."

Gabriel nodded. "Let's stay together while we're searching. If Sebastian is our guy, we know he's a killer. Keep it in mind."

They opened the heavy door that led to the attic, and the vast space yawned ahead of them, gloomy and brooding. Galina was detailed to guard the light switch to prevent an ambush.

"If he approaches you," Jonas said growled in a worried tone, "give me a shout, and I'll be right there."

"If he approaches me, you don't have to worry. I still have that little pistol."

"In the usual place?" he grinned, looking down at the top of her legs.

She nodded. "That's right. I wouldn't be dressed without it."

They left her and started to check out the huge area of the Cathedral attic, but it soon became clear that he wasn't there. They gave up and walked back toward the door.

"We could search the whole of this city and still not find him," Jonas exclaimed. "It's going to be difficult without the help of the local cops."

They reached the door. It was open, but there was no sign of Galina. Jonas erupted in anger.

"Spread out! If he attacked her, she can't be far," he shouted. "How the hell could he get the drop on her? It doesn't seem possible. I'll tear this Cathedral apart if necessary. Let's get back down and start looking."

"Jonas, you need to see this." They whirled around. Galina had just come back through the attic door.

"We thought you'd been taken," he shouted, his voice part angry and part relieved that she was okay.

"Taken? Not at all, I heard a noise and went to take a look. There's a narrow doorway that leads from the stairway halfway down to the next level. I found Brother Sebastian."

They stared at her in astonishment. "How did you manage to get the drop on him?" Gabriel asked softly.

"It wasn't difficult. He was dying. Someone slit his throat."

They were silent as they digested the implications of what she was saying. Finally, de Sade voiced what they were thinking. "So he wasn't the killer."

Galina shook her head. "Obviously not. You'd better come down and take a look at the body."

They followed her down the stairs and through the door into the tiny room where Sebastian's body lay in a broken, bloody heap. His lifeblood had leaked out around his body and formed small pools in the uneven parts of the floor.

"Was he alive when you found him?" he asked Galina.

"Yes, but unconscious. It's strange. The killer normally kills and then cuts the bodies to pieces. It's almost as if he was disturbed, or in a hurry."

Gabriel crouched down and looked at the hands. "He tried to put up a fight. It looks like skin tissue underneath his fingernails. I'll call in the local cops, and they can do some tissue DNA tests. The body is still very warm, so he was killed in the last two hours. That means the killer isn't far away, so maybe they can get on his tail."

Colonel Velasquez greeted his call with an icy chill until he heard the news of a new body in the Cathedral. After a short silence, de Sade heard him shouting orders to his men.

"Do not touch anything, Detective. My men will be there shortly to secure the crime scene."

He slammed down the phone, and Jonas grinned. "At least he'll realize there's another killer running around his city."

"We knew that before," Gabriel reminded him. "But now we're no further forward. Who the hell is this guy?"

"Look at the symbol on the floor," Faith interrupted them. She was staring at the bloody pattern. "It's a message from Brother Sebastian."

They inspected the blood trail on the wooden boards of the room.

"I can't see a symbol," de Sade replied, his voice skeptical. "It's just a random pattern where the blood spurted out all over the floor."

"No, she's right," Galina pointed out, drawing his

attention to part of the blood-smeared floor. "Look at that. It's a question mark, I believe."

He stared at the bloody pattern. "It could be a question mark, but it could be something else. And why would he make his last dying action to write a question mark on the floor?"

The tramp of feet on the stairs announced the arrival of the Policia Nacional. Velasquez led the charge, and he took them to one side.

"I want you to go downstairs, and you will stay away from my crime scene. One of my officers will take your statement, and then you will leave this investigation to us. I suggest you leave Seville. There is nothing else here for you to do. Good day."

They walked back down the stone staircase. The cop assigned to take their statements made them wait for almost an hour while he went away on some other errand, and then he returned with a clipboard and pen.

"Do any of you speak Spanish?"

They all shook their heads. He sighed with irritation. I speak little English. You must report to the police station and make your statements when there is an interpreter available."

"When will that be?" Galina asked him.

He shrugged. "Tomorrow, perhaps." Then he walked away.

"It looks like the Spanish cops are not too interested in what we have to say," Jonas muttered to Gabriel.

"No, they're probably worried we may implicate another cop."

"It's not a cop," Faith stated in a firm tone. "I think I know now who the killer is."

The three of them looked at her. "How the hell do you know that?" de Sade asked. He noticed her face was white as if she'd just had a major shock. Another dead body was hard to take, but she a veteran of many bloody and bruising encounters. Death was no stranger to her.

"Are you alright? You don't look well."

She nodded. "I'm okay, I'll tell you about it later. First of all, can we get out of here? This place is too creepy. There's been too much blood and too much killing. Then I'll tell you what I found."

They left the Cathedral and found a table back at the Café of the Indies. After they'd ordered coffee, they fixed Faith with a curious stare.

"Right, what's going on?" Galina asked her friend. "Who do you think is behind all of this?"

"Before I can answer that, I want you to think about that symbol Sebastian wrote before he died."

"The question mark?" Gabriel asked her in surprise. "What does that have to do with anything?"

"It has everything to do with it. But it's not a question mark. It's something else entirely."

They watched her and waited.

"It's a shepherd's crook."

Jonas arched his eyebrows in puzzlement. "That still doesn't make any sense, a shepherd's crook? What could it mean?"

But Galina and Gabriel both nodded. The Russian girl explained. "It's called a crozier, and it's the universal sign of a bishop. They carry a shepherd's crook as a mark of their office. In the Catholic Church, the crozier is shaped like a shepherd's crook. A bishop bears this staff as shepherd of the flock of God."

"Excuse me, I don't understand. You mean Sebastian was telling us that a bishop killed him? That's hard to believe."

Faith shrugged. "I'm only saying the symbol written in blood on that floor was the universal sign of a bishop. You can interpret that as you like."

"But you believe he meant to tell us a bishop killed him, don't you?" de Sade asked her.

"Yes, I do."

"How many bishops are there in a cathedral like Seville?" Jonas asked.

"I think the answer to that is one," Galina replied.

"Shit! He's gone, and he's running."

"Yes."

The Bishop's secretary looked up in irritation. "I'm afraid the Bishop is not here. He left several hours ago."

"Yeah, we know that," de Sade nodded. "We have to know where he went."

"I'm afraid I cannot tell you that."

He fixed her with a hard stare. "This is an emergency, life or death. We have to know where he can be found!"

"You don't understand. As a general rule, there is no secret about the Bishop's whereabouts. But on this occasion, he didn't tell me where he was going. Why don't you call back tomorrow? I have no doubt he'll be back by then."

Gabriel gave her his cell number. "If you hear from him in the meantime, would you let me know?"

"Of course," she smiled. "Is it a sick relative, is that the problem?"

"Yeah, something like that."

They were almost out of options. Except for one.

"I'm going back to see the cop, Velasquez. Whether he likes it or not, he has to know about the symbol next to the body. I doubt he's worked it out."

"I'll come with you," Faith smiled. "They say that Spanish men respond better to feminine charms."

Jonas nodded. "We'll get back to the hotel and make sure the car is gassed up ready to go. As soon as we have a lead on where he went, we'll have to go after him."

Gabriel and Faith climbed the stone stairway that led up to the Cathedral attic. Colonel Velasquez of the Policia Nacional was on his way down. He stared at them, his expression cold.

"I thought I made it clear. I require you to stay away from the crime scene."

"We came to see you," Gabriel explained. "We believe we know who the killer is."

The Colonel looked skeptical as he explained how they had come to the conclusion.

"So you are telling me that, on the basis of an ambiguous symbol that may or may not have been written by the victim, I should arrest a bishop of the Catholic Church? Are you mad?"

"No, Colonel, you don't understand. Everything points to Bishop Santiago as the most likely suspect. I'm betting that if you check his travel itinerary, you'll find he was in New York at the time of the killings over there. All that's necessary…"

Velasquez held up his hand. "Stop. Of course Bishop Santiago has traveled to New York. He is a busy man, and I know that he is an important figure in the Opus Dei organization. Their headquarters is there, so why would he not travel there? Besides which, he is a senior member of the Congregation for the Doctrine of the Faith in the Vatican. He is also a personal friend of mine, and I trust him absolutely. Your suspicions are nonsense. Bishop Santiago is one of the most highly respected members of the Catholic Church. Now, I suggest you return to your country, and leave me to get on with my work. Goodbye."

Faith looked up. "Opus Dei? He denied it."

"Denied what?"

"When we first met him, we asked him if he was a member of Opus Dei. Their headquarters is close to the site the killer used to dump the bodies in New York. We felt it was likely that there was a link to that organization, given that the murders had a strong religious motivation."

"Perhaps you were mistaken," Velasquez scoffed. "Believe me, it could not be Bishop Santiago. It is impossible. Please, I have work to do. I suggest you leave Seville. In fact, I insist. You have twenty-four hours. After that, I may be forced to place you in protective custody. In the meantime, I would ask you to leave the Cathedral. There is nothing for you here."

They returned to the hotel, and Galina was working on Jonas' laptop.

"I'm trying to get an itinerary of Bishop Santiago," she explained. "It may help us to find him if we know his usual haunts. It could also help if you contact your people at the NYPD. They can find the information much quicker than we can."

De Sade grimaced. "I'll give them a call, but it's not going to be easy. I mean, a bishop of the Catholic Church. We don't even have any direct evidence. It's all circumstantial."

He made the call and listened for ten harrowing minutes to Captain Kruger shouting down the line. When he hung up, the others were waiting expectantly.

"Velasquez has been on to him, and he made a complaint. I've been recalled, and I'm booked on a flight that leaves Seville tonight."

"I'll come with you," Faith said at once.

"Jonas, you and I had best stay here," the Russian girl added. "We can keep looking for him."

He nodded. "Yeah, I'd like to get my hands on the bastard."

"That's it then," Gabriel held up his hands. "It's all going to be down to you two. Are you sure you don't object to doing this? It should be a police operation."

"This bastard needs to be stopped," Jonas fumed. "I know it was his partner, Javier Garcia up on that mountain, but he was as guilty as if he'd been there himself. I take it very personal when people try to kill me, and it could easily have been Galina if they'd had the chance. I want him taken down."

Galina nodded. "I feel the same way. This has to end."

"Thanks," Gabriel said. "I'll do whatever I can from New York and send you any updates I get on his whereabouts. That's it, then. We may as well pack to go home."

Jonas drove them to Seville airport where they caught the local flight to Madrid. They transferred to an American Airlines 747 for the long, coach class journey across the Atlantic and arrived in New York JFK in the early hours of a Saturday morning. They took a cab to their apartment and fell into bed at ten in the morning. At one o'clock, de Sade was woken from a deep, exhausted sleep by the incessant ringing of the phone.

"De Sade? This is Captain Kruger. Can you come down here? I need to speak to you about that business in Seville."

"Cap'n, I got back a few hours ago. Can't it wait?"

"I guess I could wait. I didn't plan on coming to the Precinct today, but the Catholic Archbishop of New York has been in touch with the Mayor's office. I'm to speak to you the minute your feet touch dry land on this side of the Atlantic, if not before. They're pissed, de Sade. Very pissed. Be here in an hour!"

Faith was awake, and he explained the call.

"They won't believe it until he's caught, will they?" she exclaimed. "It's not fair. They should be hunting the bastard, not criticizing you for doing your job."

"They're criticizing me because I opened a can of worms and not for anything else. If it is the Bishop who is the killer, they'll want it quietly hushed up."

"But they can't let him run around loose," she protested.

"You know how it goes. He'll disappear, an accident maybe."

"That won't be justice for all those victims."

"No, it won't."

Kruger was not alone in his office. A priest sat in a comfortable chair next to his desk. The priest stood up when de Sade entered. Kruger remained seated, a sour look on his face.

"This is Monsignor Vincenzo. They're obviously not happy about the allegations you've been throwing around about one of their bishops. A very senior bishop, in fact."

"Of course, we do not wish to impede a serious investigation," the priest said quickly.

"That's very refreshing," de Sade replied, still suffering from jet lag and lack of sleep.

The priest flushed. "The child abuse problem is behind us, as you well know."

Neither cop replied. There were complaints still surfacing, and the Church still didn't show any signs of cooperating when their own people were in trouble.

"Monsignor Vincenzo, would you explain your take on this current problem?" Kruger asked.

He nodded. "Yes, Bishop Santiago. He is one of the most respected members of the Church. Without doubt, he will receive a red zuchetto in due course, and…"

"Red Zuchetto? Is that some kind of medal?" Kruger looked puzzled.

"It's what they give a Cardinal. The skull cap they wear on their heads, as opposed to the miter they wear when celebrating mass."

"Oh, yeah, right."

"Yes. This is due in part to the work he has done for the Holy Office, the Congregation for the Doctrine of the Faith. In addition, he is a highly respected official of Opus Dei who has its headquarters here in New York City. Quite frankly, Detective, to suggest he is some kind of mass murderer is patently absurd. We have to insist that this nonsense stops."

They glared at each other for a few moments.

"And if he is a killer?"

Vincenzo sighed. "He is not. You have my personal word on the matter. He is a man of God, I assure you."

Kruger leaned forward. "There you are, de Sade. That can be an end to it."

"Just one more thing, Captain. Monsignor, you say you are convinced of his innocence, yes?"

The priest nodded.

"In that case, you'll have no objection to me checking his itinerary for the past twelve months. We can also analyze his phone calls. If there's nothing there to find, that will be an end to it."

"For Christ's sake, de Sade, I already said…"

"No, no, the detective is quite correct. As I said, things have changed, and the Church is prepared to be totally transparent. You may examine any and all records that relate to Bishop Santiago. We will assist you in any way. But, Detective," he stared at de Sade, "after that, it must be an end to it. No more rumors, no more allegations."

His expression was hard and unrelenting. Gabriel reflected that the man would have made a good stockbroker and would make a ruthless negotiator.

"Yeah, that's fair. I'll be around tomorrow morning."

The priest smiled. "Sunday morning is a busy day for the Church, Detective. Perhaps Monday?"

He smiled back. "Yes, that'll be fine. I'll be there."

"I will see you then." The priest stood up to leave. "Captain Kruger, thank you for your help. Detective." They shook hands and he left.

"I want a word with you," Kruger snapped, as de Sade was about to walk out of the door.

De Sade turned back. "Yes, Captain?"

"Don't fuck those people around. They carry a lot of clout in this city. Enough to make or break careers."

"I hear you, Captain."

He went to leave again, but Kruger held up his hand. "One more thing. What evidence do you have?"

"Evidence? I guess it's all circumstantial, but Bishop Santiago has the means, the motive, and the opportunity. We've convicted a lot of killers for less, Sir."

Kruger sighed. "Not future Cardinals of the Catholic Church, we haven't."

"There's always a first time."

"And a last. Check out this guy's calls and anything else you can find, and put an end to it."

"Yeah, I'll do that."

"And I don't mean by breaking heads, de Sade. Do this by the book. The Church can be a powerful enemy in New York. Christ, half the cops on the force are Irish Catholic. You be careful, or you'll lose a lot of friends."

"I hear you, Captain."

When de Sade got down to the desk, Monsignor Vincenzo was talking to the sergeant, one of his parishioners. He looked up as the de Sade walked past.

"Detective, a word if I may."

He nodded to the sergeant, and the two men walked outside and down the steps.

"I meant what I said. We really will do our utmost to cooperate with you."

De Sade nodded. "I never doubted you, Monsignor."

"I see. The question I wanted to ask you is, do you have any evidence of your allegations about the Bishop?"

"Evidence? No, Sir, not direct evidence. But as I said to the Captain, he had the means, motive, and opportunity. With most people, they'd be in custody by now and answering questions about their movements."

"And you really believe the Bishop to be guilty?"

De Sade nodded. "Yes, I do. And one day he'll be caught."

"I think you're wrong, my son."

"I'm not. And if the bastard sets foot in New York City, I'll nail him myself."

Vincenzo looked puzzled. "New York City? Didn't you know?"

"Know what?"

"He is in New York City. I'm not sure exactly where he's staying, but he flew in yesterday."

"I need to talk to him."

Vincenzo nodded. "If I see him, I will tell him to contact you. One more thing, I believe you were seeking some kind of treasure. Did you ever find it?"

All of de Sade's senses came alert. "I did not go looking for any treasure, but it was my understanding that finding it was part of the killer's agenda. No, I did not find any treasure."

Which was true, he smiled to himself. Javier Garcia had found it. The rest was definitely need to know, and this priest had no need to know. Vincenzo nodded.

"I see. Should you come across anything, any Church property, would you let me know? The Archbishop had an inquiry from the Vatican, you understand."

"Yeah, I got it. I'll keep you informed if I come across anything."

"Yes. Thank you, Detective."

They shook hands. De Sade felt he must be losing his touch. He used to be able to lie on demand; it was part of being a detective. But he knew the priest hadn't believed a word of what he'd said. He knew the power of gold to excite the imagination, and the lure of treasure to fever men's brains, and to twist even dedicated priests, like Vincenzo. It was a sobering thought, and one he knew he'd have to always keep in his mind. No man was immune to the magnetic pull of hidden riches.

# CHAPTER THIRTEEN

De Sade spent all of Monday at the Diocesan headquarters of the Church. It was clear that Santiago did indeed have the opportunity to have committed the crimes. When he left to return home late Monday evening, he was working on how to persuade Kruger to put out an APB for the Bishop. He'd called Kruger earlier, but the Captain was adamant.

"I told you, de Sade, you're looking at the wrong man. Find another suspect, for Christ's sake. Finish up there today, and get back to the Precinct tomorrow. I'll assign you to another case if you haven't made any progress."

"Captain, this guy is going to kill again, I…"

"He'll kill if we don't find him, yeah. But you've got the wrong man. It's not the Bishop, for Christ's sake. Unless you've got something that directly links him to the murders, come back here. I'll see you here in the morning."

He walked into the Chinese store and said hi to Lee Fat. The Chinese owner sat behind the cash register as ever.

"Hello, Detective. Your lady, she home. Come and buy

beer, she say you need it this evening."

He smiled, so Faith knew what kind of day he'd have had.

"Thanks, Lee, there's a couple of things I need. I'll just have a look around."

"Very good. Priest come today, he very friendly. Try to convert me. I tell him we already Catholic."

"Yeah, that's good."

"He have strange accent. I thought he Hispanic, I ask him is he from Mexico, but he say no, he Spanish."

De Sade was looking at the deli counter, and he jerked around.

"Spanish? What did he look like?"

Lee shrugged. "I not sure. Tall, maybe. Thin, gray hair."

Gabriel put down the groceries. "Thanks Lee, I'll call back later for these."

Lee nodded as he rushed out of the store and into his apartment block. When he turned the key in the door and saw Faith in the living room, he breathed a sigh of relief. She looked up and smiled.

"What's up with you? You look as if you've seen a ghost."

"Not quite." He described what Lee Fat had told him.

"You think it could be Santiago?"

"I think I'm not prepared to take a chance. Make sure you carry a gun, always."

"Sure, if you think it's best. I'll take the .25 Colt Auto out of the safe. It's small enough. You think that Santiago could threaten me?"

"Yes."

He explained that the lure of the gold was enough to make the killer come after anyone he thought had it in their possession. He had a sudden thought.

"Tell me, how do you intend to get the statue back to the US?"

She smiled. "Galina has it all taken care of. She's still in Seville with Jonas, and while he was looking around, she went out and bought a small consignment of antique Spanish ironwork. She's shipping it back by special courier. I guess there's not much point in them staying over there now that the Bishop is here in the city."

"I wonder, is there any way that Santiago could know she had the statuette? As far as we know, he had no contact with Javier on that mountain."

She stared at him, her eyes wide. "His cellphone. He had it in his hand. I noticed it on the ground after he was killed."

"You mean he had a signal up there in that church in Monachil?"

She looked uncertain. "I'm not totally sure, but I picked it up to take a look at it. I seem to remember the screen was illuminated, as if he'd been trying to use it, at least."

"So we have to assume that he knows. That changes everything."

"In what way?"

"It means that we're a target, you're a target, Galina too. He won't know where the statuette is, only that we have it. That means he's not far away. It could make finding him a whole lot easier."

She looked away. "So you intend to use me as bait. He's probably waiting outside, right now."

"No, of course I'm not using you as bait." But as he said it, he realized that it was exactly what Faith would be, just bait for a trap. Waiting for one of the most vicious serial killers he'd ever encountered to fall into it. "In any case, now that we know what we're up against, that Santiago probably knows about the gold, we can take steps to protect you. Faith, come here, you know how much you mean to me."

She looked at him and came into his arms.

"I'm going to make sure you're guarded every second of every day. As well as that, you're carrying your Colt. So if she shows his face, one of us will shoot the bastard and end it."

"I hope so."

"I know so. Come to bed, we're both tired. I'll have a chat with the guys in the Precinct in the morning. See if I can rustle up some extra help."

She unwound from his arms and headed for the bedroom. He made sure the door was securely fastened and followed her. She lay on the bed, staring up at the ceiling.

"What are you thinking?"

Her eyes were wide open, but when she didn't answer he understood she saw nothing. She was staring into a deep, dark infinity. He lay beside her and waited for her to emerge from the trance she'd fallen into. It was half an hour before her head turned toward him.

"I'm sorry, I kind of went away."

"As long as it was a dream and not a nightmare."

"It was a nightmare. He's here."

"Santiago? We know he's here. It's just a question of finding him."

"Yes. I saw him outside our apartment block, and then he went away. He'll be checking out the gallery. And tomorrow, I have to go there to work."

He could hardly believe what she was saying. "Faith, you can't! Not until this is over."

"Why? Wouldn't it draw him out into the open? Isn't that what you want?"

"Not like that, no."

"That's too bad. I'm going to the gallery tomorrow."

He didn't sleep well that night. Faith's breathing was even as she dropped into a deep slumber, and he listened to the familiar night sounds of her. He smelled the odor of her body, the remnants of her fragrance, the spicy musk of a healthy young woman. An enormous well of love and concern for her welled up in him, he got out of bed and went to use his cell in the living room. He wondered if Frank would still be awake, but he was answered straight away.

"Willard here. What d'ya want?"

"Hi, Frank, it's de Sade."

"Jesus Christ, do you know what time it is? If this is anything less than an alien invasion, I'm hanging up right away."

"It's about Faith. There's a problem."

The joking stopped. "What do you need?" He'd met Faith on a few occasions and regarded her as part of the team. If anyone threatened her, they threatened everyone. He explained about Santiago being on the loose in New York.

"Isn't that the Spanish guy that Kruger was angry about, said you were chasing down the wrong perp?"

"That's the one, yes. The bishop."

"You think he's the one? The serial killer?"

"No, I don't think he is. I know he is."

"That's good enough for me. The brass doesn't know

their head from their ass anyway. How can I help?"

"I want Faith to be protected, day and night. What I could do with is, as many guys as possible who can shave some time of their regular investigations to keep an eye out. Sooner or later, he's going to come after her, and I want to be there when he does."

"Got it. That's no problem, so when do we start?"

"Tomorrow. She'll be at that little gallery she runs. I'll get her there and back, and watch her when she's at home, but I want that place covered. Say from nine tomorrow morning?"

"I'll be there, and I'll set it up with some of the guys. Don't worry, she's covered."

He put the phone down with a huge feeling of relief. He'd make certain she was safe when he was with her, here at home, or if they went out anywhere. Frank would make sure she was covered during the day while she was at work. It meant he would be able to get on with the important work of hunting down Santiago. He couldn't sleep. He felt too worried about the way the chase had come so close to their home. He got out his briefcase and looked back over the notes he'd made. He needed something, somewhere, a starting point, some place to look for the rogue bishop. He looked at the next sheet of paper and something caught his eye, an address, a building on East 34th Street, Opus Dei. That was where Santiago would be found. It was a place that was familiar to him, and a place he could go to seek shelter and aid. He wasn't officially wanted for any crime, so there was no reason why he shouldn't be welcomed as a favored member of their hierarchy. He picked up his cell again.

"De Sade, if that's you, I have to tell you that I need

some sleep if I'm to get this done tomorrow."

"Sorry, Frank. The Opus Dei building on East 34th, they don't know we're looking at him for these crimes. We need to watch that too."

There was a silence at the other end of the line. He heard Frank's breathing, and his voice came back.

"Without the Captain's okay on this, I can't get enough men. But there's a camera on the corner of Lexington Avenue, I can ask the operator in the control center to keep an eye out for this guy. You'll need to let me have a photo to show her."

"That's good, thanks, Frank. I'll send it to you by email."

"I'll see she gets it first thing in the morning. Now can I get some sleep?"

"Sure. Good night, Frank."

In the morning, he insisted on taking Faith to the gallery and made sure she'd let him know when she wanted to leave. He'd emailed the photo of Santiago to Frank and printed out several more for the detectives who would be monitoring the gallery to protect Faith. He even gave one to Lee Fat who recognized him as the man who'd come into the store. There was no sign of any of Frank's people outside the gallery, but a utility truck was parked opposite, one he knew they'd used for surveillance duties. He'd done everything he could, so he went to the Precinct for a meeting with Kruger that he knew would end in tears. Frank met him in the detectives' room.

"You saw the truck?"

"Yeah, I did. Thanks, I owe you one."

"That's okay. We do have a problem with this guy if we see him. He's not wanted for anything, so until he actually pulls a gun or does something illegal, we can't touch him.

He could get in a shot at Faith while we're still watching him."

"I thought of that, but remember, she's not defenseless. If she sees him, she'll blow his balls off."

"Let me know if anything changes."

"Like what, Frank?"

"Like you find it's somebody else."

"That won't happen. This guy is the one."

He saw Kruger waving at him to go to his office. He thanked Willard and went in. The Captain came straight to the point.

"Did you come up with anything yesterday?"

"No, Cap'n. Plenty of circumstantial…"

"We've been there, de Sade. Circumstantial is not enough for a bishop of the Catholic Church. Is there anything else?"

De Sade shook his head.

"In that case, you're assigned to another case." He handed over a file. "This came from vice. A group of working girls are rolling their clients, that's the way it looks."

"Christ, that's a case for vice. Pass it over to them."

"They passed it to us," Kruger snapped. "Some of these johns got hit for thousands of dollars. Cash, credit cards, you know the kind of thing. Get out there, interview them, and find out who's behind it. That's all."

Gabriel nodded. "Is there any sign of a replacement for Carlo?"

Normally, he'd have given the job to Carlo while he stayed with what was important. But Carlo was dead, killed by the perp de Sade was hunting. He remembered how he'd felt when he heard about his partner's tortured body, covered with burns and slashes.

"Not yet, for the time being you're on your own."

He nodded to Kruger and left the office. He knew there'd be no point in arguing. Frank was waiting for him.

"What's going down, de Sade?"

He told him about the vice job. Willard raised his eyebrows. "Sounds like he's rubbing your nose in it. How are you gonna play this?"

"By ear, Frank, by ear. You got the photo?"

"Yeah, I sent it across to Betty, my contact in the control room. She said she'll keep an eye out for him."

"Thanks, I'll put in a couple of hours on this one and write it up. Then I'll concentrate on bringing down Santiago."

"Amen to that. Don't worry about Faith. We're keeping an eye on her."

He nodded and went to his desk to work through the file. On closer examination, it was more serious that Kruger had told him. The women worked with a pair of heavies. If the johns knew they were being robbed and started to protest, the men rushed into the room and beat them, and still made off with their possessions. One of the victims was still on life support in the emergency room, and his prognosis was not good. De Sade decided to go visit another victim, Robert Clements, a New York Port Authority supervisor who'd had a hard time. He took an unmarked car and drove out to the man's place of employment. He found him at the port, amidst the bustle and debris of semi-trailers, smaller trucks and forklifts rushing around in a mad scramble. Clements was directing the unloading of cargo from a container ship. He was a short, tubby man, and his dark face populated with two days' stubble. When he took his hard hat off and exposed his balding head with a greasy comb-over, it was easy to see why he looked to the market for easy sex.

"Is there anything new on my wallet, did you get the girl who took it?"

"I'm sorry, no, Sir. I came to ask if you'd seen the girl on the street since the crime was committed."

He thought for a few moments, scratched his head. "Yeah, well, maybe. I was driving along Lexington late last night. It must have been about twelve thirty. I'm sure I saw her, and she was walking with someone, an older looking guy. It may have been her, but I'm not sure."

On an impulse, Gabriel took a photo out of his briefcase and showed it to him.

"Could this have been the guy she was with?"

He squinted at it. He nodded slowly. "It could have been, but I was looking at the girl, trying to make up my mind. If I was sure, I would have called you guys, but I wasn't. The guy I saw, yeah, I remember, he was tall, thin. Not like me," he laughed depreciatingly. "Does that help?"

"Yes, I think it might. We'll keep you informed, Mr. Clements. Anything else you see or remember, call me. Here's my card."

They shook hands and he left. So he was back in business, and the bastard hadn't even waited to slake his thirst for blood. The prostitute would be dead by now, that was certain. He drove away from the port, thinking furiously. If he had surfaced, he could be on camera - Betty, Frank's contact. He called the Precinct who transferred the call to Frank's cellphone.

"Checking on me," Willard joked. "I'm in the truck outside Faith's gallery. Nothing happening."

"Frank, I may have something. Could you ask Betty to pull up the footage around the intersection of East 34th and Lexington, around twelve thirty last night. See if there's anything on it."

He sighed. "I'll try, but she won't like it. She said her supervisor watches them, and he doesn't like them doing independent work."

"This is city business, Frank."

"Maybe, but the city doesn't know that. I'll get back to you."

"Thanks, Frank. I'm going back to the Precinct. I'll talk to you later."

He didn't reach the Precinct. Ten minutes later he took a call from Frank's contact, Betty.

"Detective de Sade? Can you get over here? I think I may have found something. I'm on the fourth floor."

"I'll be right there, give me fifteen minutes."

He drove through the traffic with the blue light flashing until he pulled up outside the grim, institutional concrete building that housed the New York City CCTV Control Center. He showed his badge at reception and went up in the elevator to the fourth floor. The room was filled with desks of monitors that covered most of the city. Betty was watching for him, and she waved him over. She had dark skin, dark curly hair and warm, liquid eyes. She'd managed to avoid the obesity that hit so many women when they went past thirty, and he wondered about her relationship with Frank Willard. Betty indicated the chair next to her.

"I've frozen the image on screen. Take a look. It sure looks like your man."

It was Santiago, or at least, it looked like him. It was hard to be sure. He was strolling along Lexington with a girl who had to be a whore. High-heeled white leather boots, mini skirt, and a boob tube. Heads were turned towards him, and his business with the woman was transparent enough to attract looks of disdain.

"Yeah, that's him. Can you see where he went?"

The guy was walking away from the Opus Dei building. Had he come from there? He asked Betty, but she shook her head.

"This is the first place I picked him up. There's nothing before then. It looks as if he climbed out of a cab next to the girl, made the deal, and started walking with her."

"Right, let's see where he goes."

She used a joystick to move the picture forward, and at one point switched to another camera. They picked him up again and tracked him along Lexington. He turned off at East 30th, and another camera was brought into focus. Then he disappeared, both him and the girl.

"What the hell happened?"

"It's the time delay on these archived films. They only show a frame every thirty seconds. Between one frame and the next, he must have turned off into some building."

He asked her to go back and then forward. There! A place lay between an electronics store and a valet car park. But what the hell kind of a building was it? He knew the area well but hadn't ever noticed the old, nondescript place. It had to be where Santiago was taking his victims, had to be. He thanked Betty and left the building, and when he was out on the street, he called Frank Willard.

"I think we have a location, East 30th, next door to the valet parking. I'm going down there."

"I'm heading to the gallery right now to take over. What do you want me to do?"

"Is there anyone watching her now?"

"My guy is about to leave. He has another assignment."

He thought furiously. It was critical to catch the killer but just as important to make sure he didn't get to Faith."

"You watch her. If I need you, I'll call."

"Roger that. Good luck, de Sade. Kick the bastard's ass."

"I intend to."

He drove back to Lexington, turned onto East 30th, and stopped in the street outside the valet parking. The attendant stared at him and came out to protest, but de Sade emerged from the unmarked, grabbed him by the scruff, and dragged him back inside the parking booth. He flashed his badge.

"See that nothing happens to my car."

"Shit, man. If you're a cop, put a sign on it. Otherwise they'll tow it."

"They'd better not. I'm on a case, and I don't want anyone to see there's a police car outside. Just watch it. Got that?"

"Yeah, sure."

He nodded and left him to walk to the building next door. It was a convent, of all places, although former convent might be a better description. The gray stone built edifice had a heavy oak door fastened with a chain to stop squatters and drug dealers getting access. But when he shook the chain, it came away loose in his hand as the padlock dropped away. He drew his Glock and walked inside. He was in a long passage that led deep into the building. The place had been empty for years. The floor was covered in dust and litter from when the building had been abandoned. Yet when he clicked on his flashlight, he could see footsteps in the dust. He followed them to a door at the end of the passage. He gently turned the doorknob and opened the door. He shone his flashlight inside. It was a small, old chapel, a darkened space with a litter of overturned wooden pews. In the beam of the light, he was sure he could see someone at the end of the chapel; at least, a body, and it was not moving. He clicked off the safety on his Glock and started forward. A stunning blow hit him on the head, and he blacked out.

When he came to, a light was shining in his face. He tried to use his limbs, but realized he was tied tightly to a wooden chair with a long length of thin line. Whoever had tied the knots was no amateur; the line was so tight it blocked his circulation so that he was already feeling numbness in his limbs.

"So you're awake, Detective. Congratulations on finding me. I wondered how long it would take you."

The voice was slightly mocking, confident, but still gentle. The accent was Spanish, but of course it was. He was hunting a Spaniard, Raul Santiago, and a bishop of the Catholic Church. Except this was not Santiago. He'd heard that voice before but couldn't place it.

"Who are you?" he shouted to the shadowy figure behind the beam of light.

"Evidently not the man thought you were hunting for," the voice replied.

"Where is he, Bishop Santiago? Is he part of this?"

"The Bishop? No, of course not. At this moment Raul is attending a retreat in the country, a Catholic Seminary at the foot of the Appalachians. I was amused when you made such strenuous efforts to link him to the killings. I even thought about sending some false information for you, but I decided that it would be easier to kill you."

So he was to die. He'd been stupid, allowing himself to make such a fatal mistake as to come in here alone after such a dangerous man. Now it could cost him his life. No, no way. He wasn't going to go that easily. How could he swing this, turn the tables? Frank knew where he was, and the unmarked was parked outside. Yes, there was a good chance of help arriving, but he needed to play for time. But who was this guy? As if reading his mind, the man came forward and stood close to him. He was gray-haired, tall, lean and elegant, and his skin had the classic Mediterranean tan. It could be Santiago, almost. But it wasn't. This man was Federico Amando. Opus Dei. And in the wash of light thrown by the flashlight, his flashlight was the body of a woman on the ground. Obviously the whore he was with in the CCTV footage.

"You recognize me, Detective? I see you do."

Amando stood over him. In his hand he held a long, thin folding knife, like Spanish hunters used for skinning.

"I see you recognize my Navaja. Which means you know what I have in store for you. Perhaps you should confess your sins, Detective. Even Orthodox Catholics should confess. After all, you have professed to follow your heretical beliefs during your lifetime. You have much to make right with God."

"How did you manage it, Amando? You were in Seville all that time?"

"Yes, I was there. Javier Garcia was careful to hide my presence from you. We both entertained ourselves, watching you chase around looking for the killer when all the time you were working with him. And then, of course, your suspicions fell on Bishop Santiago, and hilarious!

Except that Javier is now dead, which is regrettable. And something you must pay for."

"You're forgetting something," de Sade replied, trying to keep his voice calm and even. As if he was somehow in control.

"Am I? What am I forgetting, Detective Gabriel de Sade?"

"You didn't get the gold, did you?"

Amando didn't answer for a few moments. When he did, his voice was low and menacing.

"No, I did not get the gold, not yet. But you will tell me, Detective. Believe me, before you die, screaming for mercy, you will tell me everything."

"Fuck you, Amando. That gold is somewhere you'll never find it. Never! You can do what you like, but it's beyond your reach."

"In which case I will find out from your lady friend, the beautiful Faith Ward. I have no doubt she knows and will be delighted to tell me."

"She knows nothing!"

"Now I don't believe you, Detective, but never mind. If you tell me what I wish to know, it may not be necessary to subject her to unnecessary suffering. Then again, it might be enjoyable. We shall see."

He moved nearer, and the blade hovered in the air over Gabriel's face.

"Last chance, de Sade. Have you anything to say?"

"Go fuck yourself, Amando. You're a dead man. There are other people looking for you; people who don't play by the rules. They'll tear you limb from limb."

He laughed. "An empty threat. So, where shall I start?"

De Sade tensed himself as the knife came down. The

blade slashed into his chest, cutting through his jacket and shirt through to the skin. Amando dragged the blade down, opening up a long cut that started to ooze blood.

"That was just a sample, Detective, an introduction to my knife. I think perhaps a finger would be useful. I find that once a man has lost several of his fingers, he becomes even more cooperative."

Gabriel knew that nothing would stop this maniac. No matter what he did, Amando would not deviate from his determination to cause agonizing pain to his victim. Whether he told him what he wanted to know or not, it would make no difference. Amando gripped his wrist and held the fingers of his right hand splayed out on the arm of the chair.

"Are you right-handed? Yes, I think you are. Your gun was in a holster to accommodate a right-handed draw. Let's begin with your trigger finger, and I'll work back from there."

De Sade gritted his teeth as the man shifted his grip and held his finger down on the wooden arm. Amando brought the knife down, and the blade rest gently on his skin. A thin, red line appeared as the blade made a shallow cut. He saw the Spaniard's body move as the man positioned himself to put heavy pressure on the blade and slice into his finger. He could smell him, his body odor rank and stale, and under the overlay of expensive cologne was the stale, sweet stench that he associated with death. Amando started to push down, and de Sade felt the blade bite into flesh. He waited for the terrible agony of the knife cutting through his finger; but felt a cool wash of relief gush through him as a bright beam of light appeared from the direction of the doorway.

"Police! Put down that knife, and stand still where I can see you with your hands up!"

Frank Willard had arrived. Dear God, that had been close. He felt himself almost starting to black out as waves of agony surged through his brain. With an effort, he kept his consciousness. He had to be able to warn Frank about Amando. The man was much more dangerous than the veteran detective could possibly realize.

# CHAPTER FOURTEEN

Amando put his hands up, slowly and carefully. But de Sade saw the glint of the knife reflected in the beam of the flashlight, and he has his hand twisted slightly, so it was out of sight of Willard.

"Frank, the knife, he's still holding it!" he shouted.

Amando cursed, brought his hand around in a slashing motion, and it was seconds before de Sade realized that he'd been cut across the face. Then the Spaniard dropped to the floor out of the beam of light just as a shot crashed out. De Sade heard him slithering away across the floor, and Frank rushed over, using his pocketknife to free him.

"Did you see where the bastard went? He didn't go out the door. It's still shut."

"No, I couldn't see a thing," he replied. "Thanks for that, Frank, but the bastard is still on the loose somewhere. Let's take a look around here. He can't have gone far."

"Yeah. I guess he took your piece?"

"He did, and he must still have it."

"Right." Frank leaned down and slid a small backup

gun from an ankle holster. It was a Colt .25, the pistol that Faith favored. "You'd better use this. Let's try and grab him before he kills any more of these women."

Side by side, the two detectives searched the chapel. When the beam fell on the corpse, Frank grimaced. "Another one of his?"

Gabriel nodded. "He didn't get time to take her apart, but yeah, she's one of his."

"Poor kid. Where the hell has that bastard gone?"

There was nothing, no doors or exits out of the room other than the main door that was still closed. Until the beam of light fell on a metal cover in the floor.

"It's a manhole cover for the main drainage system. He must have gone down there," Frank exclaimed. "We'll need to get the city engineers to give us a plan of the system before we go down there. We don't know what we're getting into."

"I'll go down after him," Gabriel countered. "This bastard is not getting away!"

Frank sighed. "Yeah, I thought you'd say that. Okay, I'm coming with you."

\* \* \*

Faith unpacked the wooden crate that had arrived by DHL just minutes ago. There were some beautiful pieces, relics that could go on display and attract a lot of wealthy collectors to the gallery. But when she delved further into the case, her hands touched something smooth, something heavy. She lifted it out, the statuette. The solid gold contrasted with precious stones, diamonds and other gems inset into the body. She placed it in the center of her worktable. It was magnificent, a work almost beyond price. The provenance would be difficult to establish, but as it had been lost for six hundred years, and with no description in existence, she could choose whatever details she wanted. Even for just its value as gold and gems it was worth millions, and as a historical artifact, millions more. She picked it up and carried it to the safe. It would take time to work out how best to sell it, and more time to establish some kind of trust to oversee the money that would be raised. She'd wait until Galina returned. It was something they needed to work on together. As she returned to the wooden case, she suddenly felt cold. She stopped and closed her eyes. What had caused that feeling? Something dark, black, and something bad had happened, she knew that. Gabriel! Was he all right, or had he been injured, or worse? But it was more than that, and the blackness was getting nearer. She felt the approaching threat as clearly as if it was sounding an alarm bell. It meant that all of Gabriel's precautions had failed. Where was he, and where were the detectives that were supposed to be watching? She knew they weren't there. And she knew that the killer was coming here, to the gallery. She made an effort to be calm. She was no rookie, and she'd been through the FBI training courses and fought her way out of a number of scrapes. If the killer wanted the endgame to be here, she would be ready. She drew her Colt .25 and moved to the panel that controlled the circuit breakers for the gallery. When she hit the switch, the lights went off and everything was dark. She was ready.

* * *

They crawled along the dark service tunnel, both men doing their best to ignore the stench of raw sewage that permeated the air they breathed. At least the floor wasn't awash with the cities effluent as the tunnel was unused. But it was open to the main system, and the air was thick and heavy with the pungent stench. They passed a heavy iron hatch that was held up to the roof, allowing the shaft to be opened or closed at will. Frank shouted as he tripped on a length of wire, and as he did so, the hatch crashed down and locked in place. They pushed against it, but it wouldn't move.

"The bastard, he rigged it so we'd be trapped down here," de Sade said angrily.

"Yeah, but we're on his tail. All we need do is follow him," Frank replied.

"Yeah, maybe you're right."

"Christ, de Sade, do you have any idea of where we're going?"

"None at all. But if we hurry, we may just catch him."

"Or catch a dose of whatever diseases are floating around in this tunnel."

Gabriel smiled. "Have you had your shots?"

"I guess. Let's hope that perp hasn't. It'd be nice to see him die of some nasty disease."

They crawled on. In the beam of Frank's flashlight, they saw a torn piece of cloth on a piece of brickwork projecting out from the tunnel wall, expensive cloth.

"It looks like Amando's suit coat," de Sade said to his partner. "So he definitely came this way."

Willard grunted and they crawled on faster. They came to a side tunnel, but it was only twelve inches high, and not large enough to crawl down. Then they reached a shaft that led up to the street, and the purpose of the iron hatch locking behind them became obvious. There had been a ladder leaning against the side of the shaft, and the marks in the mud at the bottom of the shaft were clearly visible, but Amando had removed it. This was a preplanned escape route. They could hear the traffic sounds coming down the shaft, and Gabriel looked up at a high building that was just visible on the skyline above them. Bellevue Hospital.

"Where are we?" Frank asked anxiously. "Can you see anything?"

"We're close to Faith's gallery, and we need to get out of here fast."

"How do we do that? We're trapped."

Gabriel played the flashlight beam around the shaft. There had to be a way, had to be.

\* \* \*

She knew he was inside. He was good, and he'd made no noise. But something nudged her subconscious, and something that told her he was there. It was like a dark, evil blanket that had descended on the gallery, as if to infect it with its foulness and stench. She'd chosen her spot well. When he came nearer, she knew she'd see him, and when she did, she'd kill him. There was no other way. A shape flitted across the narrow shaft of light that came through the high, barred window. It was momentary, almost like a ghost moving. He was searching for her, so he knew that she was hiding. There was a noise by the main door.

"Hi, is anyone there? I came by to see about that icon you were offering, that darling little sixteenth century piece. I thought I'd buy it, if you can get it ready for me. Hello? Do you take credit cards?"

She could see the client now, a glamorous young trophy wife of some Wall Street millionaire. She remembered her from yesterday. She wanted something to remind her of her Orthodox religion that she felt she'd left behind in Russia. The dark form moved, behind the wealthy client. There was a shriek, and then the man spoke. It was a Spanish accent, but not Bishop Raul Santiago.

"Ms. Ward, if you want this young lady to live, I suggest you come out, and we can make a deal. You know the alternative, do I have to spell it out for you?"

She froze for a few seconds, but there was no alternative. She would have to be careful because when she spoke, he'd have an idea of where she was.

"What do you want?"

"Ah, Senorita Ward. How nice to hear from you. You know what I want. Give it to me, and I will leave. Otherwise this lady will die, and then you will die too."

She couldn't get a clear shot at him. He was no fool, holding the woman in front of his body. She would have to let him have what he wanted, or appear to let him have it.

"I need to get it from the safe. You must wait there."

"Do not take too long. I am not a patient man. I could kill this woman and then come for you, if you would prefer."

"No, no, I'll get it. Give me one minute."

She had a plan. A plan that could save the woman's life, but it would need split second timing. She went to the back of the gallery and opened the safe, took the statuette out, and looked at it. Yes, it was a beautiful piece, but he could have it if he wanted it. He mustn't see the gun. She needed that as a backup. She thought of the way her friend Galina carried it tucked under her skirt in the top of her hose, cursing the fact that she wore the old fashioned underwear because of its erotic effect on her partner Gabriel. She smiled to herself thinking of him. Where was he, and how had he allowed this maniac to get near her? No matter, she could think about that later. For the time being, she had to deal with the situation herself. She picked up a small, metal crucifix only two inches high from a display stand, holding the crosspiece between her fingers. Faith walked back through the darkened gallery toward where the killer waited. She stood a few yards away, trying to work out the best way to tackle him. He gestured with the knife.

"Bring it here quickly, or the girl dies."

"First of all, who are you? Obviously, you're not Bishop Santiago."

He laughed, a grating sound that sent shivers down her spine. "No, obviously not. Your partner already knows, so there is no more need for secrecy. I am Federico Amando, devoted officer of Opus Dei, a defender of the Holy Mother Church and saver of souls. At your service."

"So that's what you call butchering innocent women? Saving their souls?"

"They were not innocent!" he shouted. "They lived their lives in sin. They would be damned were it not for me."

"And butchering them was necessary?"

"You wouldn't understand!" he shouted again. "It had to be done. Give me that statue!"

"All right, you can have it."

She went forward, the statuette in one hand and her

other hand held up to show it was empty. But his eyes were fixed on only one thing. The gold. The culmination of many years of searching, and at last it was within his reach. He held out his hand, still staring at the gold. And she opened her fingers and dropped the crucifix.

It fell to the floor with a small, but distinct audible clatter. His eyes swiveled down to look for the new threat, and she swung the statuette, hitting him on the head. His eyes rolled, but then he recovered. She swung again, a hard, accurate blow and he crumpled, releasing the girl.

"Quickly, come with me."

She took the girl's hand and ran with her to the back of the gallery. There was a mezzanine floor where they displayed old, more valuable paintings, and they ran up the iron staircase. It was the best place to mount a defense, and already she could hear him shouting and raging.

"I have a gun. Give me the gold, and I will leave without harming you. Throw it down to me!"

They peered over the rail where they could see him on the gallery floor staring up at them.

"What do we do?" the girl whispered.

"Get down on the floor and be quiet. I'll deal with this."

"But, he has a gun."

"Yes, so have I."

She took the Colt from under her skirt, and the girl grinned as if it was a high school prank. Then Faith shouted back to Amando.

"The police are on the way. I've called them. I suggest you get out now while you're still alive. They'll shoot you like a dog. They know you're the serial killer."

The harsh, grating laugh came again. "You called no one. I cut the phone line, and I have a cellphone jammer in my pocket. Throw me the statue, and stop wasting my time." He waited a few seconds. "You had your chance. I'm coming up."

Faith took up a position behind a heavy wooden display case. She wasn't sure it would stop a bullet, but it would give her an advantage. She could get off a shot as soon as his head appeared at the top of the staircase. She could hear his footsteps on the treads as he climbed the iron stairs. A head appeared, a body, and then he was there, standing on the mezzanine floor. He had a gun in one hand and his knife in the other.

"Where are you, damn you? Give me the gold, or I will kill you."

Faith stepped out, her gun sighted and ready to fire. He twisted as he saw her. "You!"

Then she fired, aiming for his chest. She kept pulling the trigger, seeing the rounds tear through his coat and impact in his body. He staggered, fell to all fours, and incredibly, stood up again. Her pistol clicked on an empty chamber, and his face stretched into a smile.

"They're not so effective, those popguns, against a bullet-proof jacket. It's lucky you weren't firing a Glock 9mm. At this range you may have done some damage."

She could see that his coat was torn where her six tiny rounds had impacted on the ballistic vest, but other than minor bruising, she'd achieved nothing. He raised his pistol.

"It seems I can take the statuette now. There's no need for you to give it to me. I shall finish you two women, and then I can take my time traveling out of this unholy country. Goodbye, Senorita Ward."

He started to pull the trigger, and Faith tensed her

body, waiting for the smashing impact of the bullets. The report when it came was shatteringly loud, but she wasn't hit. Had he missed? He toppled forward, and as he fell, she saw the exit wound in his face where a bullet had hit him from behind. She blinked and saw Jonas standing at the top of the stairs, holding a smoking pistol. Beside him Galina watched her, holding a small automatic. Was it true? Or was it a dream?

"Jonas. Galina. You came."

Then everything went dizzy, and she plunged into darkness.

\* \* \*

When she awoke, they'd brought her home. She was lying on the bed in the apartment she shared with Gabriel. She went to get up, still not believing that she was alive. She went into the living room, and they stared at her, Galina and Jonas; and the face she wanted to see more than any other. Gabriel jumped up and came to help her to the couch.

"Are you sure you're okay?"

She nodded. "Never better, now that that bastard is dead."

She looked across the apartment as a man came into the room from the kitchen, and she felt chilled. He was tall, thin, gray haired, and with a Mediterranean color to his skin. But she recognized Bishop Raul Santiago, and she relaxed.

"How the hell did you get to the gallery so quickly?" she asked. "I thought you were in Seville, looking for leads."

Galina answered her. "Yes, we went to see Javier's

boyfriend, Diego Montalban, at the bull farm. We asked him about the Bishop, and he said Javier hardly knew him and had little time for him. But he'd seen a guy around who looked like Bishop Santiago, you know, gray haired, tall and thin. That's when we realized that you were chasing the wrong guy, and we got back here real fast."

"But how? There wasn't time to fix it all up. It's a hell of a journey from Seville to New York City."

"Not when one of the most powerful men in the Western world decided help. They tucked us into a Naval Osprey, a V22. It picked us up from Seville and dumped us on a carrier out in the Atlantic. We transferred to a pair of two seat F/A 18 Hornets, and they brought us across the Atlantic courtesy of an armada of refueling aircraft."

Faith nodded, "I understand."

They all knew that no one other than the President had the power to organize such a major logistical exercise. Except for the Director of CIA, Raymond Ward. Her father.

"You contacted him?"

Jonas nodded. "Yeah, I do contract work for the CIA, as you know. I thought he might be interested when his daughter was in serious danger. Besides, the CIA goes down on record as being a major player in the operation to take down a pair of dangerous serial killers. So everybody's happy, the White House, the Mayor of New York, and even the Spanish government. Raymond Glen earned a few favors, and all for the price of some gas and the hire of a couple of navy planes."

The Bishop looked confused. "I don't understand all of this, but I must say I'm happy that everything is resolved."

"You came close to a long prison sentence," Gabriel

told him. "I'm real sorry about that, Bishop. Except that maybe it flushed out the real killer, so maybe it was worth it."

He nodded. "I hope so. I only wanted to come here and make certain that Miss Ward is recovered. I heard that she'd been hurt during the fight at the gallery."

Gabriel looked at the man's expression. He couldn't read any ulterior motive in the man's eyes. But! There was always a but.

"She's fine, that's no problem. Tell me, how did you know that she'd been hurt?"

The Bishop hesitated. "Monsignor Vincenzo was keeping an eye on things for the Church. He has, shall I say, another matter he is looking into. He was parked opposite the gallery, writing up his notes when he saw the events unfold. He called me to let me know that Miss Ward was carried out injured, so of course I was concerned." He stood up. "I wonder if you and Miss Ward would care to have lunch with the Monsignor and me. I have to go back to Spain, but I will return in a few weeks time. If she is feeling better, we can fix it up then."

De Sade's eyes flicked to his two friends.

"And Miss Polotsova and Mr. Savage, of course," Santiago added.

Jonas and Galina nodded. He looked at Faith, and she inclined her head in the affirmative.

"We'd be delighted to, yes. Any special reason for inviting us?"

"No, no," the Bishop said quickly, too quickly. "Just a chat about the extraordinary events of the past week."

"Fine. Call in a few weeks, and we'll fix up a time and date."

They shook hands, and Santiago left.

"We know what he wants," Galina said into the silence that had descended on the apartment. "The question is how do we deal with it?"

"I have an idea," Faith murmured.

* * *

When the Bishop was invited, all expenses paid, to open a new children's hospital in a South American village, he was both puzzled and excited. Puzzled, because he couldn't think of why they'd requested that he attend the opening ceremony, and excited, because the very first expeditions to convert the natives in the New World had set off from Seville. He would be following in some very illustrious footsteps. He got off the plane at Buenos Aires and transferred to a much smaller twin prop aircraft that rattled and bumped its way across the unending plains and jungles of South America. When it landed, a white Toyota Land Cruiser, emblazoned with 'Eduardo Foundation for Sick Children' met him. The journey lasted four hours, along narrow tracks and paths that previously he would have said were impassable. Finally, he reached a large village, a mix of stone built houses and a number of poor, dilapidated huts. Except that at one end of the village was a long, low white building. The sign said 'Eduardo Foundation for Sick Children – Free Hospital'. As his driver helped him out of the vehicle, and waited politely while he massaged his stiff and aching limbs, he wondered where the money had come from to pay for such a lavish project; a billionaire philanthropist, probably. It would make a huge difference to these disease-ridden natives, and truly it was a work worthy of God. Mentally, he gave thanks for whoever had provided this wonder. When he walked into the building, four familiar faces met him. Galina Polotsova came forward and shook his hand. Jonas Savage, Faith Ward and Gabriel de Sade stood close by.

"Thank you for coming, Bishop. Would you like a tour of the hospital?"

He nodded and spent the next hour inspecting the modern equipment, the rows of neat beds, and obviously professional staff.

"It is a miracle, but tell me, how is it that the four of you are involved?"

"We helped with the fund raising," Galina explained.

"Good, good."

"So you approve?"

Why was she asking him that? "Of course I approve, it is magnificent."

"We would like you to dedicate it, in the name of God and the Catholic Church."

He was suspicious. "But, you are Orthodox Christians. Why the Catholic Church?"

"They are mostly Catholics around here."

He nodded. "Yes, that makes sense. I will certainly make the dedication."

"I already have the plaque made, Bishop."

He stared at it. The engraving stated that the hospital was opened by Bishop Raul Santiago and dedicated to God and the Catholic Church. There was nothing to object to, yet something was clearly wrong. He dismissed the thought. He must be wrong. This was a worthy project, and in the best traditions of Christianity. After the ceremony, he chatted with Gabriel de Sade, glass in hand.

"An excellent occasion, Detective, and a delightful wine."

"Glad you like it, Bishop. It's good of you to come."

"It is my honor to be invited. Tell me, who supplied the funding for this project?"

He saw that de Sade was looking at him in a peculiar way.

"You did, Bishop. You did."

He didn't understand at first, but he was not a stupid man. It took him fully ten seconds to work it all out, and suddenly, the wine didn't taste quite so good. He kept smiling. He was a senior churchman, used to keeping a pleasant expression even when it didn't match his feelings. But he spoke quietly to de Sade, so that no one overheard.

"You won't get away with it," he hissed. "You've made yourself a powerful enemy, believe me. One day, you will pay for this."

"Yeah? If I were you, my friend, I'd keep quiet about it. If they find out who paid for the hospital that you just opened and dedicated to your church, you may find they come gunning for you, and not for me. Think about it, Bishop."

Gabriel gave him a small smile and walked away to join Jonas, who stared at him.

"Any problems with the Bishop?"

"None whatsoever. That's a guy who knows how to make the most of a bad situation. He'll do the right thing."

Jonas nodded. "Good. I reckon this is winding down, so maybe we should start to make tracks."

"It's a long way in that SUV back to the airport, and it'll be dark soon."

Jonas smiled. "In that case, it's a good thing I hired a

helo to come and pick us up. It's due in about ten minutes."

De Sade nodded. "That was good thinking. I assume it's a four passenger charter with no room for the Bishop?"

Jonas' grin widened. "Now how did you work that out?"